D0239675

BLOOD

By the same author

The Tale of the Eternal Champion
*New Omnibus Editions, revised and with
new introductions by the author.*

1   Von Bek
2   The Eternal Champion
3   Hawkmoon
4   Corum
5   Sailing to Utopia
6   A Nomad of the Time Streams
7   The Dancers at the End of Time
8   Elric of Melniboné
9   The New Nature of the Catastrophe
10 The Prince with the Silver Hand
11 Legends from the End of Time
12 Stormbringer
13 Earl Aubec
14 Count Brass
Also: A Warrior of Mars

Science Fiction

The Sundered Worlds
The Shores of Death
The Winds of Limbo
The Wrecks of Time

Omnibuses

The Cornelius Quartet
A Cornelius Calendar

Behold the Man and Other Novels
*(Behold the Man,
Constant Fire,
Breakfast in the Ruins)*
Comic Capers
*(The Jerry Cornell
Stories,* w. Jack
Trevor Story)

Colonel Pyat

Byzantium Endures
The Laughter of Carthage
Jerusalem Commands
The Vengeance of Rome†

Other Novels

Gloriana; or, The Unfulfill'd Queen
The Brothel in Rosenstrasse
Mother London

Short stories and graphic novels

Casablanca
Sojan (juvenile)
My Experiences in the Third World War
Fabulous Harbours*
The Swords of Heaven, The Flowers of
   Hell (with Howard Chaykin)
The Crystal and the Amulet
   (with James Cawthorn)
etc.

Non-fiction

The Retreat from Liberty
Letters from Hollywood
   (illus. M. Foreman)
Wizardry and Wild Romance
Death is No Obstacle
   (with Colin Greenland)

Editor

New Worlds

The Traps of Time
The Best of *New Worlds*
Best SF Stories from *New Worlds*
New Worlds: An Anthology
Before Armageddon
England Invaded
The Inner Landscape

Records

With *The Deep Fix*:

The New Worlds Fair (Griffin Records)
Dodgem Dude
The Brothel in Rosenstrasse etc.

With *Hawkwind*:

Warriors at the Edge of Time
Choose Your Masques
Zones
Sonic Attack etc.
Also work with *Blue Oyster Cult,*
   Robert Calvert etc.

For further information about Michael
Moorcock and his work please send SAE
to Nomads of the Time Streams, 18
Laurel Bank, Truss Hill Road, South
Ascot, Berks, UK, or PO Box 5201,
Pinehurst, North Carolina, 28374, USA.

* In preparation (Orion Books)   † In preparation (Cape)

Michael Moorcock

BL◯◯D

A SOUTHERN FANTASY

MILLENNIUM
An Orion Book
LONDON

Copyright © Michael and Linda Moorcock 1994
All rights reserved

The right of Michael Moorcock to be identified as the author of this work has been
asserted by him in accordance with the Copyright, Designs and Patents Act 1988.

Parts of this novel were first published in slightly different form in *New Worlds*,
edited by David Garnett, © 1991, 1992, 1994, and in *The Time Centre Times*,
edited by John and Maureen Davey, Ian Covell and D. J. Rowe, © 1993.

This edition first published in 1995 by
Millennium
An imprint of Orion Books Ltd
Orion House, 5 Upper St Martin's Lane
London WC2H 9EA

A CIP catalogue record for this book is available
from the British Library

ISBN: (Csd) 1 85798 232 0
(Ppr) 1 85798 233 9

Typeset by Deltatype Ltd, Ellesmere Port, Wirral
Printed and bound in Great Britain by
Clays Ltd, St Ives plc.

To the memory of Angela Carter,
a generous heart, a brilliant mind and a great talent . . .
And for Mark and Alex, good friends

650875

MORAY COUNCIL
DEPARTMENT OF TECHNICAL
& LEISURE SERVICES
SF

The imperial ensign, which, full high advanced,
Shone like a meteor streaming to the wind,
With gems and golden lustre rich emblazed,
Seraphic arms and trophies; all the while
Sonorous metal blowing martial sounds:
At which the universal host up-sent
A shout that tore Hell's concave, and beyond
Frighted the reign of Chaos and old Night.
All in a moment through the gloom were seen
Ten thousand banners rise into the air,
With orient colours waving: with them rose
A forest huge of spears; and thronging helms
Appeared, and serried shields in thick array
Of depth immeasureable.

Milton, *Paradise Lost*

Contents

1. Colour
5

(Corsairs of the Second Ether)
47

2. Free States
57

(Corsairs of the Second Ether cont.)
89

3. Codes
95

(Corsairs of the Second Ether cont.)
133

4. Routes
139

Prologue

A year or two ago I inherited the manuscripts of Edwin Begg, the famous Clapham Antichrist, whom I had known since the 1960s. The miscellany of typescript and crudely hand-made magazines was at first entirely incomprehensible to me. It looked like the remains of a psychedelic undergraduate project which very properly had been abandoned.

Although I am known for my skills as an editor of others' work, the Begg collection seemed at first impossible. Yet I was duty-bound to prepare the papers for press and seek a publisher for them. I am doomed, I am beginning to understand, to remain a kind of eternal editor.

However, as I worked on the manuscript I began to perceive its coherence. A complex and intriguing story emerged as all the disparate elements came together to form an unfamiliar whole.

The world described in Begg's papers was not our own, nor did it appear to know of our own. It was a world in which the white races had fallen into decadence and other races had risen to build a more dynamic civilisation.

When the 'colour spots' had started to appear they were regarded as a boon – a source of free, apparently limitless, energy; raw energy which could be harnessed and used for almost any electronic purpose, but little else.

Seeking further colour as the world's other resources diminished, engineers determined to drill to what they believed to be the source of a great colour mass which had erupted one afternoon in the ocean off the port and resort of Biloxi, Mississippi and for a while provided enough electronic fuel for the whole state and much of Louisiana.

They were boring into what the engineers defined as 'ultra-reality', the Source Matter of the Universe, but they drilled for only seconds before the famous Fault emerged like a djinn from a bottle, swallowing platform crews, the pier, some beach-front buildings, gambling boats, and part of the on-shore monitoring section even as they aborted the project. All matter – living or inert – was gulped up by that hungry, uncontrollable Fault, raging and howling like a million souls in torment, vivid against the unnaturally tranquil ocean and a still, southern sky.

From then on, the process was irreversible. It seemed the fabric of reality shredded and warped, growing almost senile in its whimsicalities.

Amongst the few able to survive and thrive in such uncertain conditions were the so-called jugadors – also known as mukhamirim or, more familiarly, chocarreros – forming the famous Gambler Guilds, whose adepts played in every way for the very highest stakes, who counted it their sacred duty to take risks and did so as a matter of honour and habit, staking their lives and reputations casually.

They were called jugadors according to the patois of the day, which had developed mostly from Carib, French, Spanish, African and English sources. They knew how to calculate odds and make decisions in a world increasingly ruled by chance.

While held in superstitious suspicion by many, the jugadors and jugadoritas were the aristocratic adepts of their world and respected by the most rapacious warlords, white or black.

They looked to Africa for their models, their art, their intellectual inspiration, their morality and, to some degree, their religion. Those who had been trained in the great teaching casinos of Cairo and Marrakech were the most respected mukhamirim. These travelled freely across disputed territories, and traditionally dominated the riverboats that had again become an important means of travel.

The planet grew increasingly unstable, touched by a vast manifestation of Chaos revealed through the Biloxi Fault. Decaying energy produced sudden flurries of power blazing with an unhealthy intensity before they were tapped or disappeared. The effects of entropy were everywhere. Sometimes these effects were spectacular, miraculous and uncomfortably alien, the stuff of hectic nightmare or ecstatic vision. Few believed the Earth would ever be healed of her physical or her metaphysical wounds.

It became clear that soon the planet must perish and death consume all memory.

Perhaps fearing this inevitable end, many placed increasing value on the moment, learning to relish every remaining second of life. Amongst these were Jack Karaquazian and Colinda Dovero who were considered by many to be the king and queen of their calling, both jugadors of the highest calibre, the admiration and envy of their peers, the moral examplars of all aspirants. They were lovers and their story is told here.

This is also the story of Sam Oakenhurst and that mysterious woman who claimed to be half animal and half plant, and was known as the Rose. Mr Oakenhurst's appetites and pastimes had become, some would say, neurotic and perverse, but his love for the Rose was as honest and enthusiastic as any emotion he had ever known. Her love for him was, some think, not entirely selfless.

Two pairs of lovers, famous gamblers all— Even when Chaos threatened to engulf the multiverse, when the entire quasi-infinite was in upheaval, they staked their mortal lives and their immortal souls against all the forces of Singularity, that deadly alternative, refusing the trap of simplification and reduction.

This is a love story. It is also an adventure story. It is a tale of blind devotion, honest faith and wild risk; about honour, about codes and about a game in which the most valuable stakes are individual human souls and the prizes are all those realities for which the human spirit longs. Until the events described in this story these realities remained unattainable.

This is also a story about good luck and bad, which can never be predicted – though Jack Karaquazian made the most of his luck and in the end, it might be argued, even Sam Oakenhurst found a form of redemption.

As for the Rose, she has many titles. In Mirenburg she was the Countess von Bek but in Tanelorn she had another name, as she had in Paris, London, New York and Los Angeles. And, in Sporting Club Square, Hammersmith, where I lived for several years, she was remembered as an angel. I came to know her almost as well as I knew Una Persson who was otherwise a very different personality.

Everything about the Rose is mysterious, even her true biological makeup. Sometimes I think that she is mad, a visionary blinded by the blaze of her own imaginings. But she is too involved with others to be truly mad. I know that she weeps for the world's pain and it is this sorrow, if anything, which informs her actions. Nonetheless, there are many men who hate her with a passion I find disturbing. Though her motives are complex she has a great heart. Her enemies say she calculates too coldly, that she is a gamer without peer but a gamer without mercy. I have had a glimpse of the stakes she plays for and the risks she takes. It is altruism and hatred which help determine her actions as she moves between the spaces separating each universe from the other, walking the moonbeams between one reality and the next – the spaces which are the rich and glamorous roads uniting the worlds. 'There was never a woman,' says Wheldrake, 'as free as the Rose.'

Michael Moorcock
Hjokmok
Arctic Lapland
24 December 1993

[3]

Part 1

Colour

The very nature of our dreams is changing.
We have deconstructed the universe and are
refusing to rebuild it. This is our madness and
our glory.

   Now we can again begin the true course of
our explorations, without preconceptions or
agendas.

Lobkowitz

CHAPTER ONE

A Victim of the Game

The heat of the New Orleans night pressed against the window like an urgent lover. Jack Karaquazian stood sleepless, naked, staring out into the sweating darkness as if he might see at last some tangible horror which he could confront and even hope to conquer.

'Tomorrow,' he told his handsome friend Sam Oakenhurst, 'I shall take the *Star* up to Natchez and from there make my way to McClellan by way of the Trace. Will you come?'

(The vision of a sunlit bayou, recollection of an extraordinarily rich perfume, the wealth of the earth. He remembered the yellow-billed herons standing in the shadows, moving their heads to regard him with thoughtful eyes before returning their respect to the water; the grey ibises, seeming to sit in judgement of the others; the delicate egrets congregating on the old logs and branches; a cloud of monarch butterflies, black and orange, diaphanous, settling over the pale reeds and, in the dark green waters, a movement might have been copperhead or alligator, or even a pike. In that moment of silence before the invisible insects began a fresh song, her eyes were humorous, enquiring. She had worked for a while, she said, as a chanteuse at The Fallen Angel on Bourbon Street.)

Sam Oakenhurst understood the invitation to be a courtesy. 'I think not, Jack. My luck has been running pretty badly lately and travelling ain't likely to improve it much.' Wiping his ebony fingers against his undershirt, he delicately picked an ace from the baize of his folding table.

For a moment the overhead fan, fuelled by some mysterious power, stirred the cards. Pausing, Mr Oakenhurst regarded this phenomenon with considerable satisfaction, as if his deepest faith had been confirmed. 'Besides, I got me all the mung I need right now.' And he patted his belt, full of hard guineas — better than muscle.

'It looked for a moment as if our energy had come back.' Mr Karaquazian got onto his bed and sat there undecided whether to try sleeping or to talk. 'I'm also planning to give the game a rest. I swear it will be a while before I play at the Terminal.' They both smiled.

'You still looking to California, Jack?' Mr Oakenhurst stroked down a card. 'And the Free States?'

'Well, maybe eventually.' Jack Karaquazian offered his attention back to the darkness while a small, dry, controlled cough shook his body. He cursed softly and vigorously and went to pour himself a careful drink from the whisky on the table.

'You should do it,' said Mr Oakenhurst. 'Nobody knows who you are anymore.'

'I left some unfinished business between Starkville and McClellan.' Quietly satisfied by this temporary victory over his disease, the gambler drew in a heavy breath. 'Anywhere's better than this. Sam, I'll go in the morning. As soon as they sound the up-boat siren.'

Putting down the remaining cards, his partner rose to cross, through sluggish shadows, the unpolished floor and, beneath the fluttering swampcone on the wall, pry up one of the boards. He removed a packet of money and divided it into two without counting it. 'There's your share of Texas. Brother Ignatius and I agreed, if only one of us got back, you'd have half.'

Jack Karaquazian accepted the bills and slipped them into a pocket of the black silk jacket which hung over the other chair on top of his pants, his linen and brocaded vest. 'It's rightfully all yours, Sam, and I'll remember that. Who knows how our luck will run? But it'll be a sad year down here, I think, win or lose.' Mr Karaquazian found it difficult to express most emotions; for too long his trade had depended on hiding them. Yet he was able to lay a pale, fraternal hand on his friend's shoulder, a gesture which meant a great deal more to both than any amount of conversation. His eyes, half-hidden behind long lashes, became gentle for a moment.

Both men blinked when, suddenly, the darkness outside was ripped by a burst of fire, of flickering arsenical greens and yellows, of vivid scarlet sparks. The mechanish squealed and wailed as if in torment, while other metallic lungs uttered loud, suppressed groans occasionally interrupted by an aggressive bellow, a shriek of despair from xylonite vocal cords, or a deeper, more threatening klaxon as the steel militia, their bodies identified by bubbling globules of burning, dirty orange plastic, gouting black smoke, roamed the narrow streets in search of flesh – human or otherwise – which had defied the city's intolerable curfew. Mr Karaquazian never slept well in New Orleans. The fundamental character of the authority appalled him.

Two of a Kind

At dawn, as the last of the garishly decorated, popishly baroque mechanish blundered over the cobbles of the rue Dauphine, spreading their unwholesome ichor behind them, Jack Karaquazian carried his carpet bag to the quayside, joining other men and women making haste to board *L'Etoile d'Memphes*, anxious to leave the oppressive terrors of a quarter where the colour-greedy machinoix, that brutal aristocracy, allowed only their engines the freedom of the streets.

Compared to the conscious barbarism of the machines, the river-boat's cream filigree gothic was in spare good taste, and Mr Karaquazian ascended the gangplank with his first-class ticket in his hand, briefly wishing he were going all the way to the capital, where at least some attempt was made to maintain old standards. But duty — according to Jack Karaquazian's idiosyncratic morality, and the way in which he identified an abiding obsession – had to be served. He had sworn to himself that he must perform a particular task and obtain certain information before he could permit himself any relief, any company other than Colinda Dovero's.

He followed an obsequious steward along a familiar colonnaded deck to the handsomely carved door of the stateroom he favoured when in funds. By way of thanks for a generous tip, he was offered a knowing leer and the murmured intelligence that a high-class snowfrail was travelling in the adjoining suite. Mr Karaquazian rewarded this with a scowl and a sharp oath so that the steward left before, as he clearly feared, the tip was snatched back from his fingers. Shaking his head at the irredeemable vulgarity of the white race, Mr Karaquazian unpacked his own luggage. The boat shuddered suddenly as she began to taste her steam, her paddle-wheel stirring the dark waters of the Mississippi. Compared to the big ocean-going schooner on which, long ago, the gambler had crossed from Alexandria, the *Etoile* was comfortingly reliable and responsive. For him she belonged to an era when time had been measured by chronometers rather than degrees of deliquescence.

He was reminded, against his guard, of the first day he had met the adventuress, Colinda Dovero, who had been occupying those same adjoining quarters and following the same calling as himself.

(Dancing defiantly with her on deck in the summer night amongst the mosquito lamps to the tune of an accordion, a fiddle, a Dobro and a bass guitar, while the Second Officer, Mr Pitre, sang 'Poor Hobo' in a sweet baritone . . . *O, pauvre hobo, mon petit pierrot, ah, foolish hope, my grief, mon cœur . . . Aiee, no longer, no longer Houston, but our passion she never resolves. Allons dansez! Allons dansez!* The old traditional elegies; the pain of inconstancy. *La musique, ma tristesse . . .* They were dancing, they were told in turn, with a sort of death. But the oracles whom the fashion favoured in those days, and who swarmed the same boats as Karaquazian and his kind, were of proven inaccuracy. Even had they not been, Karaquazian and Mrs Dovero could have done nothing else than what they did, for theirs was at that time an ungovernable chemistry . . .)

As it happened, the white woman kept entirely to her stateroom and all Karaquazian knew of her existence was an occasional overheard word to her stewardess. Seemingly, her need for solitude matched his own. He spent the better part of the first forty-eight hours sleeping, his nightmares as troubled as his memories. When he woke up, he could never be sure whether he had been dreaming or remembering, but he was almost certain he had shouted out at least once. Horrified by the thought of what he might reveal, he dosed himself with laudanum until only his snores disturbed the darkness. Yet he continued to dream.

Her name, she had said, was West African or Irish in origin, she was not sure. They had met for the second time in the Terminal Café on the stablest edge of the Biloxi Fault. The café's sharply defined walls constantly jumped and mirrored, expanding space, contracting it, slowing time, frantically dancing in and out of a thousand mirror matrixes; its neon sign (LAST HEAT ON THE BEACH), usually lavender and cerise, drawing power directly from the howling chaos a few feet away, between the white sand and the blue ocean, where all the unlikely geometries of the multiverse, all the terrible wild colours, that mælstrom of uninterpretable choices, were displayed in a smooth, perfect circle which the para-engineers had sliced through the core of all-time and all-space, its rim edged by a rainbow ribbon of vanilla-scented crystal. Usually, the Terminal Café occupied roughly the area of space filled by the old pier, which itself had been absorbed by the vortex during the early moments of an experiment intended to bore into the very marrow of ultra-reality and extract all the energy the planet needed.

The operation had been aborted twenty-two seconds after it began.

Since then, adventurers of many persuasions and motives had made the sidestep through the oddly coloured flames of the Fault into that inferno of a billion perishing space-time continua, drawn down into a maw which sucked to nothingness the substance of whole races and civilisations, whole planetary systems, whole histories, while Earth and sun bobbed in some awkward and perhaps temporary semi-parasitical relationship between the feeding and the food; their position in this indecipherable matrix being generally considered a fluke. (Or perhaps the planet was the actual medium of this destruction, as untouched by it as the knife which cuts the throat of the Easter lamb.)

Even the least fanciful of theorists agreed that they might have accelerated or at least were witnesses to a universal destruction. They believed the engineers had drilled through unguessable dimensions, damaging something which had until now regulated the rate of entropy to which human senses had, over millions of years, evolved. With that control damaged and the rate accelerating to infinity, their perceptions were no longer adequate to the psychic environment.

The multiverse raced perhaps towards the creation of a new sequence of realities, perhaps towards some cold and singular conformity; perhaps towards unbridled chaos, the end of all consciousness. This last was what drew certain people to the edge of the Fault, their fascination taking them step by relentless step to the brink, there to be consumed.

On a dance floor swept by peculiar silhouettes and shifts of light, Boudreaux Ramsadeen, who had brought his café here by rail from Meridian, encouraged the zee-band to play on while he guided his tiny partners in the Cajun steps. These professional dancers travelled from all over Arcadia to join him. Their hands on their swaying hips, their delicate feet performing figures as subtly intricate as the Terminal's own dimensions, they danced to some other tune than the band's.

Boudreaux's neanderthal brows were drawn together in an expression of seraphic concentration as, keeping all his great bulk on his poised left foot, describing graceful steps with his right, he moved his partners with remarkable tenderness and delicacy.

(Jack Karaquazian deals seven hands of poker, fingering the sensors of his kayplay with deliberate slowness. Only here, on the whole planet, is there a reservoir of energy deep enough to run every machine, synthetic reasoner, or cybe in the world, but not transmittable beyond the Terminal's peculiar boundaries. Only those with an incurable addiction to the past's electronic luxuries come here, and they are all gamblers of some description. Weird light saturates the table; the light of Hell. He is waiting for his passion, his muse.)

Colinda Dovero and Jack Karaquazian had met again across the blue,

[11]

flat sheen of a mentasense and linked into the wildest, riskiest game of 'Slick Image' anyone had ever witnessed, let alone joined. When they came out of it, Dovero was eight guineas up out of a betting range which had made psychic bids most seasoned players never cared to imagine. It had caused Boudreaux Ramsadeen to rouse himself from his mood of ugly tolerance and insist thereafter on a stakes ceiling that would protect the metaphysical integrity of his establishment. Some of the spectators had developed peculiar psychopathic obsessions, while others had merely become subject to chronic vomiting. Dovero and Karaquazian had, however, gone into spacelessness together and did not properly emerge for nine variations, while the walls expanded and turned at odd angles and the colours saturated and amplified all subtleties of sensation. There is no keener experience, they say, than the act of love during a matrix shift at the Terminal Café.

'That buzz? It's self-knowledge,' she told the Egyptian, holding him tight as they floated in the calm between one bizarre reality and another.

'No disrespect, Jack,' she had added.

CHAPTER THREE

Il Fait Chaud

Karaquazian found her again a year later on the *Princesse du Natchez*. He recognised, through her veil, her honey-coloured almond eyes. She was, she said, now ready for him. They turned their stateroom into marvellous joint quarters. Her reason for parting had been a matter of private business. That business, she warned him, was not entirely resolved but he was grateful for even a hint of a future. The old Confederate autonomies were lucky if their matrixes were only threadbare. They were collapsing. There were constant minor reality meltdowns now and yet there was nothing to be done but continue as if continuation were possible. Soon the Mississippi might become one of the few geographical constants. 'When we start to go,' he said, 'I want to be on the river.'

'Maybe chaos is already our natural condition,' she had teased. She was always terrifyingly playful in the face of annihilation, whereas he found it difficult even to confront the idea. She still had a considerable amount of hope in reserve.

They began to travel as brother and sister. A month after they had established this relationship, there was some question of her arrest for fraud when two well-uniformed cool boys had stepped aboard at New Auschwitz on the Arkansas side as the boat was casting off and suddenly they had no authority. In midstream they made threats. They insisted on entering the ballroom where she and the Egyptian were occupied. And then Karaquazian had suffered watching her raise promising eyes to the captain who saluted, asked if she had everything she needed, ordered the boys to disembark at Greenville, and said that he might stop by later to make sure she was properly comfortable. She had told him she would greatly appreciate the attention and returned to the floor, where a lanky zee-band bounced out the old favourites. With an unsisterly flirt of her hands, she had offered herself back to her pseudo-brother.

Jack Karaquazian had felt almost sour, though gentleman enough to hide it, while he took charge of the unpleasant feelings experienced by her cynical use of a sensuality he had thought, for the present at least, his preserve. Yet that sensuality was in no way diminished by its knowing employment, and his loyalty to her remained based upon profound respect – a type of love he would cheerfully have described as feminine, and through which he experienced some slight understanding of the extraordinary individual she was. He relished her lust for freedom, her optimism, her insistence on her own right to exist beyond the destruction of their universe, her willingness to achieve some form of immortality in any terms and at any cost. She thrilled him precisely because she disturbed him. He had not known such deep excitement since his last two-and-a-half weeks before leaving Egypt and his first three weeks in America; and never because of a woman. Until then, Mr Karaquazian had enjoyed profound emotion only for the arts of gaming and his faith. His many liaisons, while frequently affectionate, had never been allowed to interfere with his abiding passion. At first he had been shocked by the realisation that he was more fascinated by Colinda Dovero than he had ever been by the intellectual strategies of the Terminal's ranks of Grand Turks.

The mind which had concentrated on gambling and its attendant skills, upon self-defence and physical fitness, upon self-control, now devoted itself almost wholly to her. He was obsessed with her thoughts, her motives, her background, her story, the effect which her reality had upon his own. He was no longer the self-possessed individual he had been before he met her; and, when they had made love again that first night, he had been ready to fall in with any scheme which kept them together. Eventually, after the New Auschwitz incident, he had made some attempt to rescue his old notion of himself, but when she revealed her business had to do with a potential colour strike valuable beyond any modern hopes, he had immediately agreed to go with her to help establish the claim. In return, she promised him a percentage of the proceeds. He committed himself to her in spite of his not quite believing anything she told him. She had been working the boats for some while now, raising money to fund the expedition, ready to call it quits as soon as her luck turned bad. Since Memphis, her luck had run steadily down. This could also be why she had been so happy to seek an ally in him. The appearance of the cool boys had alarmed her; as if that evening had been the first time she had suffered any form of accusation. Besides, she told him, with the money he had they could now easily meet the top price for the land, which was only swamp anyway. She would pay the fees and expenses. There would be no trouble raising funds once the strike was claimed.

At Chickasaw, they had left the boat and set off up the Trace together.

She had laughed as she looked back at the levee and the *Princesse* outlined against the cold sky. 'I have made an enemy, I think, of that captain.' He was touched by what he perceived as her wish to reassure him of her constancy. But in Carthage, they had been drawn into a flat game, which had developed around a random hot-spot no bigger than a penny, and played until the spot faded. When the debts were paid, they were down to a couple of guineas between them and had gambled their emergency batteries. At this point, superstition overwhelmed them and each had seen sudden bad luck in the other.

Jack Karaquazian regretted their parting almost immediately and would have returned to her, but by the time he heard of her again she was already lost to Van Beek, the planter. It had been Van Beek that time who had sent his cool boys after her. She wrote once to Mr Karaquazian, in care of the Terminal. She said she was taking a rest but would be in touch.

Meanwhile Mr Karaquazian had a run of luck at the Terminal which, had he not cheated against himself and put the winnings back into circulation, would have brought a halt to all serious gambling for a while. Jack Karaquazian now played with his back to the Fault. The sight of that mighty appetite, that insatiable mystery, distracted him these days. He was impatient for her signal.

CHAPTER FOUR

La Pointe à Pain

Sometimes Jack Karaquazian missed the ancient, exquisite colours of the Egyptian evening, where shades of yellow, red, and purple touched the warm stone of magnificent ruins, flooded the desert and brought deep shadows, as black and sharp as flint, upon that richly faded landscape, one subtle tint blending into the other, one stone with the next, supernaturally married and near to their final gentle merging, in the last, sweet centuries of their material state. Here, on the old *Etoile*, he remembered the glories of his youth, before they drilled the Fault, and he found some consolation, if not satisfaction, in bringing back a time when he had not known much in the way of self-discipline, had gloried in his talents. When he had seemed free.

Once again, he strove to patch together some sort of consistent memory of when they had followed the map into the cypress swamp; of times when he had failed to reach the swamp. He had a sense of making progress up the Trace after he had disembarked, but he had probably never reached McClellan and had never seen the Stains again. How much of this repetition was actual experience? How much was dream?

Recently, the semi-mutable nature of the matrix meant that such questions had become increasingly common. Jack Karaquazian had countless memories of beginning this journey to join her and progressing so far (usually no closer than Vicksburg) before his recollections became uncertain, and the images isolated, giving no clue to any particular context. Now, however, he felt as if he were being carried by some wise momentum allowing his unconscious to steer a path through the million psychic turnings and cul-de-sacs this environment provided. It seemed to him that his obsession with the woman, his insane association of her with his luck, his Muse, was actually supplying the force needed to propel him back to the reality he longed to find. She was his goal, but she was also his reason.

CHAPTER FIVE

Les Veuves des la Coulee

They had met for the third time while she was still with Van Beek, the brute said to own half Tennessee and to possess the mortgages on the other half. Van Beek's red stone fortress lay outside Memphis. He was notorious for the cruel way in which his plantation whites were treated, but his influence among the eight states of the Confederacy meant he would inevitably be next Governor General, with the power of life and death over all but the best protected machinoix or guild neutrals, like Jack Karaquazian and Colinda Dovero. 'I am working for him,' she admitted. 'As a kind of ambassador. You know how squeamish people are about dealing with the North. They lose face even by looking directly at a whitey. But I find them no different, in the main. A little feckless. Social conditioning.' She did not hold with genetic theories of race. She had chatted in this manner at a public occasion where, by coincidence, they were both guests.

'You are his property, I think,' Mr Karaquazian had murmured without rancour. But she had shaken her head.

Whether she had become addicted to Van Beek's power or was merely deeply fascinated by it, Mr Karaquazian never knew. For his own part, he had taken less and less pleasure in the liaison that followed while still holding profound feelings for her. Then she had come to his room one evening when he was in Memphis and she in town with Van Beek, who attended some bond auction at the big hotel, and told him that she deeply desired to stay with him, but they must be so rich they would never lose their whole roll again. Mr Karaquazian thought she was ending their affair on a graceful note. Then she produced a creased read-out which showed colour sightings in the depths of Mississippi near the Tombigbee not far from Starkville. This was the first evidence she had ever offered him, and he believed now that she was trying to demonstrate that she trusted him, that she was telling the truth. She had intercepted the report before it reached Van Beek. The airship pilot who sent it had crashed in flames a day later. 'This time we go straight to it.'

She had pushed him back against his cot, sniffing at his neck, licking him. Then, with sudden honesty, she told him that, through her Tarot racing, she was into Van Beek for almost a million guineas, and he was going to make her go North permanently to pay him back by setting up deals with the white bosses of the so-called Insurgent Republics. 'Van Beek's insults are getting bad enough. Imagine suffering worse from a white man.'

Within two weeks, they had repeated their journey up the Trace, got as far as McClellan, and taken a pirogue into the Streams, following, as best they could, the grey contours of the aerial map, heading towards a cypress swamp. It had been fall then, too, with the leaves turning; the tree-filled landscapes of browns, golds, reds and greens reflected in the cooling sheen of the water. The swamp still kept its heat during the day.

'We are the same,' he had suggested to her, to explain their love. 'We have the same sense of boredom.'

'No, Jack, we have the same habits. But I arrived at mine through fear. I had to learn a courage that for you was simply an inheritance.' She had described her anxieties. 'It occasionally feels like the victory of some ancient winter.'

The waterways were full of birds which always betrayed their approach. No humans came here at this time of year, but any hunters would assume them to be hunting, too. Beautiful as it was, the country was forbidding and with no trace of Indians, a sure sign that the area was considered dangerous, doubtless because of the snakes.

She foresaw a world rapidly passing from contention to warfare; from warfare to brute struggle, from that to insensate matter, and from that to nothingness. 'This is the reality offered as our future,' she said. They determined they would, if only through their mutal love, resist such a future.

They had grown comfortable with one another, and when they camped at night they would remind themselves of their story, piecing it back into some sort of whole, restoring to themselves the extraordinary intensity of their long relationship. By this means, and the warmth of their sexuality, they raised a rough barrier against encroaching chaos.

CHAPTER SIX

Mon Cœur et Mon Amour

It had been twilight, with the cedars turning black and silver, a cool mist forming on the water, when they had reached the lagoon marked on the map, poling the dugout through the shallows, breaking dark gashes in the weedy surface, the mud sucking and sighing at the pole. Each movement tired Mr Karaquazian too much, threatening to leave him with no energy in reserve, so they chose a fairly open spot, where snakes might not find them, and, placing a variety of sonic and visual beacons, settled down to sleep. They would have slept longer had not the novelty and potential danger of their situation excited their lusts.

In the morning, sitting with the canvas folded back and the tree-studded water roseate from the emerging sun, the mist becoming golden, the white ibises and herons flapping softly amongst the glowing autumn foliage, Jack Karaquazian and Colinda Dovero breakfasted on their well-planned supplies, studying their map before continuing deeper into the beauty of that unwelcoming swamp. Then, at about noon, with a cold blue-grey sky reflected in the still surface of a broad, shallow pond, they found colour – one large Stain spread over an area almost five feet in circumference, and two smaller Stains, about a foot across, almost identical to those noted by the pilot.

From a distance, the Stains appeared to rest upon the surface of the water, but as Mr Karaquazian poled the boat closer, they saw that they had in fact penetrated deeply into the muddy bottom of the pond. The gold Stains formed a kind of membrane over the openings, effectively sealing them, and yet it was impossible to tell if the colour were solid or a kind of dense, utterly stable gas.

'Somebody drilled here years ago and then, I don't know why, thought better of it.' Colinda looked curiously at the Stains, mistaking them for capped bores. 'Yet it must be of first quality. Near pure.'

Jack Karaquazian was disappointed by what he understood to be a note of greed in her voice, but he smiled. 'There was a time colour had to come out perfect,' he said. 'This must have been drilled before Biloxi – or around the same time.'

'Now they're too scared, most of them, to drill at all!' Shivering, she peered over the side of the boat, expecting to see her image in the big Stain, and instead was surprised, almost shocked.

Watching her simply for the pleasure it gave him, Jack Karaquazian was curious and moved his own body to look down. The Stain had a strangely solid, unreflective depth, like a gigantic ingot of gold hammered deep into the reality of the planet.

Both were now aware of a striking abnormality, yet neither wanted to believe anything but some simpler truth, and they entered into an unspoken bond of silence on the matter. 'We must go to Jackson and make the purchase,' he said. 'Then we must look for some expert engineering help. Another partner, even.'

'This will get me clear of Van Beek,' she murmured, her eyes still upon the Stain, 'and that's all I care about.'

'He'll know you double-crossed him as soon as you begin to work this.'

She shrugged.

At her own insistence she had remained with the claim while he went back to Jackson to buy the land and, when this was finalised, buy a prospecting licence without which they would not be able to file, such were Mississippi's bureaucratic subtleties; but when he returned to the cypress swamp, she and the pirogue were gone. Only the Stains remained as evidence of their experience. Enquiring frantically in McClellan, he heard of a woman being caught wild and naked in the swamp and becoming the common possession of the brothers Berger and their father, Ox, until they tired of her. It was said she could no longer speak any human language but communicated in barks and grunts like a hog. It was possible that the Bergers had drowned her in the swamp before continuing on up towards Tupelo where they had property.

CHAPTER SEVEN

Valse de Cœur Casser

Convinced of their kidnapping and assault upon Colinda Dovero, of their responsibility for her insanity and possibly her death, Jack Karaquazian was only an hour behind the Bergers on the Trace when they stopped to rest at The Breed Papoose. The mendala tavern just outside Belgrade in Chickasaw Territory was the last before Mississippi jurisdiction started again. It served refreshments as rough and new as its own timbers.

A ramshackle, unpainted shed set off the road in a clearing of slender firs and birches, its only colour was its sign, the crude representation of a baby, black on its right side, white on its left, and wearing Indian feathers. Usually Jack Karaquazian avoided such places, for the stakes were either too low or too high, and a game usually ended in some predictable brutality. Dismounting in the misty woods, Mr Karaquazian took firm control of his fury and slept for a little while before rising and leading his horse to the hitching post. A cold instrument of justice, the Egyptian entered the tavern, a mean, unclean room where even the sawdust on the floor was filthy beyond recognition. His weapon displayed in an obvious threat, he walked slowly up to the mendala-sodden bar and ordered a Fröm.

The two Bergers and their huge sire were drinking at the bar with every sign of relaxed amiability, like creatures content in the knowledge that they had no natural enemies. They were honestly surprised as Jack Karaquazian spoke to them, his voice hardly raised, yet cutting through the other conversations like a Mason knife.

'Ladies are not so damned plentiful in this territory we can afford to give offence to one of them,' Mr Karaquazian had said, his eyes narrowing slightly, his body still as a hawk. 'And as for hitting one or cursing one or having occasion to offer harm to one, or even murdering one, well, gentlemen, that looks pretty crazy to me. Or if it isn't craziness, then it's dumb cowardice. And there's nobody in this here tavern thinks a whole lot of a coward, I believe. And even less, I'd guess, of three damned cowards.'

At this scarcely disguised challenge, the majority of The Breed Papoose's customers turned into discreet shadows until only Mr Karaquazian, in his dusty silks and linen, and the Bergers, still in their travelling kaftans, their round Ugandan faces bright with sweat, were left confronting one another along the line of the plank bar. Mr Karaquazian made no movement until the Bergers fixed upon a variety of impulsive actions.

The Egyptian did not draw as Japh Berger ran for the darkness of the backdoor convenience, neither did his hand begin to move as Ach Berger flung himself towards the cover of an overturned bench. It was only as Pa Ox, still mildly puzzled, pulled up the huge Vickers 9 on its swivel holster that Mr Karaquazian's right hand moved with superhuman speed to draw and level the delicate silver stem of a pre-rip Sony, cauterising the older Berger's gun-hand and causing his terrible weapon to crash upon stained, warped boards – to slice away the bench around the shivering Ach, who pulled back withering fingers with a yelp, and to send a slender beam of lilac carcinogens to ensure that Japh would never again take quite the same pleasure in his private pursuits. Then the gambler had replaced the Sony in its holster and signalled, with a certain embarrassment, for a drink.

From the darkness, Ach Berger said: 'Can I go now, mister?'

Without turning, Karaquazian raised his voice a fraction. 'I hope in future you'll pay attention to better advice than your Pa's, boy.' He looked directly into the face of the wounded Ox who turned, holding the already healing stump of his wrist, to make for the door, leaving the Vickers and the four parts of his hand in the sawdust.

'I never would have thought that Sony was anything but a woman's weapon,' said the barkeep admiringly.

'Oh, you can be sure of that.' Jack Karaquazian lifted a glass in cryptic salute.

CHAPTER EIGHT

Les Flammes d'Enfer

It had been perhaps a month later, still in the Territory, that Mr Karaquazian had met a man who had seen the Bergers with the mad woman in Aberdeen a week before Jack Karaquazian had caught up with them.

The man told Mr Karaquazian that Ox Berger had paid for the woman's board at a hotel in Aberdeen. Berger had made sure a doctor was found and a woman hired to look after her 'until her folks came looking for her'. The man had spoken, in quiet wonder, of her utter madness, the exquisite beauty of her face, the peculiar cast of her eyes.

'Ox told me she had looked the same since they'd found her, wading waist-deep in the swamp.' From Aberdeen, he heard, she had been taken back to New Auschwitz by Van Beek's people. In Memphis, Mr Karaquazian learned she had gone North. He settled in Memphis for a while, perhaps hoping she would return and seek him out.

He was in a state of profound shock.

Jack Karaquazian refused to discuss or publicly affirm any religion. His faith in God did not permit it. He believed that when faith became religion it inevitably turned into politics. He was firmly determined to have as little to do with politics as possible. In general conversation he was prepared to admit that politics provided excellent distraction and consolation to those who needed them, but such comfort was usually bought at too high a price. Privately, he held a quiet certainty in the manifest power of Good and Evil. The former he personified simply as the Deity; the latter he called the Old Hunter, and imagined this creature stalking the world in search of souls. He had always congratulated himself on the skill with which he avoided the Old Hunter's traps and enticements, but now he understood that he had been made to betray himself through what he valued most: his honour. He was disgusted and astonished at how his most treasured virtues had destroyed his self-esteem and robbed him of everything but his uncommon luck at cards.

She did not write. Eventually, he took the *Etoile* down to Baton Rouge and from there rode the omnus towards the coast, by way of McComb and Wiggins. It was easy to find Biloxi. The sky was a fury of purple and black for thirty miles around, but above the Fault was a patch of perfect pale blue, there since the destruction began. Even as continua collided and became merely elemental, you could always find the Terminal Café, flickering in and out of a thousand subtly altering realities, pulsing, expanding, contracting, pushing unlikely angles through the after-images of its own shadows, making unique each outline of each ordinary piece of furniture and equipment, and yet never fully affected by that furious vortex above which the solar system bobbed, as it were, like a cork at the centre of the mælstrom. They were not entirely invulnerable to the effects of chaos, that pit of non-consciousness. There were the hot-spots, the time-shifts, the perceptual problems, the energy drains, the odd geographies. Heavy snow had fallen over the Delta one winter, a general cooling, a coruscation, while the following summer, most agreed, was perfectly normal. And yet there remained always that sense of borrowed time. She had seen the winter as an omen for the future. 'We have no right to survive this catastrophe,' she had said. 'Yet we must try, surely.' He had recognised a faith as strong as his own.

She spoke one night of the Nation of Angels and of worlds ruled by all that was best and wisest, Law and Chaos balanced and harmonious. 'You must learn to find harmony, Jack,' she said.

'I believe I have it.' He had responded seriously, without a hint of irony. 'I believe I have conquered what is dishonourable or base within me.'

'It is not conquest I mean,' she said. 'There is a jackal in you, ma joli. That jackal is a symbol of all that you believe, the noblest of your instincts, and it is your greatest aid to survival. Don't listen to the jackal, darling. You must listen only to your heart . . .'

He had heard the singing rhythms of her words, almost swooning in the seductive music of them, the thrilling delight of the sound alone. The meaning came vaguely to him, but he guessed it to be some reciprocated sentiment that would be modified by morning light.

'One day, Jack, you will have to leave the beast behind.'

Boudreaux Ramsadeen brought in a new band, electrok addicts from somewhere in Tennessee where they had found a hot-spot and brained in until it went dry. They had been famous in those half-remembered years before the Fault, and they played with extraordinary vigour and pleasure, so that Boudreaux's strange, limping dance took on in-creasingly complex figures and his partners, thrilled at the brute's exquisite grace and gentleness, threw their bodies into rapturous invention, stepping in and out of the zig-zagging after-images, sometimes dancing with twin selves, their heads flung back and the colours of Hell reflected in their duplicated eyes. And Boudreaux cried with the joy of it, while Jack Karaquazian, on the raised game floor, where the window looked directly out into the Fault, took no notice. Here, at this favourite flat game, his fingers playing a ten-dimensional pseudo-universe like an old familiar deck, the Egyptian still presented his back to that voracious Fault. Its colours swirling in a kind of glee, it swallowed galaxies while Mr Karaquazian gave himself to old habits. But he was never unconscious.

Mr Karaquazian remained in the limbo of the Terminal Café. Up in Memphis, he heard, bloody rivalries and broken treaties would inevitably end in the Confederacy's absolute collapse, unless some sort of alliance was made with the reluctant Free States. Either way, wars must begin. Colinda Dovero's vision of the future had been clearer than most of the oracles.

Mr Karaquazian had left Egypt because of civil war. Now he refused to move on or even discuss the situation. He kept his back to the Fault because he had come to believe it was the antithesis of God, a manifestation of the Old Hunter. Yet, unlike most of his fellow gamblers, he still hoped for some chance of reconciliation with his Deity. His faith had grown more painful but was not diminished by his constant outrage at his own obscene arrogance, which had led him to ruin innocent men. Yet something of that arrogance remained, and he believed he would not find any reconciliation until he had rid himself of it. He knew of no way to confront and redeem his action. To seek out the Bergers, to offer them his remorse, would merely compound his crime, shift the moral burden and, what was more, further insult them. He remembered the mild astonishment in Ox's eyes. At last he understood the man's expression as Ox sought to defend himself against one whom he guessed must be a psychopath-blood looking for a coup.

Sam Oakenhurst wondered, in the words of a new song he had heard, if they were not 'killing time for eternity'. Maybe, one by one, they would get bored enough with the game and stroll casually down into the mouth of Hell, to suffer whatever punishment, pleasure or annihilation was their fate. But Mr Karaquazian became impatient with this, and Sam apologised. 'I'm growing sentimental, I guess.'

Mr Oakenhurst and Brother Ignatius had borrowed two of his systems for the big Texas game. They had acted out of good will, attempting to re-involve him in the things which had once pleased him. Mr Oakenhurst had told of an illegal acoustic school in New Orleans. Only a few people still had those old cruel skills. 'Why don't you meet me down there, Jack, when I get back from Texas?'

'They're treacherous dudes, those machinoix – outlaws or otherwise.'
'What's the difference, Jack? It'll make a change for you.'

When he had first entered the American interior, Jack Karaquazian found a familiar world in which all the details were alien. The bird cries were exotic. The greens of the live oaks and the pecans, the magnolias, elms and black walnuts were subtly awry. The smells were too simple and then too complex. The animals were primitive in some species, highly evolved in others. The olive trees were actually mesquite, the blackberries had the bite of loganberries, the ibis were twice the size, while certain crows were vivid crimson or royal blue.

Even in Africa, even in the Revered City, the Red City of Marrakech, whose mountains were glazed with silver, whose palms were the most elegant in all Islam, whose palaces and mosques rivalled those of Egypt or Istamboul – even there the world had not seemed so thoroughly familiar or so utterly strange. It was unlike any Christian or Islamic world he had ever experienced; yet a peculiar combination of them both.

It had not taken Jack Karaquazian long to adapt to the easier, more formal, manners of the Americans. Americans had a reverence, he perceived, for archetypes and were slow to change. He was glad of this respite from the hurry and machismo of the Mediterranean cities, where politics had grown almost unbelievably volatile, never stabilising long enough for an idea to be tested, but must ultimately simplify under longed-for dictatorship: the popular will over there was now a fascist will. The class struggle was already lost for the likes of himself. His class, the aristocratic gambling adepts, had dreamed itself out of power. When the civil war came he had had no choice but to sail to New Orleans and take professional passage aboard a Mississippi steamboat, prepared to lose a fair percentage of his savings upon a study of the particular game played in those parts. He had learned quickly and brought such a strange new perspective to his games that for a while he could do nothing but win, until they began to study him and then, at last, he was playing with equals.

Mr Karaquazian did not always win, but he was one of a select number. *Los jugadors*, the master gamblers, tended out of custom to keep company together when not engaged with the tables, and, according to their preference, enjoy a miraculous kind of sexual congress in which their skills and experience were delightfully engaged. There was much to be said, he had decided, for such customs.

The culture suited him, though he had a distaste for whites which was hard to overcome. Many of these Americans treated their whites almost as friends. It seemed to him a dishonest relationship, perversely sentimental at best. But it was not his business to judge his hosts and he was glad that the majority rarely judged him. He had a talent for adaptability, on certain levels. All he required were the fundamental mathematics of the game, then he could enjoy playing. In his distant way, Jack Karaquazian relished profoundly all life's experiences.

Mr Karaquazian was blessed with what his mentor had once described as a holy curiosity. He was also lucky that he had arrived in the region at a time when it was prosperous, liberal, ruled by an aristocratic intelligentsia which had a tradition of social conscience, enabling it usually to hold that important balance of power which kept society vital. But as rapidly as had happened in Spain, their paternalism had eventually decayed and lost power to a petite bourgeoisie which, in the first waves of its conquest, was violently anti-intellectual and which all but destroyed the old intellectual tradition. Then, having gained wealth, this new power began to cultivate the manners and traditions of its defeated rivals, until in no time at all the old aristocracy was returned to power. When this sudden upheaval had first occurred, Jack Karaquazian and his friends saw their skills devalued, imitated in crude forms in a million arcades, as simplified and as vulgar as such imitations always are, until, on another turn of the wheel, back the traditional standards came again and Mr Karaquazian and his kind were heroes, able to re-establish all their old privileges. So familiar was this cycle that, when their luck changed again, Jack Karaquazian and the others took almost no notice, but withdrew to weather the phenomenon.

That was when the colour-greedy power barons had been talked into a crank experiment, designed to bore into the very soul of the universe, the deepest core of inexhaustible energy, and live forever free on the proceeds of their profits. With a great deal of swagger and smart authoritative language, the engineers set up equipment to put their slick theory into practice.

And with alarming speed they had created the Biloxi Fault which, when it did not seem to be doing harm to this particular loop in the great web of time and space, drew tourists of every kind until Boudreaux Ramsadeen saw a business opportunity and, having imagination only for music and catering, went up the line to Meridian and bought the Terminal Café and Hotel, bringing it back in three parts on the monstrous flatbeds designed to move boats and homes across America. The massive gauges of the trains, the vast power of her steamers, enabled him to obey such whims. He thought the title of the place would bring him luck. It brought him luck, and music, and the legendary gamblers. After a while the power ran out everywhere, except in Biloxi. Some subtle change had occurred which altered the nature of electricity and made power sources difficult to find and unfamiliar in appearance.

It would have seemed that the adepts, mostly deprived of their complex electronics, would cease to play their games. But the adepts, flexible of mind, bit by bit discovered and invented unimaginable substitutes for their electronics that conjured the same rich variety of invention, the same spiritual, intellectual mathematical and emotional levels of play, with the use of touch and minute variations of sound to create communicable codes. It was an astonishing act of disciplined imagination on their part. Their skills and their brains adapted within a matter of years, evolving in ways which, any scientist would insist, must take millennia.

Faced with such profound changes in the nature of things, Jack Karaquazian had had no choice but to continue acting upon his habitual assumptions. He played his hands and proceeded with his games as he had done since a youth amongst the great teachers of Alexandria and Marrakech. There, they had never doubted that God was a God of love and justice, of equity and logic; yet they taught him how to give himself up to Chaos, to the laws of chance, to play those complex electronic games in which whole universes, species and nations were created, sometimes down to the most ordinary individual, and then manipulated in a game which sometimes took decades of subjective time, yet only a few minutes of the real time used by the mukhamirim, the jugadors, the master gamblers of the Holy Order of Akmaten, who stood against and together with all the other great gambling guilds. These were games of such complexity and subtle creativity, using the most exquisitely delicate electronics (or more recently pseudo-electronics) to create realities whose responsibilities and mathematics sometimes terrified even the most experienced of gamblers. It was not for nothing that they debated at the schools and in their gathering places the moral assumptions and burdens of those who followed their calling. Were they, themselves, no more than the creation of some other intelligence's momentary whim?

Sometimes Jack Karaquazian would walk away from a game and go to an abandoned cabin about a mile inland, on one of the old bayous. Sitting on the porch and enjoying the peace of the Mississippi evening he might consider how the Egyptians had conquered nature so thoroughly that in the end they had poisoned the very source of their existence, the Nile. Jack Karaquazian would give himself up to the music of the birds, the rhythms of the grasshoppers, the insects and reptiles which man's hand might never now eradicate.

The adepts frequently discussed amongst themselves whether the reality they created in their games was any different from the reality they experienced. Were they themselves mere counters in some game played amongst the angels? Or had they also created the angels?

They made worlds, universes, and then set events in motion which depended upon the actions of billions of pseudo-individuals.

Did those individuals possess souls? Some thought so. Mr Karaquazian did not. He created histories which were challenged by rival histories from the other players. The winner was the adept whose reality withstood all assaults upon it, every test, random or calculated, the other gamblers could marshal against them.

But was there a place where their games continued to be played out beyond their control, beyond their very imagining? A place of Chaos? Mr Karaquazian's metaphysics and maths were more practical and applied directly to his trade. He had no use for such unprovable speculation.

After playing a few more hands on the edge of eternity, Mr Karaquazian joined Mr Oakenhurst in New Orleans. Brother Ignatius was gone, taken out in some freak pi-jump on the way home, his horse with him. Mr Karaquazian discovered the machinoix to be players more interested in remorseful nostalgia and the pain than the game itself. It had been ugly money, but easy, and their fellow players, far from resenting losses, grew steadily more friendly, courting the jugadors' company between games, offering to display their most intimate scarifications.

Jack Karaquazian had wondered, chiefly because of the terror he sensed resonating between them, if the machinoix might allow him a means of salvation, if only through some petty martyrdom. He had nothing but a dim notion of conventional theologies, but the machinoix spoke often of journeying into the shadowlands, by which he eventually realised they meant an afterlife. It was one of their fundamental beliefs. Swearing he was not addicted, Sam Oakenhurst was able, amiably, to accept their strangeness and continue to win their guineas, but Mr Karaquazian became nervous, not finding the dangers in any way stimulating.

When his luck had turned, Mr Karaquazian had been secretly relieved. He had remained in the city only to honour his commitment to his partner. He felt it might be time to try the Trace again. He felt she might be calling him.

CHAPTER NINE

Louisiana Two-step

'The world was always a mysterious dream to me,' she had told him. 'But now it is an incomprehensible nightmare. Was it like this for those Jews do you think?'

'Which Jews?' He had never had much interest in anthropology.

She had continued speaking, probably to herself, as she stood on the balcony of the hotel in Gatlinburg and watched the aftershocks of some passing skirmish billow over the horizon: 'Those folk, those Anglo-Saxons, had no special comfort in dying. Not for them the zealotry of the Viking or the Moor. They paraded their iron and their horses and they made compacts with those they conquered or who threatened them. They offered a return to a Roman Golden Age, a notion of universal justice. And they gradually prevailed until chaos was driven into darkness and ancient memory. Even the Normans could not reverse what the Anglo-Saxons achieved. But with that achievement, Jack, also vanished a certain wild vivacity. What the Christians came to call "pagan".' She had sighed and kissed his hands, looking away at the flickering ginger moon. 'Do you long for those times, Jack? That pagan dream?'

Mr Karaquazian thought it astonishing that anyone had managed to create a kind of order out of ungovernable chaos. And that, though he would never say so, was his reason for believing in God and also, because logic would have it, the Old Hunter. 'Total consciousness must, I suppose, suggest total anti-consciousness – and all that lies between.'

She told him then of her own belief. If the Fault were manifest Evil, then somewhere there must be an equivalent manifestation of Good. She loved life with a positive relish, which he enjoyed vicariously and which in turn restored to him sensibilities long since atrophied.

When he left the steamboat at Greenville, Mr Karaquazian bought himself a sturdy riding horse and made his way steadily up the Trace, determined to admire and relish the beauty of it, as if for the first time. Once again, many of the trees had already dropped their leaves.

Through their skeletons, a faint pink-gold wash in the pearly sky showed the position of the sun. Against this cold, soft light, the details of the trees were emphasised, giving each twig a character of its own. Jack Karaquazian kept his mind on these wonders and pleasures, moving day by day towards McClellan and the silver cypress swamp, the gold Stains. In the sharp, new air he felt a strength that he had not known, even before his act of infamy. Perhaps it was a hint of redemption. Of his several previous attempts to return, he had no clear recollections; but this time, though he anticipated forgetfulness, as it were, he was more confident of his momentum. In his proud heart, his sinner's heart, he saw Colinda Dovero as the means of his salvation. She alone would give him a choice which might redeem him in his eyes, if not in God's. She was still his luck. She would be back at her Stains, he thought, maybe working her claim, a rich machine-baron herself by now and unsettled by his arrival; but once united, he knew they could be parted only by an act of uncalled-for courage, perhaps something like a martyrdom. He felt she was offering him, at last, a destiny.

Mr Karaquazian rode up on the red-gold Trace, between the tall, dense trees of the Mississippi woods, crossing the Broken and New rivers, following the joyfully foaming Pearl for a while until he was in Chocktaw country, where he paid his toll in piles noires to an unsmiling Indian who had not seen, he said, a good horse in a long time. He spoke of an outrage, an automobile which had come by a few days ago, driven by a woman with auburn hair. He pointed. The deep tyre tracks were still visible. Mr Karaquazian began to follow them, guessing that Colinda Dovero had left them for him. At what enormous cost? It seemed she must already be tapping the Stains. Such power would be worth almost anything when war eventually came. He could feel the disintegration in the air. Soon these people would be mirroring the metaphysical destruction by falling upon and devouring their fellows. Yet, through their self-betrayal, he thought, Colinda Dovero might survive and even prosper, at least for a while.

He arrived in McClellan expecting to find change, enrichment from the colour strike. But the town remained the pleasant, unaltered place he had known, her maze of old railroad tracks crossing and recrossing at dozens of intersections, from the pre-Biloxi days when the meat plants had made her rich, her people friendly and easy, her whites respectful yet dignified.

Jack Karaquazian spent the night at the Henry Clay Hotel and was disappointed to find no one in the tidy little main street (now a far cry from its glory) who had heard of activity out around the streams. Only a fool, he was told, would go into that cypress swamp at any time of year, least of all during a true season. Consoling himself with the faint hope that she might have kept her workings a secret, Mr Karaquazian rented himself a pirogue, gave an eager kiddikin a guinea to take care of his horse, and set off into the streams, needing no map, no memory – merely his will and the unreasoning certainty that she was drawing him to her.

CHAPTER TEN

Sugar Bee

'I had been dying all my life, Jack,' she had said. 'I decided I wanted to live. I'm giving it my best shot. If we are here as the result of an accident, let us take advantage of that!'

The swamp fog obscured all detail. There was the sharp sound of the water as he paddled the pirogue; the rustle of a wing, a muffled rush, a faint shadow moving amongst the trunks. Jack Karaquazian began to wonder if he were not in limbo, moving from one matrix to another. Would those outlines remain the outlines of trees and vines? Would they crystallise, perhaps, or become massive cliffs of basalt and obsidian? There was sometimes a clue in the nature of the echoes. He whistled a snatch of 'Grand Mamou'. The old dance tune helped his spirits. He believed he must still be in the same reality.

'Human love, Jack, is our only weapon against chaos. And yet, consistently, we reject its responsibilities in favour of some more abstract and therefore less effective notion.'

Suddenly, through the agitated grey, as if in confirmation of his instinct, a dozen ibises winged low beneath the branches of the cypresses and cedars, as silvery as bass, so that Mr Karaquazian in his scarlet travelling cloak felt an intruder on all that exquisite paleness.

When at last the sun began to wash across the west and the mist was touched with the subtle colours of the tea-rose, warming and dissipating to reveal the tawny browns and dark greens it had been hiding, he grew more certain that this time, inevitably, he and Colinda Dovero must reunite. He was half prepared to see the baroque brass and diamonds of the legendary Prosers, milking the Stains for his sweetheart's security, but only herons disturbed the covering of leaves upon the water; only ducks and Perpetua geese shouted and bickered into the cold air, the rapid flutter of their wings bearing eerie resemblance to a mechanish engine. The cypress swamp was avoided by men, was genuinely timeless, perhaps the only place on earth completely unaffected by the Biloxi error.

Why would such changelessness be feared?

Or had fundamental change already occurred? Something too complex and delicate for the human brain to comprehend, just as it could not really accept the experience of more than one matrix. Jack Karaquazian, contented by the swamp's familiarity, did not wish to challenge its character. Instead, he drew further strength from it so that when, close to twilight, he saw the apparently ramshackle cabin, its blackened logs and planks two storeys high, riveted together by old salt and grit cans that still advertised the virtues of their ancient brands, and perched low in the fork of two great silvery cypress branches overhanging the water and the smallest of the Stains, he knew at once that she had never truly left her claim; that in some way she had always been here, waiting for him.

For a few seconds, Jack Karaquazian allowed himself the anguish of regret and self-accusation, then he threw back his cloak, cupped his hands around his mouth, and with his white breath pouring into the air, called out:

'Colinda!'

And from within her fortress, her nest, she replied:

'Jack.'

She was leaning out over the verandah of woven branches, her almond eyes the colour of honey, bright with tears and hope; an understanding that this time, perhaps for the first time, he had actually made it back to her. He was no longer a ghost. When she spoke to him, however, her language was incomprehensible; seemingly a cacophony, without melody or sense. Terrible yelps and groans burst out of her perfect lips. He could scarcely bear to listen. *Is this*, he wondered, *how we first perceive the language of angels?*

The creosoted timbers lay in odd marriage to the pale branches which cradled them. Flitting with urgent joy, from verandah to branch and from branch to makeshift ladder, she was a tawny spirit.

Naked, yet unaffected by the evening chill, she reached the landing she had made. The planks, firmly moored by four oddly plaited ropes tied into the branches, rolled and bounced under her tiny bare feet.

'Jack, my *pauvre hobo!*' It was as if she could only remember the language through snatches of song, as a child does. '*Ma pauvre pierrot.*' She smiled in delight.

He stepped from the pirogue to the landing. They embraced, scarlet engulfing dark gold. It was the resolution he had so often prayed for; but without redemption. For now it was even clearer to him that the mistake he had made at The Breed Papoose had never been an honest one. He also knew that she need never discover this; and what was left of the hypocrite in him called to him to forget the past as irredeemable. And when she sensed his tension, a hesitation, she asked in halting speech if he had brought bad news, if he no longer loved her, if he faltered. She had waited for him a long time, she said, relinquishing all she had gained so that she might be united with him, to take him with her, to show him what she had discovered in the Stain.

She drew him up to her cabin. It looked as if it had been here for centuries. It seemed in places to have grown into or from the living tree. Inside it was full of magpie luxury – plush and brass and gold-plated candelabra, mirrors and crystals and flowing muralos. There was a little power from the Stains, she said, but not much. She had brought everything in the car long ago. She took him on to the verandah and, through the semi-darkness, pointed out the burgundy carcass of an antique Oldsmobile.

'I thought . . .' But he was unable either to express the emotion he felt or to comprehend the sickening temporal shifts which had almost separated them forever. It was as if dream and reality had at last resolved, but at the wrong moment. 'Some men took you to Aberdeen.'

'They were kind.' Her speech was still thick.

'So I understand.'

'But mistaken. I had returned to find you. I went into the Stain while you were gone. When I tried to seek you out, I had forgotten how to speak or wear clothes. I got back here easily. It's never hard for me.'

'Very hard for me.' He embraced her again, kissed her.

'This is what I longed for.' She studied his dark green eyes, his smooth brown skin, the contours of his face, his disciplined body. 'Waiting in this place has not been easy, with the world so close. But I came back for you, Jack. I believe the Stain is not a sign of colour but a kind of counter-effect to the Fault. It leads into a cosmos of wonderful stability. Not stasis, they say, but with a slower rate of entropy. What they once called a lower chaos factor, when I studied physics. I met a woman whom I think we would call "the Rose" in our language. She is half-human, half-flower, like all her race. And she was my mentor as she could be yours. And we could have children, Jack. It's an extraordinary adventure. So many ways of learning to see and so much time for it. Time for consideration, time to create justice. Here, Jack, all the time is going. You know that.' She sensed some unexpected resistance in him. She touched his cheek. 'Jack, we are on the edge of chaos here. We must eventually be consumed by what we created. But we also created a way out. What you always talked about. What you yearned for. You know.'

'Yes, I know.' Perhaps she was really describing Heaven. He made an awkward gesture. 'Through there?' He indicated, in the gathering darkness, the pale wash of the nearest Stain.

'The big one only.' She became enthusiastic, her uncertainties fading before the vividness of her remembered experience. 'We have responsibilities. We have duties there. But they are performed naturally, clearly from self-interest. There's understanding and charity there, Jack. The logic is what you used to talk about. What you thought you had dreamed. Where chance no longer rules unchecked. It's a heavenly place, Jack. The Rose will accept us both. She'll guide us. We can go there now, if you like. You must want to go, *mon cheri, mon cheri*.' But now, as she looked at him, at the way he stood, at the way he stared, unblinking, down into the swamp, she hesitated. She took his hand and gripped it. 'You want to go. It isn't boring, Jack. It's as real as here. But they have a future, a precedent. We have neither.'

'I would like to find such a place.' He checked the spasm in his chest and was apologetic. 'But I might not be ready, *ma fancy*.'

She held tight to his gambler's hand, wondering if she had misjudged its strength. 'You would rather spend your last days at a table in the Terminal Café, waiting for the inevitable moment of oblivion?'

'I would rather journey with you,' he said, 'to Paradise or anywhere you wished, Colinda. But Paradise will accept you, *ma honey*. Perhaps I have not yet earned my place there.'

She preferred to believe he joked with her. 'We will leave it until the morning.' She stroked his blue-black hair, believing him too tired to think. 'There is no such thing as earning. It's always luck, Jack. It was luck we found the Stains. It's luck that brought us together. Brought us our love. Our love brought us back together. It is a long, valuable life they offer us, *mon papillon*. Full of hope and peace. Take your chance, Jack. As you always did.'

He shook his head. 'But some of us, my love, have earning natures. I made a foolish play. I am ashamed.'

'No regrets, Jack. You can leave it all behind. This is luck. Our luck. What is it in you, Jack, this new misery?' She imagined another woman.

He could not tell her. He wanted the night with her. He wanted a memory. And her own passion for him conquered her curiosity, her trepidation, yet there was a desperate quality to her lovemaking which neither she nor he had ever wished to sense again. Addressing this, she was optimistic: 'This will all go once we enter the Stain. Doesn't it seem like heaven, Jack?'

'Near enough,' he admitted. A part of him, a bitter part of him, wished that he had never made this journey, that he had never left the game behind; for the game, even at its most dangerous, was better than this scarcely bearable pain. 'Oh, my heart!'

For the rest of the night he savoured every second of his torment, and yet in the morning he knew that he was not by this means to gain release from his pride. It seemed that his self-esteem, his stern wall against the truth, crumbled in unison with the world's collapse; he saw for himself nothing but an eternity of anguished regret.

'Come.' She moved towards sadness as she led him down through the branches and the timbers to his own pirogue. She refused to believe she had waited only for this.

He let her row them out into the pastel brightness of the lagoon until they floated above the big gold Stain, peering through that purity of colour as if they might actually glimpse the paradise she had described.

'Your clothes will go away.' She was as gentle as a Louisiana April. 'You needn't worry about that.'

She slipped over the side and, with a peculiar lifting motion, moved under the membrane to hang against the density of the gold, smiling up to him to demonstrate that there was nothing to fear, as beautiful as she could ever be, as perfect as the colour. And then she had re-emerged in the shallow water, amongst the lilies and the weeds and the sodden leaves. 'Come, Jack. You must not hurt me further, sweetheart. We will go now. But if you stay I shall not return.' Horrified by what she understood as his cowardice, she fell back against the Stain, staring up at the grey-silver branches of the big trees, watching the morning sun touch the rising mist, refusing to look at Jack Karaquazian while he wept for his failures, for his inability to seize this moment, for all his shame, his unforgotten dreams; at his unguessable loss.

She spoke from the water. 'It wasn't anything that happened to me there that turned me crazy. It was the journey here did that. It's sane down there, Jack.'

'No place for a gambler, then,' he said, and laughed suddenly. 'What is this compensatory Heaven? What proof is there that it is real? The only reason for its existence appears to be a moral one!'

'It's a balance,' she said. 'Nature offers balances.'

'That was always a human illusion. Look at Biloxi. There's the reality. I'm not ready.'

'This isn't worthy of you, Jack.' She was frightened now, perhaps doubting everything.

'I'm not your Jack,' he told her. 'Not any longer. I can't come yet. You go on, *ma cherie*. I'll join you if I can. I'll follow you. But not yet.'

She put her fingers on the edge of the boat. She spoke with soft urgency. 'It's hard for me, Jack. I love you. You're growing old here.' She reached up her arms, the silver water falling upon his clothes, as if to drag him with her. She gripped his long fingers. It was his hands, she had said, that had first attracted her. 'You're growing old here, Jack.'

'Not old enough.' He pulled away. He began to cough. He lost control of the spasm. Suddenly drops of his blood mingled with the water, fell upon the Stain. She cupped some in her hand and then, as if carrying a treasure, she slipped back into the colour, folding herself down until she had merged with it entirely.

By the time he had recovered himself, there was only a voice, an unintelligible shriek, a rapidly fading bellow, as if she had made one last plea for him to follow.

'And not man enough either, I guess.' He had watched the rest of his blood until it mingled invisibly with the water.

'Mon ange.'

CHAPTER ELEVEN

Pourquoi m'Aimes-tu Pas?

He remained in her tree-cabin above the Stain for as long as the food she had stored lasted. She had prepared the place so that he might wait for her if she were absent. He forced himself to live there, praying that through this particular agony he might confront and perhaps even find a means of lifting his burden. But pain was not enough. He began to suspect that pain was not even worth pursuing.

More than once he returned to the big Stain and sat in the pirogue, looking down, trying to find some excuse, some rationale which would allow him this chance of paradise. But he could not. All he had left to him was a partial truth. He felt that if he lost that, he lost all hope of grace. Eventually he abandoned the cabin and the colour and made his way up the Trace to Nashville, where he played an endless succession of reckless games until at last, as fighting broke out in the streets between rival guilds of musician-assassins, he managed to get on a military train to Memphis before the worst of the devastation. At the Van Beek Hotel in Memphis, he bathed and smoked a cigar and, through familiar luxuries, sought to evade the memories of the colour swamp. He took the *Etoile* down to Natchez, well ahead of the holocaust, and then there was nowhere to go but the Terminal Café, where he could sit and watch Boudreaux Ramsadeen perform his idiosyncratic measures on the dance floor, his women partners flocking like delicate birds about a graceful bull. As their little feet stepped in and around the uncertain outlines of an infinite number of walls, floors, ceilings and roofs, expertly holding their metaphysical balance even as they grinned and whooped to the remorseless melodies of the fiddles, accordion and tambourines, Jack Karaquazian would come to sense that only when he lost interest in his own damaged self-esteem would he begin to know hope of release.

Then, unexpectedly, like a visitation, Ox Berger, a prosthesis better than the original on his arm, sought Mr Karaquazian out at the main table and stood looking at him across the flat board, its dimensions roiling, shimmering and cross-flashing within the depths of its singular machinery, and said, with calm respect, 'I believe you owe me a game, sir.'

Jack Karaquazian looked as if a coughing fit would take control of him, but he straightened up, his eyes and muscles sharply delineated against a paling skin, and said with courtesy, almost with warmth, 'I believe I do, sir.'

They agreed on a boyhood favourite: 'Desdemona's Luck'. The object was to arrive inevitably at a sequence of events in which, through the recreation of history from the age of the Prophet, with particular emphasis on Venetian society at the appropriate time, Desdemona is inevitably and inadvertently responsible for the death of Othello and the reformation and conversion to Islam of Iago. A game with a fundamentally simple result, the subtleties of its moves and the complexities of its sub-sets were famous. The object must be achieved elegantly and surprisingly, offering no clue to rival players as to the means. Novices trained on the short forms and learned to translate a relatively small number of human emotions and ambitions into the logical language of their choice. The requisite societies were created, together with individuals and the relevant sub-plots, then translated into symbolic form, to be retranslated at the last moments of the game. These forms had to be understood and countered with rival mathematics to block attempts at producing the endgame and to produce one's own. One thoughtless simplification of the mathematics, and the game was lost.

Ox Berger opened with a classic Mandelbrot gambit.

For the following days they played the long forms, sign for sign, commitment to commitment, formula for formula; the great classic flat-game schemes, the logic and counter-logic of a ten-dimensional matrix, rivalrous metaphysics, a quasi-infinity held in a metre-long box in which they dabbled minds and fingers and ordered the fate of millions, claimed responsibility for the creation, the maintenance, and the sacrifice of whole semi-real races and civilisations, not to mention individuals, some of whom formed cryptic dependencies on an actuality they would never directly enjoy. And Ox Berger played with grace, with irony and skill which, lacking the experience and recklessness of Jack Karaquazian's style, could not in the end win, but showed the mettle of the player.

As he wove his famous 'Faust' web, which only Colinda had ever been able to identify and counter, Jack Karaquazian developed a dawning respect for the big farmer who had chosen never to exploit a talent as great as the gambler's own. And in sharing this with his opponent, Ox Berger achieved a profound act of forgiveness, for he released Mr Karaquazian from his burden of self-disgust and let him imagine, instead, the actual character of the man he had wronged and so understand the true nature of his sin. Jack Karaquazian was able to confront and repent, in dignified humility, his lie for what it had truly been.

When the game was over (by mutual concession) the two men stood together on the edge of the Fault, watching the riotous death of universes, and Mr Karaquazian wondered now if all he lacked was courage, if perhaps the only way back to her was by way of the chaos which seduced him with its mighty and elaborate violence. But then, as he stared into that university of dissolution, he knew that in losing his pride he had not, after all, lost his soul, and just as he knew that pride would never earn him the right to paradise, so, he judged, there was no road to Heaven by way of Hell. And he thanked Ox Berger for his game and his charity. Now he planned, when he was ready, to make a final try at the Trace, though he could not be sure that his will alone, without hers, would be sufficient to get him through a second time. Even should he succeed, he would have to find a way through the Stain without her guidance. Mr Karaquazian shook hands with his opponent. By providing this peculiar intimacy, this significant respect, Ox Berger had done Mr Karaquazian the favour not only of forgiving him, but of helping him to forgive himself.

The gambler wished the map of the Stain were his to pass on, but he knew that it had to be sought for and only then would the lucky ones find it. As for Ox Berger, he had satisfied his own conscience and required nothing else of Jack Karaquazian. 'When you take your journey, sir, I hope you find the strength to sustain yourself.'

'Thanks to you, sir,' says Jack Karaquazian.

The olive intensity of his features framed by the threatening madness of the Biloxi Fault, its vast walls of seething colour rising and falling, the Egyptian plays with anyone, black, white, red or yellow, who wants his kind of game. And the wilder he plays, the more he wins. Clever as a jackal, he lets his slender hands, his woman's hands, weave and flow within the ten dimensions of his favourite flat game, and he is always happy to raise the psychic stakes. Yet there is no despair in him.

Only his familiar agony remains, the old pain of frustrated love, sharper than ever, for now he understands how he failed Colinda Dovero and how he wounded her. And he knows that she will never again seek him out at the Terminal Café.

'You're looking better, Jack.' Sam Oakenhurst has recovered from the machinoix's torments. 'Your old self.'

Jack Karaquazian deals seven hands of poker. In his skin is the reflection of a million dying cultures given up to the pit long before their time; in his green eyes is a new kind of courtesy. Coolly amiable in his silk and linen, his raven hair straight to his shoulders, his back firmly set against the howling triumph of Satan, he is content in the speculation that, for a few of his fellow souls at least, there may be some chance of paradise.

'I'm feeling it, Sam,' he says.

Corsairs of the
Second Ether

Warwick Colvin Jnr.

NOTE: This serial can be read now
or at any time the reader feels ready.

THE STORY SO FAR:

In common with most of the others who explore the Second Ether, CAPTAIN WILHELMINA ROBERTA BEGG and the crew of the *Now The Clouds Have Meaning* are searching for Ko-O-Ko, the legendary Lost Universe, said to be the single naturally habitable location of its kind in the whole of the bizarre space-time continuum, itself the sole level of the multiverse so far discovered which is not wholly inimical to humankind. 'Humes' have divided the multiverse into a number of planes or branches – or perhaps facets of a near-infinite prism – calling our own division the First Ether and those with which we most frequently intersect the Second Ether, Third Ether and so on. Thus far we have found *only* the Second Ether responsive to our logic and therefore navigable (though legends abound of captains like AYESHA VON ABDUL, who found a means of sailing through the Third and Nineteenth facets to discover Paradise and determine that it should never be corrupted by the crazed sinonauts who roam the burst fractals and twisted reality folds of the Initial Circuits, forever bathed in a spectrum of unimaginable and unreproducible light). Alone, Captain Billy-Bob Begg has tested the million roads, one by one, and imprinted herself with a map of the multiverse only she will ever be able to read. She is the greatest of the so-called Chaos Engineers who, using the principles of *self-similarity*, pilot their peculiar craft up and down the scales. They call this process 'folding', a kind of blossoming movement which enables their ships to progress in a series of 'folds' in which they 'lock scale' with a number of proscribed multiversal levels. 'Actually,' as PROFESSOR POP, Captain Billy-Bob's deputy, explains, 'we are dissipating and concentrating mass in ratio to size and so on – we can go "up" scale or "down" scale. And if we "up" scale for two hundred and five calibrations or "folds", we reach, if we're lucky, the wonder of the Second Ether.'

Opposed to the CHAOS ENGINEERS is the dominant culture known as the SINGULARITY which is bent on 'taming' the Second Ether and conquering Ko-O-Ko, the Lost Universe. The Singularity has discovered a method of Hard Warping which allows its ships to 'drop' through the multifaceted planes of the multiverse and emerge, if *they* are lucky, in the Second Ether. It is believed by some that the power of the Singularity to put its stamp on Chaos is so considerable that the Second Ether in some odd way scales herself to its laws. Rather than adapting, as do other travellers, to the sometimes whimsical conditions of Chaos, the Singularity imposes its own reality. The only power great enough to challenge the natural order of Creation, the Singularity is, in the eyes of most intelligences, the personification of pure Evil, an instrument of the ORIGINAL INSECT, while OLD

REG, first Voice of the Singularity, is Satan incarnate. As both groups of humes continue to search for Ko-O-Ko, the Lost Universe, this great clash of philosophies is fought largely within the relative stillness of the Second Ether, that quasi-infinity of pearly rainbows, millennia of light years long, and curtains of violent, jewellish colour rising like sudden walls ahead or behind.

The slogan of the wild-eyed Chaos Engineers, who cruise the Second Ether for adventure, curiosity and massive profit, is 'Ride With The Tide', while the Voice of their opponents bellows forever that 'The Singularity Must Hold: One Refuses To Fold'. So clever are these mad creatures, arrogant enough to defy the fundamental logic of the multiverse, that they have built themselves a kind of false universe in which to dwell. Enclosed within a vast, stabilised crystal of carbon woven to infinite strength and able to resist the combined power of the multiverse, the Singularity is not merely defiant, it is determined to triumph. To it, Chaos is anathema, threatening the ultimate, destruction of all humes. Each individual unit of the Singularity sees it as its duty to aid in the conquest of Chaos. Yet, equally, the multiverse – chaotic and swift to adapt to any threat – shifts, multiplies and modifies so rapidly that the status quo can never entirely be broken, though sometimes the balance might tilt first to the Singularity, next to Chaos, so radically that it might seem that one had conquered at last, yet it is never so. The two philosophies will war for eternity or else be reconciled. Reconciliation is ever the hope of the Chaos Engineers but the idea is utterly loathsome to all units of the Singularity.

While the bleak metaphysics of the Singularity, never better represen-ted than in the person of her bravest Ether-traveller CAPTAIN HORACE QUELCH and his ship *The Linear Bee*, permits only Victory, Chaos, rich with choice and tolerance, accepts and respects all philosophies, perceiving co-dependent variety to represent the 'true' nature of the multiverse. The Chaos Engineers – that great family of freebooters, normally only connected through their communications systems – have noted a step-up in the Singularity's impositions – while areas of the Second Ether are being colonised. The search for Ko-O-Ko, the Lost Universe, has become more intense. During their mutual adventuring in the infamous Field of Saffron, Captain Billy-Bob learns, via Captain Quelch, that the Singularity has begun to fall away from our gravity – ripping horribly through the layers of the multiverse, pulled either by some other force or by its own unnatural weight, they cannot tell. The fact is, as Captain Quelch admits, it has become crucial for the Singularity to colonise and dominate the Second Ether. During an enforced sojourn upon Earth, core world of the Singularity, young MANDY BEGG learns that Captain Quelch and his supporters are fighting a new tendency amongst their own kind – for the

Lure of Isolation is very strong amongst their doubters, while the ethic of the pure Singularity is Victory or Noble Death! Captain Quelch still represents the dominant faction which demands the total conquest of the Second Ether. Against these powerful centralists, Captain Billy-Bob Begg and her crew of crazed solipsippers, high on super-distilled carbons and a craving for curious experience, swear loyalty to the Great Mood, whom they worship, and pledge themselves to the freeing of the Second Ether from these 'unnatural and perhaps cancerous intrusions'.

Escaping at last from the quasi-universe the Singularity calls *The Statement of Truth*, Captain Begg and her 'buckobusters' are unable to stop the process as their ship, *Now The Clouds Have Meaning*, goes into rogue fold – scaling up towards infinity and a kind of death – though to these brave souls that is no more than a welcome reunion with the Great Mood itself.

Meanwhile the *I Don't Want To Go To Chelsea* and the *Plum Blossom Local*, captained by RAIDER MILES of the Gulf Star and MY CHIN TOLLY respectively, have emerged safely into home scale above the main Martian scaling station which had held entry until twilight, when Mars is a little more hospitable to Chaos Engineers not used to the stomach-turning bleakness of raw singularity, only to find, contrary to all agreements, that *The Statement of Truth* quasi-universe has engulfed the First Ether and has ordered their capture. In attempting to back-fold without co-ordinates, the *Plum Blossom Local* irredeemably dissipates while the *I Don't Want To Go To Chelsea* escapes with the evil news that the Chaos Engineers have lost a Chief Attractor. The struggle has ceased to be wholly metaphysical!

Meanwhile, within the groaning, sweating innards of a Singularity ship, *Definitely Sagittarius*, LITTLE RUPOLDO BEGG has crucial news of Old Reg's next plan. Creeping through corridors whose every massive seam appears perpetually at bursting point, listening to the deep distress of the bulging bulkheads, Little Rupoldo searches for a communications room while the ship's captain, MRS KRONA, concentrates on her relationship with DUNGO, her partner. 'I am weary,' she says, 'of your dismissive mockery.' The ship falls relentlessly towards the Second Ether. At last Little Rupoldo comes upon a communications room, only to discover Mrs Krona dead on the floor, the rejected posy of ratweed and lady's fist telling the whole story. On the screen another tragedy manifests itself.

Now read on . . .

CHAPTER NINETY-SEVEN

Scale Sickness Again!

As universes, scale upon scale, formed and re-formed, dissolved and re-dissolved behind them at a rate suggesting they must ride this fractal up to infinity before they could ever hope to be reunited entirely with the Great Mood, the famous Chaos Engineers gathered around their revered Main Type.

'Fargone,' said Captain Billy-Bob, a tear or two in her distant eye, 'it's a flat tyre, I think, sweethearts.'

But they were swift to deny it. 'You were always a lucky captain until now, dear Main Type,' said Pegarm Pete with an awkward slap to her shoulder (all obsidian carapace, these days), 'and you're still lucky, we'd opine!' He had long since ceased to question the intensity of his love for the captain.

'Fast agreement!' The other Engineers rushed to confirm.

'This is how we learn *if* the music goes round and round *or*, if not, where it comes out!' Corporal Organ raised her granitesque head in a massive gesture of joy, her wide, wide eyes steady on the front screens and the great shimmering black and yellow globe appearing just at the moment it disappeared, at the next scale, behind them.

But 'Oh,' despaired Captain Billy-Bob, 'this looks unending. My instruments! Have you spoken to them recently?' There was no cheering her. She insisted she had failed them.

CHAPTER NINETY-EIGHT

Codependency Theories Aft

Captain Quelch had yet to experience the exhilaration he had expected to accompany his old enemy's defeat. Yet defeated she surely was. And with the greatest of the Chaos Captains blown to infinity, there would be no stopping the Singularity's holy expansion into the Second Ether. If, like Lucifer, he was prepared to defy the Definitive Logic of the Universe, he expected the securities of Lucifer – a knowledge that the Singularity was IN CONTROL forever. Now the others must think twice before pursuing their perverse adventures and celebrations.

'He died of a busted bladder, marm. I told him not to take that last bottle of port. He wasn't exactly a gent, if you know what I mean. *Ubi beni, ibi patria*, ha, ha!' Captain Quelch swung in his brochette, his eyes full of mild and faraway madness. 'As they say.'

MaMa Singh ignored him. Her anxieties involved, as always, the efficiency of their weapons. 'My crown is a crown of feathers formed from the rarest of lights, the scarcest of spectra. I am trapped in the power of a devastatingly unimaginative political and academic Orthodoxy. And *because* the Orthodoxy is so powerful, no one in it will listen to the truth. They deny the very Orthodoxy they worship. There is no addressing them! I need new weapons, but will they listen?'

Each Unit is lost in their own-ness, always a noted paradox of the Singularity, which It, of course, furiously denies. Paradox is an obscenity which cannot be permitted to any part of Its philosophy.

She sights aggressively at the sweating metal of their walls, the in-bulging plates, the re-folded rivets threatening to burst into the control room, the greenish steams and vivid gases. And everything moaning and squealing in protest at this unnatural means of progress through the multiverse, drowning the boombooms of Afrikaner Tom's dreadful discosound as the pale disciplinarian boogies in the comforting shadows of the big oven. He at any rate is relishing some sort of victory.

'Captain Quelch!' comes the voice of Roman Romanescu from the bowels. 'Has anyone seen my antique manual? There's something boiling on the E-line and I don't think we have the shot to suit it.'

'Exactly my point!' squeaks MaMa Singh, astonished by this confirmation and glad as a bell. 'I have an ally, I know, in you, dear Roman Romanescu. We need new weapons!'

She shudders her bronze and copper quills, her pleasure out of all proportion, and it is as well Roman Romanescu has no vision on this, only the delicious sounds; so he wets his lips. 'More and better weapons, good MaMa. Smarter, warmer, kinder weapons, marmy boombooms, suck, suck.'

She is cackling with delight, taking some control of herself as she hurries to the down-shaft.

'What sublime decision! What maley ways!'

CHAPTER NINETY-NINE

Phoneouts At Last!

'They have lost their main fractal and are off-scale. They claim this is under control but Old Reg knows it means the destruction of their whole quasi-universe and the First Ether with it. Perhaps,' added Little Rupoldo into the dolly's mouth, 'the Second Ether, also. I heard this from the First Voice Itself, Old Reg.'

He was at last communicating with Wire Ears of the *Pulsing Blood*, in a crisis of her own involving Kaprikorn Schultz, the half-hume, Banker to the Homeboy Tong, who had attached himself freehand to their outer folds and made it impossible to drive anywhere but down-scale. Even at the dolly Little Rupoldo could hear some of the mathematical obscenities yelled by the half-hume through the ship's marrow, not to mention the other stuff. Little Rupoldo felt bile rise in his throat.

'I are half-skimling, half-hume – comb my spikes. Lick my tips. Taste my flumes . . . Eff farping parentheses zed equals zed farping squared and squeezed like a wopper!'

Everyone had heard how Kaprikorn Schultz, the half-hume, had singlehandedly climbed half a thousand scale fields and countless textures to spread his brilliant blue wings against the hazy serenity of the Second Ether. He disdained all protection and lived entirely upon his own twisted wits, using skimling techniques to hitch rides through the scale fields. Or so he claimed. For no hume had ever set eyes on a skimling.

'SOS the Chaos Engineers! SOS the Chaos Engineers!' The cry went out across the Ether as Wire Ears sought help for herself and Little Rupoldo.

'We're heading out to where the ether's silvery white, lit by the light of countless galaxies, the farping very hub of the multiverse and the best and most dangerous, believe me juicy pals, gateway directly into the Second Ether. I know! I am Kaprikorn Schultz, Banker to the Homeboy Tong! There is no more respectable voice in the multiverse! Didn't you ever wonder what mainlining was really all about, pretty bodies, pretty bodies? Oh, we'll tittle together in that fold-away-from-fold! I am it and I am more than it.'

'SOS THE CHAOS ENGINEERS!'

'What's to do, Cap'n?' demands the ever-cheerful Sto-Loon. 'More grub for the hands, is it, or must we be lean for what's a-comin'?' He smells a storm as fast as any other old Second Ether hand and he squares up reluctantly, for he believes he's too old to weather another like the last one. 'Hell's glaciers, there's a slim chance yet for the Balance to correct herself, but I can't seem to get back on to the crew. Are they frozen already?'

Captain Otherly says this was nowt to a Yorkshireman when he was a boy, in the days when Buggery Otherly ran things like a kakatron. But is he rattled? Maybe, thinks the youngest hand, Monkeygirl, who hopes she will soon settle down. It is her duty to keep the gardens at peace. She had done so for gone fifteen years and the *Pulsing Blood* had always responded well to her harmonies, but with the onset of Kaprikorn Schultz, the gardens were showing signs of restlessness and it would take little to send these vibrations throughout every fold of the great, old-fashioned Bloomer as she made her stately way up the scales.

Captain Otherly readily admits he let his ship fall towards a mirage attractor, the most feared phenomenon in the multiverse, and that only this put them in the power of the legendary Banker (whose greatest strength lay in his pseudo-reality weaving). Yet he was damned if he wasn't going to try to get out of the trap in spite of the filth pouring everywhere into the ship from Schultz's barkbox.

'Try them with some more Mozart and if that doesn't work give 'em the last of your Messiaen,' he tells Monkeygirl. 'It's all we can do now.' And he throws himself deep into his brass legs, a brave smile on his big face as the massive prosthenics hiss into union with his flesh.

'Captain Otherly's ready to give that half-hume bastard a run for his money!'

(To be continued)

Part 2

Free States

Thou still unravish'd bride of quietness!
  Thou foster-child of Silence and slow Time,
Sylvan historian, who canst thus express
  A flowery tale more sweetly than our rhyme;
What leaf-fringed legend haunts about thy shape
  Of deities or mortals, or of both,
In Tempe or the dales of Arcady?
  What men or gods are these? What maidens loth?
What mad pursuit? What struggle to escape?
  What pipes and timbrels? What wild ecstasy?

Keats, *Ode on a Grecian Urn*

CHAPTER ONE

Llamada de las Lejanas Colinos

'You're looking better, Jack.' Sam Oakenhurst has recovered from the machinoix torments. 'Your old self.'

Jack Karaquazian deals seven hands of poker. His skin reflects a million cultures given up to the pit long before their time; his green eyes reveal a new kind of courtesy. Coolly amiable in his black silk and white linen, his raven hair hanging straight to his shoulders, his stoic back set firmly against that howling triumph of Satan, he is content.

'I'm feeling it, Sam,' he says.

Mr Oakenhurst picks up his bags. All around him the outlines and shadows of the Terminal Café shift and caper while Boudreaux Ramsadeen practises a graceful figure with Fathima Panosh, the tiny dancer currently favoured by the Terminal's regulars who come to hear real old-fashioned zee and witness the purity of the high games. Only at Biloxi, where the Fault yells and ululates, can enough colour be tapped to push new limits. And for those who lose too much, there is always the Fault itself, restless and demanding, greedy for energy and offering, perhaps, an ultimate wisdom.

'On your way, Sam?' Jack Karaquazian sits back from his game. His fellow players know him as Al-Q'arcen. Many are shades, men and women ready to risk everything to win nothing but the company of their peers. They have the dedicated, ascetic appearance of a strict order. The Egyptian smiles, a kindly jackal.

'On my way.' Mr Oakenhurst sets his broad-brimmed pale Panama, dusts at his fine cord travelling coat, his buckskin riding boots, his blue cotton shirt and breeches. 'So long.'

'Nobody knows what's going on up there now,' says Boudreaux Ramsadeen from the dance floor, his brutish face clouded with concern. 'They say it's nothing but vapour up in the Frees. Turned all to steam, mon ami. You be better off staying here.'

Mr Oakenhurst lifts a hand to show appreciation. 'Estrella errante, vieux pard. You know how it is.'

But Boudreaux Ramsadeen will never know how that is. He brought his café on the train from Meridian to take advantage of the tourist trade. Now he and the Terminal are married to the Fault until the end of time.

(We are all echoes of some lost original, she would tell him. But we are not diminished by this knowledge. Rather, we are strengthened by it.)

CHAPTER TWO

Se Eres Rapido Dispara

When Mr Sam Oakenhurst took off for the Free States he had it in mind
to heal the memories and still the cravings of his last six seasons at the
mercy of New Orleans' infamous machinoix, whose final act of trust
was to introduce him to the long, complex mutilation rituals they
believed to be the guarantee of continuing existence in the afterlife.

Ending his stopover at the Terminal Café, where Jack Karaquazian
still wagered the highest psychic stakes from what had become known as
the Dead King's Chair, framed by the whirling patterns of Chaos
ceaselessly forming and reforming, Mr Oakenhurst was at last able to
ask his old friend how things went for him.

'Not so bad now, Sam, pretty good.'

'You're looking better, Jack. Your old self.'

'I'm feeling it, Sam.' The Egyptian's fingers moved abstractly around the
dormant dimensions of a waiting flat game. The other players were
unhappy with this interruption but unwilling to risk Mr Karaquazian's
displeasure. He toyed with the dealing plates, himself anxious to begin the
next hand. And his eyes looked upon so many simultaneous memories.

Before he walked to the door, Sam Oakenhurst said: 'Come up there
with me, Jack. They got some famous spots in Texas and New Mexico.
They're finding colour every day in California. Don't you want to visit
San Diego while she's still burning? They say you can walk in and out of
those flames and feel no heat at all. There's people living in the city,
completely unhurt. That's something to see, Jack.'

Mr Karaquazian wished his friend luck in the West but reckoned he
had a game or two left to play at the Terminal. In answer to Sam
Oakenhurst's glare of honest surprise, he recalled the old intimacy of
their friendship and said, in words only Mr Oakenhurst heard, 'I can't
go yet.' He was not ready to speak of his reasons but if his friend were to
ride by again at a later time he promised he would tell what happened
after they had parted in the Quarter, when the Egyptian had gone
upriver on the Memphis boat.

Mr Oakenhurst tipped his hat to his friend and went to collect his horse from Boudreaux's makeshift stables.

(Have you heard of the conspiracy of the Just? she would ask. Once the likes of us become aware of this conspiracy, we are part of it. There's no choice in the matter. We are, after all, what we are. And you and I, Sam, are of the Just. You don't have to like it.)

In common with most who chanced their luck at the gambling trade, Sam Oakenhurst had left his will with the Terminal's neanderthal proprietor. He took the one good horse he had ridden in on, the sound of Boudreaux's zee-band still marking the rhythm of his actions.

He was almost in the ruins of Picayune before the tunes had left his head. On his way up, he had seen two corpses, a man's and a woman's, half buried in the shallow of the beach; behind them was the distant wail of the Biloxi Fault, howling and groaning and never still.

Picayune was the closest Mr Oakenhurst would let himself get to New Orleans. He had no fear of machinoix enmity. They regarded him as one of their own. But he had found a dark new greed in himself which tempted him back to their stronghold.

Mr Oakenhurst did not feel in any way free of the hunger until he entered the twilight fern forests beyond Nouveaux Iberie. His horse followed a broad, dry road, well-marked and patrolled by the local security committees who guaranteed the safety of all who lived there, or passed through peacefully, and swift death to any aggressor.

Sam Oakenhurst's plan was to take the road right up past Sulphur. He stopped for the night at a lodging house just above Lake Charles where he was met by the landlord, a veteran of the First Psychic War, his skin scaled with pale unstable colour. Lieutenant Twist said that the road now ran up to De Quincey, beside the Texas Waters, a recent series of connected lochs populated by islands stretching almost as far as Houston and nearly up to Dallas. There were a few paddle-wheelers carrying passengers through the lakes but they were infrequent and unscheduled. Mr Oakenhurst was advised to return to New Orleans and buy a ticket on a coastal schooner to Corpus Cristi. 'There's a weekly run. Calmest and safest waters in the world now. They say all the ocean around the Fault's like that.'

Mr Oakenhurst said he had decided to take his chances. 'In that case,' said Lieutenant Twist, 'you would be better trying for De Quincey and hope a boat or a colour rider come in soon.' He shook his head in admiration of what he understood to be Mr Oakenhurst's bravery. '*Somebody help me out of Louisiana, help me get to Houston town!*' Whistling, he led Sam Oakenhurst to the choice individual accommodation behind the old main building.

Making himself presentable Mr Oakenhurst went, after half-an-hour, to join an acoustic game in a corner of the hotel's bar, but after a few minutes he grew bored and deliberately let the other players win back most of their stakes, keeping five piles noires as payment for his time. On his way to his cabin he saw a movement high up where the fronds were thinnest and the moonlight was turned to pale jade – some sort of owl. Its eyes were huge and full of hope.

Sam Oakenhurst's chamber was clean and well-kept, though the furniture was old and the bedding darned. A useless V cabinet stood in the corner. Converted to hold magazines, it dispensed them in return for a few pennies. The magazines were hand-coloured, crudely stencilled versions of old-time V programmes. Mr Oakenhurst put in the coins and the screen opened to offer him a selection.

They were chiefly magazines detailing the escapades of various unfamiliar heroes and heroines – *The Merchant Venturer, Pearl Peru –* *Captain Billy-Bob Begg's Famous Chaos Engineers – Karl Kapital –* *Professor Pop – Fearless Frank Force – Bullybop – Corporal Pork –* violently coloured attempts to reproduce the interactive video melo-dramas some addicts still enjoyed at the Terminal Café. All the characters seemed engaged in perpetual war between Plurality and Singularity for the domination of a territory (possibly philosophical) called the Second Ether. These unlikely events were represented as fact. The gambler, finding their enigmatic vocabularies and queer storylines too cryptic, replaced them in the dispenser, blew out his lamp and slept, dreaming a familiar dream.

(He had talked to Jack Karaquazian when they were still in New Orleans. He had asked his friend if he would care if he spoke of something that was on his mind.

'Not at all,' the Egyptian had said.

I had this dream, said Sam Oakenhurst. I was standing on this cliff with a pack of dogs and killer blankeys at my back and nothing but rocks and ocean far below and nowhere to go but down when suddenly out of the blue this golden limo pulls up in the air right where I'm standing on the edge and the driver's eye-balling me. She's a beautiful woman, real elegant, and she says, 'Hop in, Sam. Where do you want to go?'

'Where are you going?' I ask.

'Any place you like,' she says.

'Well,' I say, 'I guess in that case I'll stick here and take my chances.'

'Please yourself,' she says and she's ready to start up when I say, 'Hey, what's your name, lady?'

'Luck,' she says, puts the car in gear and vanishes. I turn around and the dogs and the men are gone. What do you make of that, Jack?

'Well,' said Jack Karaquazian after some considerable thought, 'I guess it means that luck is luck. That's all.'

'I guess so,' said Mr Oakenhurst. 'Well, goodnight, Jack.'

Next morning they played a game of 'Joli Jean' before breakfast and talked about going up to the Frees.)

He had the dream again, exactly as before, but this time he stepped into the limo.

(Jack Karaquazian kept a room above the main casino of the Terminal Café. You could feel the zee coming up through the floor. The room was filled with shadows and flames, ragged holes of verdigris and kidney. 'It's home,' he had said.)

CHAPTER THREE

Erase una Vez en la Oueste

'I had a dream,' says Precious Mary as she moves against Sam Oakenhurst's arm. 'I dreamed I was lying in this field of silver poppies, looking up at the moon. I stretched my arms and legs wide and the Moon Goddess smiled. She had a wonderful round pale face like a Buddha. Is that a Buddhess, Sam? And she came down from the midnight blue and pursed her silver lips and she sucked my pussy, Sam, like nobody but you.' She grins and laughs and slaps at him in his flattered embarrassment.

They had been here at Ambry's for almost a month. Precious Mary was on her way to join a closed order in Laredo. She collected mosquitoes and her little clear envelopes were full of the different types, including the hybrids. Her pride was a great dragon mosquito, rainbow carapace over two inches long, able to drain a small rodent dry of blood in less than a minute. 'They thought it carried A,' she said. 'But now they ain't so sure.'

She had cornrows beaded with tiny precious stones – emeralds, rubies, sapphires, diamonds – large green eyes, a refined Watutsi face. She wore a silk shift which swam on the blackness of her skin like milk over marble. Her head, she said, was worth a million guineas, but her body was priceless. She lived, like everybody in De Quincey, at Ambry's big Gothic timber house just by the jetty which jutted over the flat sheen of a lake revealed below the surrounding yellow and black mist. The lake was never entirely at rest. Shapes just under the surface were mysterious and alarming. Every once in a while a tiny spot of colour would float by. 'They find big ones out there and milk them,' she said. 'There's nothing but rigs once you get twenty kays over that horizon.' She pointed to the north. 'Do you believe in God, Sam?'

Mr Oakenhurst admitted that he did.

'You believe in a just God, Sam?'

'I believe God deals you a fair hand.' He became thoughtful. 'What you do with it after that is a question of luck and judgement both. And luck is what other people are making of *their* hands. It's a complicated game, it seems to me, Mary. Only a few of us are willing to accept the kind of odds it offers. But what else can you do? This is reality, I think. I look at the game. I work out the odds. And then I decide if I want to play or not. I hope I'm doing no more or less with my mind and time than God expects of me.'

'You're crazy,' she said.

That was the last Sam Oakenhurst and Precious Mary ever spoke of religion.

In Milton he had lost his horse to a tall pile broker from Natchez who had proved to be so much better than the table's other partners that Mr Oakenhurst suspected him of being a secret professional. But he had played a fair game. The broker let Sam take his place on the coach to De Quincey. That trip to the lake shore had been Mr Oakenhurst's first real experience of the practical realities of the Free States, where whites were supposed to be his equals. He found it awkward to be travelling in a horse-drawn coach with a black man driving and a white man riding inside. On the seat across from him the 'blanco' showed no similar embarrassment and chatted amiably on the tandem subjects of fluke attractors and the availability of piles noires. Mr Oakenhurst did his best to converse without seeming to condescend, but he was still suffering from a strong desire to stare in wonder at this educated and self-confident whitey much as one would regard a clever circus animal. His name was Peewee Wilson and he had owned property up in Haute Country, he said, until it had popped one morning, all of a piece, and left him 'wiv a weird damned hole coloured like dirty bottly-glass an' radiatin' coldness so damned bad ah'd felt mahse'f chillered to mah soul.' He had moved his wife and kids to his sister in San Diego and was on his way to join them. He had never been to Biloxi ('Ah have not chosered vat pilgrimage, sah, as yet') but was eager to hear Mr Oakenhurst's account of it and the jugador loved to tell a tale.

So the time had passed pleasantly enough between Milton and De Quincey. Peewee informed Mr Oakenhurst about the famous Colossus of Tarzana, one of the wonders of their new world – a huge figure some two hundred feet high and apparently consisting of living flame, which gave off a soft heat filling most observers with a sense of calm and well-being. A tent town had grown around the feet of the Colossus, populated by those who had become hooked on the phenomenon's influence.

(Let us have the body, the machinoix would demand. We need it for our science. Its soul has dissipated. What use is it to you? But Sam Oakenhurst would refuse to give it up. He would take it all the way to the Fault and pitch it in. The machinoix would not be offended. He was of their number. He could do no wrong, save betray another of their own.)

Mr Oakenhurst waded through the shallow mud of the lake shore. There seemed no end to it. At present the flat, troubled liquid reflected nothing, but every so often a shape threatened to break through the surface. The sky had become a solid monochrome grey. Once in a while a long thread of bright scarlet would rise from below the horizon and give the sky a lizard's lick. Mr Oakenhurst ran secret fingers over his most intimate scars. His longing for the terrible satisfactions of the past was like physical hunger. A madness. He prayed for a vessel to rescue him.

Mr Oakenhurst walked through the mud. Sometimes his legs would begin to tremble, threatening to give out completely, and he would panic, turning slowly to look back at Ambry's and the long, dark jetty whose far point penetrated the mist.

'Darling.' Precious Mary led him home on these occasions.

'Darling, Sam.'

Sam Oakenhurst decided that if he stayed another week he would take it as a sign and let New Orleans call him back. He shivered. He was suffering a profound greed. He had made no real decision at all. He glared at the grey water. The sky, he thought, had turned the colour of rotten honey.

CHAPTER FOUR

La Muerte Terrio un Precio

Precious Mary was not impatient to leave. She had discovered an interest in the vegetable garden and, with another woman called Bellpaïs, was planting in the assumption there would be some kind of new season. The garden lay behind the house, where it was most sheltered. Mary complained about the lack of sunlight, the clouds of dust which swam forever out of the north. 'It seems like it's the same clouds keep coming around,' she said. 'Like everything's on repeat.'

'Hope not,' said Sam Oakenhurst, thinking of New Orleans and licking salty lips. As a child he had played his favourite records until the phonograph's machinery had started to show the strain. Gradually the voices grew sluggish and the music became a mixture of whines and groans until finally the records brought only depression, a sense of loss, a distorted memory of harmony and resolution. He sometimes thought the whole world was running down in a series of ever-widening, steadily dissipating circles. 'I cannot believe that one thing cancels out another,' he admitted to Precious Mary.

'It's like a roof.' She looked at the sky. 'Like a cave. We could be underground, Sam. Lying on the innards of the world.'

Across the surface of measureless grey, past the end of their jetty, a couple of spots of colour floated. The spots moved as if with purpose but both Mr Oakenhurst and Precious Mary knew they drifted more or less at random around the perimeter of the lake, carrying with them an assortment of organic flotsam. Bones, feathers, twigs, tiny corpses, made a lattice through which gleamed the dull gold and silver of the colour, blank round eyes staring out from a void. The colour seemed like a magnet to certain vegetable and animal matter. Other material it repulsed violently, not always predictably.

(We are the whole within the whole, Sam. Your ancestors knew that. And we are unique.)

'I reckon Jack Karaquazian struck colour up on the Trace,' mused Sam Oakenhurst. 'But something happened that didn't suit him. What the hell is that, Mary?' He pointed out over the lake. Through the twilight a slow bulky shape was emerging. At first the jugador thought it might be the tapering head of a large whale. Then as it came nearer he realised it was not a living creature at all but a ramshackle vessel, shadowing the shore, a great broad raft about ninety by ninety, on which was built a floating shanty-town, a mélange of dull-coloured shacks, tents, barrels and lean-tos. In the middle of this makeshift fortress stood a substantial wooden keep with a flat roof where other tents and packing-case houses had been erected so that the whole had the appearance of an untidy ziggurat made of animal hides, old tapestries, painted canvases, upholstery and miscellaneous pieces of broken furniture.

Observing what distinguished this floating junkpile, Precious Mary said: 'Ain't that queer, Sam. No metal, not much plastic . . .'

'And there's why.' Sam showed her the dull gleam of colour spilling up from under the raft's edges. 'She's moving on a big spot. She's built to cover it. You saw it. That kind of colour won't take anything much that's non-organic. It's kind of like anti-electricity. They haven't figured any real way of conducting the stuff. It can't be refined or mined. It moves all the time so it's never claimed. I guess those types have found the only use there is for it. Ahoy!'

CHAPTER FIVE

Muchos Gracias, Mon Amour

The idea of being trapped on a raft which would put the Texas Waters between him and New Orleans was immensely attractive to Mr Oakenhurst just then. There was no way of stopping the spot, only of slowing it down with metal lures floated out from the shore on lines. As soon as the goods had been thrown aboard, he jumped from the jetty to the slow-moving deck, shook hands with Captain Roy Ornate, master of *The Whole Hog*, and thanked him for the opportunity to take passage with him. He did not bother to announce his trade.

He had been allowed to carry no arms aboard *The Whole Hog*, no razor, no metal of any kind except alumite, and so glad was he to be on his way that he had accepted the terms, leaving his gold, his piles noires, his slender Nissan 404 and all other metal goods with Precious Mary. She had loaded the raft with so much collateral in the form of fresh provisions that she had put him in excellent credit with Captain Ornate. The bandy-legged, pig-faced upriver rafter had lost his original trade to the Colorado Gap. 'Took the river and half the State with it. You can still see the spray fifty kays away.' He was a cheerful man who apologised for his rules. His methods were the only practical ones for the service he offered, which was, he admitted, not much. 'Still, chances are this spot'll carry us round to Waco and then you're halfway to Phoenix, or wherever it is you're heading, mister. You won't be old when you get there, but I can't guarantee how long it will take . . .

'You won't be bored, either, mister. There's a couple of jugadors in the main saloon glad to make room for another. This is an easy vessel, Mr Oakenhurst, and I hope you'll find her comfortable. She's rough and ready, I'll grant, but we have no power weapons aboard and hardly any violence, for I don't tolerate trouble. Those who make it I punish harshly. We have, as last resort, a duelling field.'

'A man of my own principles, captain,' said Sam Oakenhurst, conscious of the loss of his fancy links. His shirt was heavier on the wrists, the cuffs now decorated with antique Mickey and Minnie Mouse figures his daughter had given him for his twenty-fifth birthday, almost exactly forty-four seasons ago, and which he had never expected to wear in public. Now that the need had arisen he welcomed it. Wearing the links felt like some sort of confirmation. Serdia and Ona had died together on the Hattiesburg Roar, trying to escape an army of half-wild blankeys released by a shiver from the nearby pens. Unable to resist the chance, he had been in Memphis, running a powered game for Van Beek and his fellow barons who were rich enough to command all the necessary colour.

Mr Oakenhurst had never known the detailed circumstances of his wife's and daughter's deaths and time had put that particular pain behind him. He sensed some link between his grief and his self-destructive taste for machinoix torments. He had never, after all, thought to blame himself for the deaths. They had wanted to remain in Hattiesburg where everyone agreed it felt pretty stable. For a while he had wished he could die too, that was all. Maybe he felt guilty for not following them.

He let Roy Ornate's little kiddikin lead him up the rickety outside staircase to his room. The urge to live was very strong in Sam Oakenhurst but not quite equalled by his hunger for pain which he only barely governed these days. With relief he watched the jetty and the Ambry House slip away behind, but the look he turned on the kiddikin, even as the skinny white kid glowingly accepted a whole guinea bill for his trouble, was one of vicious and unjust hatred.

Sam Oakenhurst came out of his room and looked down at the smoking stoves and basket fires of a floating slum. Roy Ornate was waiting at the bottom of the stairs. 'Why do these people live in such squalor, captain, when on land they have a better chance of dignity?' Were they all power addicts?

Captain Ornate cleared his throat. 'If you're trying to fathom the pilgrims, Mr Oakenhurst, you'll have poor luck. If you're dining this evening, I'd welcome your company.' He spoke with no great enthusiasm. Sam Oakenhurst guessed that Roy Ornate was not really his own man and suspected that there was another power aboard *The Whole Hog* greater than the master.

CHAPTER SIX

Mi Buena Suerte

The saloon was on the lower floor, a big, bright room full of old-fashioned wooden Kenya-lamps and carved candelabra. On the other side of the archway, in relative gloom, five people were absorbed in a complex game of 'Hunt the Moth', their eyes golden with concentration as they fanned their acoustic hands with practised pseudo-electronic signals, listening intensely to the subsonics.

(In times like these, when hope fades and our expectations of reality become uncertain, people develop a keen interest in an afterlife, the Rose would say. She would sing to him in a language he did not know until he begged her to translate. '*We are trapped in the glare of their headlights*.')

Elsewhere in the saloon men and women in couples or groups sat together drinking and talking, but taking pains not to disturb the five gamblers as they strove to simulate with a multitude of devices the serial linking, the empathetic convolutions, the exquisite arabesques of the electronic original.

Amongst those chocarreros it was at once evident who was the real power aboard *The Whole Hog*: fat body pulsing, the creature faced and dominated the room. The head, fallen to one side, was hidden by a queerly shaped mask and old dust seemed to fall from its folds. The pale eyes glittered like over-polished diamonds. The top of the player's head was scarred and pitted, as if by fire, and a few tufts of grey-black hair sprouted here and there, while a little multicoloured bead curtain, some bizarre *chadurrah*, hung from the bottom edge of its mask, obscuring the jaw. The only flesh visible was the ruined crown and a pair of large, white hands which also bore the grey scars of fire and sat poised on their tips like obscene tarantulas, pale with menace.

The masked figure was, on its right, flanked by a light-skinned, but otherwise handsome, half-caste woman with greased black ringlets and hard Irish eyes. Her name was Sister Honesty Marvell. She was *persona non grata* at the Terminal, for taking out an amateur in a massive psychic gambit which even broke the high limits Boudreaux Ramsadeen set for the professionals. When he had made her go for good she had sworn she would return and the second Boudreaux saw her would be the second he died.

(*En la playa, amigo*, replied Amos Gallibasta when Sam Oakenhurst found him again and asked how he was. The thin giant had grinned, death's triumph, and snapped his huge fingers. *En la playa terminante, eh? Joli blanc! Joli blanc!* He had no similar desire to return to New Orleans. The very breathing of the word 'machinoix' sent him into uncontrollable fits of vomiting.)

Next to Sister Honesty sat Carly O'Dowd. Mr Oakenhurst also knew her. Mrs O'Dowd sported a man's suit in the Andalusian style and as always bore an air of disdainful self-sufficiency. Her Moorish good looks reminded Mr Oakenhurst of some legendary toreador. He tipped his hat when she looked up but she could not see beyond her strategies. The two players at the other side of the enmascarado were people Sam Oakenhurst recognised, but he could name only one. Popper Hendricks, sagging with the weight of a thousand indulgences, had once been a famous zee star in the days when touring was still possible, when the population was considerably larger and records were still being made. Fifty per cent at least of the white minority had fled north or west after the Fault's effects began to be felt. Even many middle-class people had preferred to go west into the Frees to take their chances on equal terms with the whites, but mostly got caught by the quakes. Hendricks had the sybaritic, bloated look of a heavy oper. The other man, with his huge square head, had the features of an Aztec god. Even his body seemed made of granite. He moved now, slowly. It was as if ten years went by. Mr Oakenhurst found the Aztec disturbing but the masked man at the centre of the game horrified him.

In shape the mask resembled a map of the old US. Each State, cut out of an alumite can, had been soldered to the next. Washington bore the distinctive logo of Folger's Coffee, Texas offered RC Cola and Pennsylvania advertised EXXON. Hanging from the patchwork of pseudo-metal the curtain of heavy beads veiled a suggestion of red, wet lips, skin as burned and scarred as the hands and skull.

Mr Oakenhurst turned his back on the table to order a Fröm from the bartender, a round-faced whitey who proved unduly surly. To be civil Sam Oakenhurst asked, 'What's your name, boy?'

'Burt,' said the whitey curtly. 'You want anything else, mister?'

Mr Oakenhurst kept his own counsel. After all, he could soon be facing much more of this behaviour in the Free States and he had best get used to it. He intended to relax. For the first time since he had left the Terminal he no longer depended upon his own will. Whatever problems he found on the raft, he thought, must seem minor. He was glad there were no power weapons permitted, though he missed the comfort of his Nissan.

From the shadows in the back of the big room came a sudden wheeze, a whine, and an accordion began to play *Pierrot, Pierrot, le monde est fou.* Some of the passengers swayed to the old tune, singing the poet Armangal's sad, ironic words. *Le monde est fou, my carazon d'or. Le monde est fou, el mundo c'est moi!*

A voice from the table, soft and threatening, said: 'Play something else, dear.'

The tune changed almost instantly to 'Two-Step de Bayou Teche' and a few of the couples got up to dance.

The masked man returned his attention to the game.

CHAPTER SEVEN

Desafio

'Mr Minct and me came aboard at Carthage,' said Carly O'Dowd. She referred to the masked man, still at the table. 'Nice to see you, Sam.'

'And you, Carly. How's the game?'

'Worth your time, if you're interested.' She was taking a break and joined Captain Ornate and Mr Oakenhurst at the bar. 'Some rough edges you could smooth out.' She reached for his long right hand and drew it to her mouth. 'Lucky, Sam?' She kissed the tip of his index finger.

'Maybe,' he said. 'I don't know.'

Roy Ornate had grown expansive on his big pipe of ope. His cheeks glowed, his eyes bulged with bonhomie. 'I can think of no better pleasure than swinging your feet over the edge of the Abyss and contemplating the damnation of the entire universe,' he confided. 'Ha, ha, Mr Oakenhurst. You'll do!' His confidences became increasingly mysterious. 'What a thrill, eh? To take the whole horrible vessel to the edge – cargo, crew and passengers – and hang upon the lip of some hellish niagara – every day gambling the same stake against a thousand new disasters – all the devil's winning hands – and every day carry back from the brink – what? Playing dice with God and not a damned thing any of you fellows can do about it. I know the only man good enough to stop this planet going the way of the rest and that's Paul Minct, and he won't do it. I would, but I can't. And that, sir, should permit me a few privileges . . .'

Neither Mr Oakenhurst nor Mrs O'Dowd could follow his reasoning.

'You have a great admiration for this Mr Minct,' said Sam Oakenhurst.

'He's my hero,' admitted Captain Ornate with a confiding gesture.

Now the Aztec Carly O'Dowd had identified as Rodrigo Heat divorced himself from the game and moved heavily over the floor to stand beside an empty chair next to Captain Ornate.

Sam Oakenhurst received the impression that the masked man had sent Heat to him. The Aztec's massive head inclined towards the seat but his eyes were on Carly O'Dowd. 'You have a high price, lady, but that don't scare me.'

Sam Oakenhurst knew only one way of responding to such boorishness and his words were out before he had properly calculated the situation. He said evenly that if Mr Heat pursued that thread of conversation he would be obliged to invite the Aztec outside to the place familiarly known as – and here he looked to Captain Ornate to tell him the name again . . .

'Bloody Glade,' said Roy Ornate, still benign. 'But we discourage its use. This M & E is better than my own.' He was trying a mixture, he said, recommended by Paul Minct. He displayed a garish package: *Meng & Ecker's Brandy Flake.*

'Bloody Glade,' said Mr Oakenhurst, 'and settle the matter alla gentilhombres.'

Whereupon Mr Heat laughed open-mouthed, exuding nutmeg, and asked what was wrong with his conversation.

Understanding, now, that he was being provoked, Sam Oakenhurst could only continue. His honour gave him no choice. 'It demeans a lady,' he explained.

Mr Heat continued to laugh and asked where the lady in question happened to be, which led to a silence falling in the room, since Mr Oakenhurst's principles, if not his courage, were shared by the majority of the floor's diamentes brutos.

'Very well,' said Mr Oakenhurst after a moment. 'I will meet you in the usual circumstances,' and as if he had settled some minor matter he turned back to signal the surly whitey for more drinks and enquire of Carly O'Dowd how her brother was doing in the Border Army. 'Ain't they romantic, Carly? I heard they're winning big new tracts of restabilised up above Kansas.'

'You're a man after my own heart, sir,' suddenly says Captain Ornate, puffing on his churchwarden's. 'Would you care for a dip from my special mixture?' He reached into his coat.

'*Give him my Meng & Ecker's, Captain Ornate.*'

Paul Minct's cruel voice chilled the house into irredeemable silence.

'Give Mr Oakenhurst a dip of my own ope and ask him if, at his convenience, he would come and join me later for a chat. It's rare to meet an equal, these days. One grows so starved of intellectual cut and thrust.'

CHAPTER EIGHT

Gracias Nada Mas

'Caballero and mukhamir you may be, Mr Oakenhurst, of the highest principles and most excellent suba', but Captain Ornate allows no desafio aboard *The Whole Hog* and so your affair must be abandoned until such time you are both ashore. Those are Captain Ornate's rules.' Paul Minct speaks with a certain weariness.

'*Honour* and *blood*, Mr Oakenhurst. Aren't they the last resort of those who yearn for stability and cannot achieve it? But they are no substitute for common law. It is surely a measure of a society's decadence when it reverts to such primitive means to maintain order and self-esteem. I am one of those who still believes the Court to be a more effective guarantee of social stability than the duelling field.'

Sam Oakenhurst murmurs that he does not at heart hold with duelling and all that goes with it, particularly the endless blood-feuding which often results.

'When a custom, sir, ceases to achieve its object, it is no longer a useful virtue but a self-destructive vice. But the human yearning for certainty means we all cling to institutions that no longer function for our benefit, eh? None doubts your integrity or courage, Mr Oakenhurst.'

Sam Oakenhurst understands that he has been tested, that his honour is not at issue. He shrugs the matter off.

They sit together in the snug in the black shadows, a candle burning on the table giving unsteady life to Paul Minct's geographic mask.

Mr Oakenhurst finds himself reading the fragments of words – ELMONTE, OLA, AXWELL HOU, CRISCO, CASTRO, ONT MAID, OHNSONS WAX and others – remembering his childhood when such brands were vital and had complex and casual meaning to everyone. The world's realities changed, he thinks, long before the advent of the Fault. The Fault is perhaps the result of that change, not the cause. He cannot give his entire attention to Paul Minct's words. The man disturbs and fascinates him. He gathers Paul Minct respects him, which is why he has been taken aside like this and not admonished in public, and he is relieved. But he knows he could never trust the enmascarado. Paul Minct could change his mood at a moment's notice and casually kill him. Sam Oakenhurst is close to admitting he made a mistake. He should have found the nerve to stick it out at Ambry's until the stern-wheeler came by. His self-disgust only serves to fuel his discomfort. He wishes the enmascarado would leave him alone, but already guesses Mr Minct plans somehow to use him.

(Paul Minct had been a blankey-chaser in the old days, Carly O'Dowd would say. Mr Minct had gone after bounty boys, always willing to take a dead-or-alive. One day he had crossed the big bridge into Louisiana with six red scalps on his belt, all that was mortal of the Kennedy pack which ran wild for a while up near Texarcana and announced they'd founded a 'white republic'.

Captain Ornate retired. Mrs O'Dowd called for more drinks. 'Paul Minct's a man who gets what or who he wants, one way or another. He was Van Beek's main chaser. He hates whiteys with a passion and would wipe them all out if he could. He loathes them so bad some of us think maybe he's a blankey himself, or anyway a breed, who was fortunate enough to be burned in a fire – like the blankey who went to hell, got burned black and thought he'd gotten to heaven! Loosen up, Sam. Nothing much ever happens on *The Whole Hog*.')

'I was in a bad fire or two in my time, Mr Oakenhurst.' Paul Minct fingers the tufts of hair on his skull. 'You should hear my wife complain. But someone must bring home the bacon. We're the chaps who have to get out there in the world, eh? Nobody will do it for us. We are never allowed nor encouraged to the best. That's the shame of it. We must seek the best for ourselves. It is what drives us, I suspect. Almost secretly. Will you be joining our little pasatiempo? You'd be very welcome.'

When Mr Oakenhurst accepts the veiled order with the same grace with which it is given, one of Paul Minct's unsightly hands reaches into his and welcomes him to the school.

('He told me he had been in and out of the Fault five times. He says he knows secret trails which only he had the courage to discover. It is true that in the main he has no fear.'

'Does he fear anything, Carly?'

'Something. I don't know. Is there a jugador brave enough to find out?')

Paul Minct offers his own pouch: 'A cut above the Brandy Flake. It's M & E's Number Three. They'll try to tell you it's extinct, but they're still making it down in Mexico.'

Against his better judgement, Sam Oakenhurst fills his long-stemmed pipe.

'Señor Heat is an old colleague of mine.' Paul Minct receives the ope again and puts it away. 'Volatile and blunt, as you know, and a little uncouth, but one of the world's great people. He discovered the factory. The last Meng & Eckers is in a place called *Wadi-al-Hara*, the River of Stones, in Arabic. The Indian dialects give it a similar name. Guadalajara, the Spanish say. Mr Heat made his second fortune bringing it back. This stuff's what the old days were about, Mr Oakenhurst. Not much of a vice compared to some we hear of. That's what I remind my wife. She's overly worried. My health. That's women for you, isn't it? My health, as matter of fact, has never been better. But there you are. Now, Mr Oakenhurst, I know your credentials and I must say I'm impressed. How would you like to come in on a small venture I'm organising?'

'Well, sir,' says Sam Oakenhurst. 'I guess it depends on the game.'

'Very good, Mr Oakenhurst. I take your point. This is in the nature of an exploratory expedition. But only the likes of us can even contemplate the kind of adventure I have in mind. Only a trained jugador has the patience, the experience and the gumption for it. And Mrs O'Dowd says you're one of the best. Played evens with Jack Karaquazian.'

'Once,' agrees Sam Oakenhurst.

'Quite enough for me, sir. I'm recruiting, Mr Oakenhurst, a few brave souls. Outstanding individuals who will join an expedition to accompany me into the Biloxi Fault.'

Sam Oakenhurst has a taste for pain but not for death. He resolves to play along with this madman, whose pale unblinking eye awaits his acceptance, but if the time comes he will never go with him. That would be suicide. He will jump off the raft the first moment they sight land and put this fresh lunacy behind him.

He shakes Paul Minct's hand.

CHAPTER NINE

Escudo d'Oro

Mr Sam Oakenhurst did not immediately join the game but claiming weariness retired early and stood on the little landing outside his door taking the ill-smelling air and staring over the dark water. No light escaped the spot on which they rode, but through the dirty cloud a little moonlight fell, making the water sinister with half-seen shapes.

In seeking to avoid the machinoix temptations Mr Oakenhurst had put himself into an equally unwelcome predicament. Paul Minct had a horrible authority and, taken unawares, Sam Oakenhurst had been unable to resist it.

Tomorrow he would test Mr Minct's metal, if he could, in that acoustic game they played, and get some notion of the man's resonances. He had not been manipulated so expertly since he was fourteen. He believed Paul Minct to be a charlatan, probably crazy, perhaps even messianic in some way. Frequently a secret faith, too insane to risk upon the air, fuelled such aggressive solipsism. The man appeared to have the tastes of a Torquemada and the savage appetites of a European warlord. Always a strong hand, thought Mr Oakenhurst. His lies would therefore be complicated and self-convincing. Mr Oakenhurst had lived for months at a time beside the Fault and knew it well. He had seen a woman from Jackson walk in at the semi-permanent section known as The Custard Bowl and disintegrate, bawling for help, as soon as she reached the so-called East Wall, a turbulent tower sometimes emerging within the Bowl, usually coloured deep red and black. On another occasion he had held a rope for Cab Ras, the famous daredevil, as he went in through the glistening organic scarlet of Ketchup Cove. He had vanished. The rope had fallen to the surface as if cut and Ras was gone for good. Everything was consumed by the Biloxi Fault. Was Paul Minct merely reluctant to die alone?

Mr Oakenhurst did not doubt the enmascarado's courage or ferocity, the man's murderous determination, but could not fathom Paul Minct's objectives. Perhaps Mr Minct had actually convinced himself that he could survive the Fault, and others with him. It was not a belief Sam Oakenhurst wished to put to the test. Yet, for all his evident insanity, the man continued to terrify Sam Oakenhurst who wondered if Paul Minct already had his measure, as he did not have Paul Minct's. A game would answer most of his questions. He was no Jack Karaquazian or Colinda Dovero, but he had held his own with the rest.

Most of the lights were now extinguished to conform with Captain Ornate's tough curfew, enforced by a gang of breed blankeys under their own vicious leaders.

The raft rocked a little in the water and a powerful shaft of moonlight broke through full on *The Whole Hog* as if God for a moment had turned his undivided attention on them. A voice came up to him out of the shadows. 'Time for bed, Sam?'

'Good evening, Carly.' Sam Oakenhurst wanted to learn all she knew of Paul Minct. 'I've a bottle of Ackroyd's I know you'll taste.'

Carly O'Dowd had little more real information. She remembered a story that Paul Minct's hatred of whites could be relatively recent, following a fire started by his own relatives from Baton Rouge. But there was a different story, of how Paul Minct had been a member of the Golala sect which understood death by fire to be a guarantee of heaven. She asked Sam if he believed in an afterlife.

'I have a hunch your soul has a home to go to.' That was all Sam Oakenhurst would say on the matter, but when she asked if he thought God dealt everyone a square hand, he shook his head. He had considered that lately, he said, and had to admit God's dealing sometimes seemed a little uneven.

'But I don't think he plays dice, Carly. He plays a hand of poker against the devil and some of us believe it's our job to help him. Some of us even do a little bit about it.' He shrugged.

'Jesus,' said Carly O'Dowd. 'I never heard anyone describe gambling as a moral duty before. Ain't this the end of everything, Sam? Ain't it over for us?'

'Maybe,' said Sam Oakenhurst, 'but I got a feeling it evens out. Like luck, you know.'

Carly O'Dowd took a long pull on the pipe and sipped her winking Ackroyd's.

'*Quid pro quo*,' said Mr Oakenhurst.

'*Allez, los tigres*,' she sang softly. '*Ma bebé sans merci, il est un majo sin comparé. O, bebé, you bon surprise, you darling ease.*'

In the morning she insisted he come to the open window to look over the ragged shanty town, towards the east where the cloud had cleared and red sunlight rose in broad rays from the watery horizon, staining the whole lake a lively ruby. Against this redness a single black outline moved.

'It's coming closer.' Sam Oakenhurst squinted to improve his focus. 'It's a big heron, Carly.' He shivered. He took her slight body to his. 'Bigger.'

It was an aircraft. A beautiful white flying boat with six pairs of wing-mounted roaring engines and whistling airscrews, moving to make a preliminary pass at the water, intending to land. The flying boat was turned a sudden, subtle pink by the sun.

Everyone on the raft was up and out in haste to see the splendid craft. Pilgrims and jugadors all wondered at the wealth it took to squander so much colour upon an antique conceit.

And then, throttling down to a confident thud, the flying boat came to settle, light as a gull, upon the surface. The big engines fell silent. Water lapped at her ivory hull. Almost at once a door above the lower wing opened and a figure stepped out, dragging a small inflatable. The yellow rubber boat blended with the sulphurous waters as black and yellow cloud drew itself around the sun like a cloak. Through the gloom of the new day the figure began to row, calling out in a melodious, ringing voice: 'Ahoy, the raft! Is this *The Whole Hog* and Captain Roy Ornate?'

Just up from his quarters in his Monday whites and weak-kneed with wonderment, Captain Ornate could barely lift his megaphone to utter an unsteady: 'I am Captain Roy Ornate, master of *The Whole Hog*. Be warned that we accept no metal. Who calls the ship?'

This was a formal exchange, as between river captains. The rower replied, 'Mrs Rose von Bek, lately out of Guadalajara with a package for Mr Paul Minct. Is Mr Minct aboard, sir?'

The weight of the curious crowd began to tilt the raft dramatically. The shanty dwellers were set upon by the blankeys, led by a plague-pocked overseer, and beaten back into order. To add to their humiliation they were forced into their windowless dwellings, denied any further part of the miracle.

'Mr Minct is one of our passengers,' agreed Roy Ornate, his own curiosity undisguised. 'What's the nature of your goods, ma'am?'

Before the rower could answer, Paul Minct, massively fat, his body wrapped in lengths of multi-coloured velvet, rolled up to Captain Ornate's side to stand stroking his beaded veil as another might stroke a beard. He took the megaphone from the grateful master and spoke in a wet, amplified soprano. 'So you found me at last. Is that my M & E come up from Mexico, dear?'

Any answer Mrs von Bek might have made was drowned by six

bellowing engines as the flying boat began to taxi out over the endless yellow lake and, with a parting shriek, vanished into the air.

The inflatable came up against embarking-steps thick with mould. A slim, athletic woman stepped aboard, her features disguised by a cowl on her cape which fell in blue-green folds almost to the deck. Maybe a white woman. She had a small oilskin package in her left hand.

By now Mr Oakenhurst and Mrs O'Dowd, fully dressed, stood on the landing listening to the silence returning.

'I'm much obliged, ma'am.' Paul Minct reached for his package. 'One would have to be Scrooge himself to begrudge that extra little bit it takes to get your M & E delivered.' He turned, his mask on one side, as if in apology to Sam Oakenhurst. 'I'll admit it's a terrible extravagance of mine. You should hear my wife on the subject.'

Had he arranged this whole charade merely to demonstrate his power and wealth?

The woman pushed her cowl back to reveal a most wonderful dark golden pink skin, washed with the faintest browns and greens, some kind of sensitive North African features, reminding Mr Oakenhurst of those aquiline Berbers from the deep Maghribi desert. Her auburn hair reflected the colour of her cloak and her lips were a startling scarlet, as if they bled. She was as tall as Sam Oakenhurst. Her extraordinary grace fascinated him. He had never seen movement like it. He found himself staring at her, even as she took Paul Minct's arm and made her way to the main saloon. Her perfume was delicious.

'What would you call that colour skin?' murmured Carly O'Dowd.

CHAPTER TEN

Los Belles du Canada

'I tasted a thousand scales to reach this place.' Mrs von Bek had been joined at her table by Sister Honesty Marvell, Mrs O'Dowd and Rodrigo Heat, but she kept a seat beside her empty and this she now offered to Mr Oakenhurst who bowed, brushed back his tails and wished her good morning as he sat down beside her. He wondered why she seemed familiar. At close quarters the greenish blush of her hands, the pink-gold of her cheeks, had a quality which made all other flesh seem unnatural. He had never before felt such strong emotion in the presence of beauty.

In amused recognition of his admiration, she smiled. Clearly, she was also curious about him. 'You are of the jugadiste persuasion, Mr Oakenhurst?'

'I make a small living from my good fortune, ma'am.' Had he ever felt as he did now, at the centre of a concert while the music achieved some ecstatic moment? Was he looking on the true face of his lady, his luck? Where would she take him? Home?

He realised to his alarm that he was on the verge of weeping.

'Well, Mr Oakenhurst,' Mrs von Bek continued, 'you would know a flat game, I hope, if one turned up for you. And "Granny's Claw"? Is that still played in these parts?'

'Not to my knowledge, ma'am.'

I need an ally, she said in an urgent signal, which marked her as his peer. *Paul Minct is my mortal enemy and will destroy me if he recognises me. Will you help?*

He returned her signal. *At your service, Mrs von Bek.*

No sworn jugador could have refused her. Their mutual code demanded instant compliance. Only in extreme need did one of his kind thus address a peer. But he would have helped her anyway. He was entirely infatuated with her. He began to wonder what other allies, and of what calibre, he might find here. Did fear or some profound sense of loyalty bind Rodrigo Heat to Paul Minct? Carly O'Dowd, given to sudden swings of affection, would be unreliable at best. Roy Ornate was clearly Paul Minct's man. Sister Honesty Marvell might side with them, if only out of an habitual need to destroy potential rivals. Meanwhile, Mr Oakenhurst would have to follow Mrs von Bek's lead until she told him to do otherwise.

Her fingers dropped from the grey-green pearls and coral at her throat while his own hands lost interest in his links. Their secret exchange was for a moment at an end.

It had been seven years – twenty-eight seasons by current reckoning – since Mr Oakenhurst had been in a similar situation and that had been the start of his friendship with Jack Karaquazian. On this occasion, however, the intellectual thrill, the thrill of the big risk, was coupled with an overwhelming desire for the Rose, given extra edge by his own anxious guess that perhaps she was a little attracted to him. Even the chemistry with Serdia, his wife, had not been so strong. The sensation attacked his mind as well as his flesh while the cool part of him, the trained jugador, was taking account of this wonderful return of feelings he had thought lost forever. He considered new odds.

'Do you think it will be long before we reach the Frees, Mr Ornate?' She looked up as the skipper returned with a tray on which stood an oak cafetière and some delicate rosewood cups. 'Here you go, ma'am, here you go. I fixed it myself. You can't trust these blankeys to fix good coffee.' The man was blushing like a rat on a hot-spot, oblivious of the open derision on Rodrigo Heat's old-fashioned head.

Mr Oakenhurst relaxed his body and settled into his chair. Paul Minct would make his entrance at any moment.

'Shall we play?'

Corsairs of the
Second Ether

Warwick Colvin Jnr.

THE STORY SO FAR:

After successfully 'Rhyming the Balance' and at the same time restoring the Singularity to its former power (but no more) CAPTAIN BILLY-BOB and her buckobusters in their ship, *Now The Clouds Have Meaning*, set course into the Second Ether again, for the Mountains of Palest Blue and Deepest White, where they believe the SWIPLING swarm must pass.

In common with most others who explore the Second Ether, Captain Billy-Bob and her crew are searching for Ko-O-Ko, the Lost Universe. In that section of the Second Ether known as Blue and White Mountain Country, where the ships of all four exploring races drift against vast semi-stable masses of curling, frozen lava which float like icebergs, half in and half out of the continua, they await the coming of the swipling swarm. The swipling is a kind of bird capable of flying between the various spheres or planes of the multiverse and said to migrate between the Nineteenth Ether and Ko-O-Ko, the Lost Universe. It is the intention of the various ships waiting 'at anchor' in the Blue and White Mountain Field to track the swipling swarm back to Ko-O-Ko.

There are two rival types of HUMES: THE CHAOS ENGINEERS who delight in all forms of experience and are hugely tolerant of all other logics – and the followers of THE SINGULARITY, which rules the large part of the humes' home continuum and still dreams of imposing full linearity upon what it perceives as the 'unformed' Chaos of the far greater part of the multiverse.

Two other rivals, as indistinguishable to humes as humes are to them: THE SKIPLINGS and THE SKIMLINGS have (or assume) corporeal forms which are not entirely stable. The two races both claim to be descendants of the many different peoples who inhabit their home spheres across a band of continua still inaccessible to hume ships of either persuasion. The humes know little of the skiplings or skimlings while those people seem to have an intimate knowledge of all things hume.

All seek to find the legendary Lost Universe, Ko-O-Ko.

One of the ships lying uneasily in stasis in the Blue and White Mountain Country is Billy-Bob Begg's famous old rival, CAPTAIN HORACE QUELCH, commanding *The Linear Bee*, together with a scratch fleet including *The Straight Arrow*, *The Definite Article*, *The Absolute Truth* and *The Only Way*.

They plan to claim Ko-O-Ko, the Lost Universe, in the name of the Singularity. The other hume ships are all of the Chaos persuasion, a loose confederation of merchant-adventurers, including *Ruby Dances*, *I Don't Want To Go To Chelsea*, *My Memories* and *The Blue Gardenia*.

Many events have led to this moment; many adventures amongst the participants, frequently involving the Singularity's implacable hatred of the Chaos Engineers.

Every afternoon in the Blue and White Mountain Field, Captain Billy-Bob and her ship are forced to leave for a few relative hours – in pursuit of her famous 'hopping legs', stolen by scraplings for their brass, and once to aid Captain Quelch when *The Linear Bee* was holed by a SLIPLING between continua. The sliplings are the so-called 'Corsairs of the Second Ether' (though others call them carrion rats), preying on all continua-travellers at their weakest transitions. Although related to skiplings and skimlings, the sliplings are hated by both. It is on this matter that the First Beast of the Skimlings, RA, has called a conference attended by the Skipling First Beast RO-RO, by Captain Quelch and Captain Billy-Bob Begg, elected main types for their respective camps. Now read on . . .

CHAPTER TWO HUNDRED AND FOUR

Skipling Courtesies

'There is no war between skiplings and skimlings – we simply refuse to communicate. Yet both races shun sliplings, for they are unnatural and immoral carrion. These so-called Corsairs are no better than a cancer which should be treated or eradicated. It is your duty, Captain Begg, to support us in this policy.'

So spoke Sterling the Skipling, Second Beast of *The Power in Contemplation*, with all authority, for he was equal to the extraordinarily beautiful Chief Engine. He illustrated his words with broad movements of his fiery arms. 'We travel—' swing, undulation, 'sometimes we go with you—' fold, unfold, 'sometimes with the heavy ones. We fall with them, Captain Quelch, ho, ho! And this is very thrilling for us and also dangerous.' What might have been mammalian eyes moved behind the lattice of insectoid prisms – two sets of eyes at least, perhaps more (Captain Quelch had heard a claim for seven or eight layers of specialised eyes and five graduated sets of independently articulated teeth). 'Nar! To your equations – Nar! Nar! Nar! We *are* humes. We are humes, *too*. We are *everything*.'

'What are you NOT?' demanded the sneering, unconvinced Quelch. A pause.

'We are not God.'

'They are ANGELS!' says Romantic Minnie. 'Warring angels. War in Heaven!' She pointed to the R. 'Look. It's proof.' But her theory is disliked. Corporal Organ takes her aside.

'It is your duty not to warn the living but to comfort the dead and the soon-to-be-dead. You have no function to alarm, no need. Yours is a gentler destiny, if sadder.'

Suddenly they looked back at the aft screens and the black and yellow sphere, once the hiding place of *The Linear Bee*, but for now Quelch's whereabouts were known to them.

Or were they?

CHAPTER TWO HUNDRED AND FIVE

Heavy Duties All Round

'Slit my beak!' Kaprikorn Schultz, Banker to the Homeboy Tong, made a fist of his right wing. 'Slime my quills! Farping Z equals z^2 plus farping c. You await your diamond allies, but your Carbon Chief is far, Captain Q, wherever you slip. I cough up your Great Idea, skimpling possers, dirty tips. Skimplings are too discreet about their origins. I could lead the world there.'

'Foolish hume, with your filthy bone! 'Tis no skimpling you address, but a slipling weed. Ach! Insidious creeper. Stamp on it!' His reluctant ally, Big Ball, the skimpling renegade, backs away. He has no defences against sliplings of any size. Kaprikorn Schultz often asks him why one so sickly chose the buckoniring trade, which was nothing, after all, if not strenuous. But all Big Ball would allow was that it was a family calling.

Kaprikorn Schultz does not need to remind him of the fate of his sister merchant-adventuress. He had last made out the deep shadows, black and white, of *The Scarab's Son*, embedded in hard space while the rest of the insect legs and carapace waved in the bitter freedom of the Second Ether. Hers had not been a scale-fault but a problem of misleading pseudo-attractors. Nonetheless, he had thrown up as the significant mathematics clarified on his screen. Those mathematics had, he had known even then, been none other than Kaprikorn Schultz's, for only Schultz lacked all conscience and was a well-known wrecker, an illusionist capable of creating pseudo-attractors almost indistinguishable from the real thing. Yet there was always the slight possibility that Schultz was blameless. *The Scarab's Son* would not, after all, be the first victim to a mirage-attractor.

The strains of Duke Ellington and Jimi Hendrix drifted up from the old gardens and filled Big Ball with comfortable nostalgia, for which he was grateful.

He was convinced that, by throwing in with Kaprikorn Schultz, he had shorted his scale rather badly.

CHAPTER TWO HUNDRED AND SIX

Green Dragon Country

Bibby-Boo Begg sprawls before the R as she attunes herself to the voice. 'Here,' she trills now, 'is the tale according to my understanding and my art, of the Turbulence Bucko-Roos and their raidings in the Second Ether, before the multiverse was tame and music was indistinguishable from matter, in the grand past when forever faded to aft and the easy future forever loomed for'ard, all a single golden moment, a scale apart.'

Dungo the Murderer is poised at the pod, unbeknownst to Bibby-Boo, who has had no education in the classics. Is this innocence? Or ignorance? In the confusion, nobody has thought to educate her. Who is morally to blame for what happens next?

(To be continued)

Part 3

Codes

'The joy and the sorrow the letters bring is all we have left.'

—Woman in Sarajevo
26 January, 1994

CHAPTER ONE

Las Bon Temps Arrivée

'Mr Oakenhurst informs me that you might be willing to come in on our special play, Mrs von Bek.' Paul Minct brushed dust from his mask. One of his pale eyes peered from the ragged hole in the Rocky Mountains where Quaker marked Colorado. It was as if he brushed a tear.

After an exhausting week-long game in which the three of them had emerged equals in all but specific skills and appetites, Paul Minct, Rose von Bek and Sam Oakenhurst believed they had learned almost everything they would ever know about one another. All were prepared, in appropriate circumstances, to risk everything on the flick of a sensor, the turn of a card, an instinctive snap judgement.

Paul Minct's topological half-face glittered in the flamelight and behind his whispering curtain of beads his ruined lips twisted in an involuntary grin, as if flesh remembered pain his mind refused.

Sam Oakenhurst cursed his own quickened blood, the vast emotions he seemed to be riding like a vaquero on a runaway bronc, barely able to haul hard enough on the reins to avoid the worst disasters as they approached.

'I take it you are considering some unusually high stakes, Mr Minct.' Her voice had grown warmer, more musical, like a well-practised instrument. She was all of a piece, thought Sam Oakenhurst admiringly, a perfect disguise. There was, however, no evidence that Paul Minct had been deceived by either of them.

The week's play had left the Rose and Sam Oakenhurst uncertain lovers, but it was of no interest to Paul Minct how they celebrated their alliance. He appeared to be under the impression that a more reckless Rose von Bek had persuaded Mr Oakenhurst to let her join him.

'Here's my say in the matter,' declared Sam Oakenhurst, to open the bidding. 'Your luck and mine, Paul Minct. Even shares. Try it once? Double our luck or double our damnation, eh?'

Sam Oakenhurst knew Mr Minct viewed treachery as a legitimate instrument of policy and that nothing he offered would guarantee Mr

Minct's consistency. But he was hoping to appeal to Paul Minct's gambler's soul, to whet his appetite for melodrama and catch him, if possible, in a twist or two before the main game began. At present it was the only strategy he could pursue without much chance of detection.

'You'll stake your life on this, Mr Oakenhurst?'

'If you'll give us some idea of the odds and the winnings, sir.'

'Good odds, limitless reward. My word on it. And your word, Mr Oakenhurst. How do you value it?'

'I value my word above my life, sir. In these troubled times a jugador has nothing but honour. I will need to know a little more before I stake my honour. So I'll fold for the moment. Save to say this, sir – you play an honest game and so will I.'

'And you, Mrs von Bek?' Paul Minct made an old-fashioned bow. 'Do you also offer an honest game?'

'I have played no other up to now, Mr Minct. I'll throw in all I have, if the prize suits me. We can triple our luck, if you like. We all have some idea of the size of the stakes, I think. But not the size of the *bonanza*. Whatever it shall be, I'll put in my full third and take out my full third – or any fraction decided by any future numbers.'

'You can't say fairer than that, ma'am. Very well, Mr Oakenhurst. We have another pard.'

Sam Oakenhurst could not fathom her style, but he recognised that she was a peerless mukhamir. It was as if she had trained in the very heart of Africa. She was his superior in everything but low cunning, that instinctive talent for self-preservation which had proven so useful to him and which had resulted in his becoming kin to the machinoix, rather than their prey. He had never underestimated this useful flaw in his character. But now it could only serve his honour and help him keep his word to the Rose. He had no other choice.

She had played Paul Minct well so far. Mr Minct's weakness was that he had less respect for a woman than he had for a man. Yet the enmascarado was in no doubt about her worth to their enterprise, so long as, in his view, Mr Oakenhurst kept her under control.

'I have always preferred the company of ladies,' said Paul Minct. 'It will be a pleasure to work with you, my dear.'

'I like the feel of the game,' she said. As yet she had given Sam Oakenhurst no clue as to the nature of her quarrel with Mr Minct or why the masked man did not recognise her. (Or did not choose to recognise her. He was the master of any five-dimensional bluff on the screen and a few more of his own invention.)

'We shall form a family as strong as our faith in our own strengths,' said Paul Minct. For once his eyes looked away from them, as if ashamed. 'We are peers. We need no others. The three of us will take our sacrifice to the Fault and reap the measureless harvests!'

'You anticipated my sentiments, Mr Minct,' said the Rose, almost sweet, and Sam Oakenhurst thought he caught a swiftly controlled flicker of emotion in Paul Minct's bleak eyes.

CHAPTER TWO

Un Homme de Pitie

The rules at last agreed, Paul Minct promised to tell them more after they reached the Frees and were off the raft. Then the three of them settled down to an easy companionship, playing a hand or two of old flat and a simulated folded paper version of 'Henri's Special Turbulence' which could only be modified with difficulty and which they eventually abandoned by mutual consent, having failed to discover mutually communicable harmonics.

One evening, as Captain Ornate pumped his melancholy squeezebox in a corner and a couple of whiteys capered to the old familiar zee tunes, the conversation turned to the subject of animals and whether it was possible to have significant conversation with them.

Mrs von Bek spoke of the famous Englishman, Squire Begg, a cousin of hers, and his affinity with crows. He believed they possessed a primitive wisdom enabling them to talk in some way with humans, but first one had to learn and obey their language and customs, which were simple enough, though immutable. It was by these customs that, down the long millennia, crows survived. Assured of your courtesy, the crow would give full attention to your thoughts and desires. 'Crows,' she said, 'came from all over the world to his London mansion in Sporting Club Square, and he was frequently sketched in the company of Egyptian, Amazonian or Antipodean crows, mostly hooded, who would mysteriously leave, returning without warning to their native grounds.'

'I was once an initiate of my tribe's Crow Cult.' Rodrigo Heat's words were thick as Mississippi mud. 'My totem was the crow. I was sworn to protect the crow and all his kind, even with my life, even above my family. In return the crow offered us his wisdom. But this advice was not always suited to modern times.'

'I heard of a young buckaree from up in Arizone who had his eyes pecked out by a crow. He went crazy in the sun, they said, and jumped off that old London Bridge up there, straight down until he hit the granite, thinking he *was* a crow,' said Sister Honesty Marvell. 'Nobody ever found out why.'

Sam Oakenhurst suggested a game of 'Mad John Parker', but Honesty Marvell favoured 'Doc Granite', so in the end they made it a tambourine game and shouted like kiddikins over it. That night the Rose told Sam Oakenhurst that they might have to kill Paul Minct.

At your service, he signalled, but bile came up in his throat.

(We are not *fragments* of the whole, the Rose would insist, but *versions* of the whole. Mr Oakenhurst had told her of the last time he had stood in a ploughed field, full of bright pools of winter rain, on a fine, pale blue evening, with the great orange sun bleeding down into the horizon, and watched a big dog fox, brush high as he picked his way amongst the furrows, circling the meadow where he was hidden by the lattice of the hedge, sniffing the wind for the geese who had begun to honk with anxious enquiry. All of it disappeared, Mr Oakenhurst said, in the Hattiesburg Roar. 'I had thought that, at least, must endure. Now, even our memories are becoming suspect.')

He had no qualms about killing the man, if he proved actively dangerous to them, but he was not at all sure he could play this. He had given his word to something for which he might not possess the necessary bottom. By now he was as nervous of losing her approval as he was terrified by Paul Minct's displeasure. The irony of this amused and sustained him.

'*Ma romance,*' she sang, '*nouvelle romance. Ma romancier, muy necromancier. Joli boys all dansez. Joli boys all dansez – But they shall not have muy couleur.*'

CHAPTER THREE

El Bueno, el Feo y el Malo

The three left *The Whole Hog* when she ran aground on a mudbank near Poker Flats but not before Sister Honesty Marvell had butchered Roy Ornate in a quarrel over the nature of things. Paul Minct had finished her with a glass spike whereupon the swamp people, some devolved survivalists, had tried to crawl aboard, to be repulsed and mostly blown apart by the violent anti-gravity reaction of the colour to their metal. They were extinguished by the power of their ornaments. Carly O'Dowd was dead, too, from a poison she had picked up somewhere, and there was reasonable fear of a whitey uprising until Rodrigo Heat put himself in charge.

Almost as soon as they were ashore they came upon a scattering of the swamp people's weapons, flung this far into the reed beds by the colour. Sam Oakenhurst had never held an original Olivetti PP6 before and he treasured the instrument in his hands, to the Rose's open amusement.

'Take up one of these weapons for yourself, ma'am.' Paul Minct became proprietorial, motioning with his wicked fingers. 'It will almost certainly prove useful to you.' He bent and his arms, encased in hide, again emerged from their velvet wrappings to examine the scattered hardware. 'I have made this journey before. Many times, this journey. Yes. This time we will go on.' He straightened, turning the glittering weapon in her direction and, gasping at sudden pain, examined his pricked wrist. He watched the wand that had wounded him disappearing back into her cloak at the same moment as she apologised.

'She is sometimes hasty in my defence.'

'Swift Thorn,' he said.

The wind was ugly in their ears. A grey whine from the north.

'You would not prefer to pack this OK9?' continued Paul Minct. 'Some kind of back-up?' He dangled the thing by its flared snout, as if tempting a whitey gal to a piece of pie. But she had stirred a memory in him and he turned away, looking out to where the saplings shivered. To Sam Oakenhurst she flashed a fresh play, then she gathered her *gravitas* so that when, also controlled, Mr Minct turned back, she seemed proudly insouciant of any slight.

Again Sam Oakenhurst recognised a game beyond his usual experience.

'She is all I shall need,' said the Rose, almost distantly, while Paul Minct retreated, having apologised with equal formality. He took the OK9 for himself and also hid a Ryman's 32/80 ('a beastly, primitive weapon') in his pack.

They were walking up a well-marked old road which followed the edge of the lake. The road had run between Shreveport and Houston once. They could follow it, Paul Minct assured them, as far as San Augustine. 'I have heard or read of a weapon called Swift Thorn,' he added as he lengthened his gait to lead them south. 'The subject of some epic.'

'Not the subject,' she said. Oh, he is easily clever enough to kill me, Sam. He tricked me into a show.

He doesn't know that he succeeded. He will not dare risk a move on you until he's sure of me. Sam Oakenhurst fell in beside her.

I must take risks, Sam. He must not escape me. I am pledged to his destruction.

'*Hey, hola! Les bon temps rolla! Ai, ha! The good times pass! Pauvre pierrot, muy cœur, mon beau soleil,*' sang out Paul Minct up ahead. 'What a day, pards! What a day!'

A tremor moved the ground and the reed beds rippled.

Around them suddenly boiled the cloudy landscapes, the powerful mirages, of the Free States, all in a condition of minor agitation, as if not fully in focus. Crazy tendrils erupted into a bewildering kaleidoscope, each fragment a fresh version of its surroundings and of the people inhabiting them. A thousand images of themselves, in a variety of rôles and identities, poured away down fresh cracks in the fabric of their histories.

Sam Oakenhurst found this a depressing illusion.

'They refused to search for the centre and hold to it against all attacks and temptations. There must be sacrifices. Lines drawn. And faith. You're familiar with *The Pilgrim's Progress*, Mr Oakenhurst, you being a preacher's son? There's a book, eh? But if only life were so simple. We must press on, holding together, through this valley of desolation, to our just reward. We must know complete trust. And what a reward, my dears!'

Orange and yellow pillars pissed like egg yolk into the sky and splashed upon a gory firmament.

'Here we are,' sang Paul Minct. 'This is it!' He paused before the yelling pillars and threw back his head as if to drink them up: his crude cartographic visor flickered and flashed and made new reflections. 'We are about to pass into the Free States. This is the malleable world indeed! This, or one like it, must bend to our will. Do you not think?'

The Rose was unimpressed. Not as malleable as some, she told Sam Oakenhurst. She moved with an extra grace as if until now her blood had hardly quickened. She had the alertness of an animal in its natural element. Sam Oakenhurst thought they were walking into the suburbs of Hell and he told her that while he remained at her service he was also entirely in her hands. This experience was too unfamiliar. He had thought the stories only legends.

'Here is what all matter should aspire to,' Paul Minct continued. 'Here is true tolerance. Everything is free.'

'Tolerance without mercy,' murmured Sam Oakenhurst, willing to reveal this fear if only to disguise his other, more profound, anxieties.

'We shall find further allies here!' Paul Minct appeared to have forgotten his earlier pledge as he led them between the columns. 'I will guide you.'

But it was soon left for the Rose to lead them, with miraculous confidence, through the vivid shadows, through volatile matter and corrupted time. Perspective, gravity and the seasons were all unstable and Sam Oakenhurst felt he must throw up as Paul Minct, with angry gestures of refusal, had done after they had walked the Bridge of Rubies for uncountable hours. Mr Minct, expecting to be the most experienced of them, clearly resented the Rose's easy pathfinding. Generally he managed to hide his feelings. It was as if, with the sureness of one who knew such waters well, she steered their boat through the wildest rapids.

Agitated scratchings came from within Paul Minct's mask and swaddlings. Occasionally the enmascarado uttered a little, shrill bubbling sound which added to Sam Oakenhurst's own fearful nausea. For a while it seemed they passed between fields of stars, crossing by silver spans of moonbeams, but the Rose told them it was the abandoned forecourt of The Divided Arabia which at one time had been the largest shopping mall in the Western Hemisphere. What they witnessed was what it had become.

'That stuff scares the devil out of me,' Sam Oakenhurst admitted as they emerged from a forest of bright metallic greenery into a wide relief of desert dominated by the brazen stability of a tiny sun.

'Now, my dears, this is more *like* Texas,' said Paul Minct.

CHAPTER FOUR

No me Entierres en la Pradera

The first town they reached was Poker Flats, built in a wide yellow plain in what had been, Paul Minct told them, the old mustard-growing region. Her streets were full of whiteys and mixed couples and she was clearly a town given over almost entirely to licence. Poker Flats announced herself as the Theater Capital of the Southwest and her main boardwalk was nothing but vivid marquees and billboards advertising simulatings, using living actors, of the great local V heroes, whose adventures Sam Oakenhurst had already skimmed at Lieutenant Twist's. These were elaborate dramas concerning the love triangle of Pearl Peru, Bullybop and Fearless Frank Force or the Quest for the Fishlings, featuring Professor Pop, Captain Billy-Bob Begg and her Famous Chaos Engineers. Many of the protagonists were white. White barkers stood outside their booths and called to the newcomers. 'So true you'd think it was V! – "Dallas Horizon". / It's the net! – "Ontario Outer". / Virtually V! – "Laramee Deadlock". / Frank Force Face to Face – "Ludoland".' Their words were echoed overhead in the baroque calligraphy of the day. Power paint growled with all the brilliant vulgar bellicosity of the old circus towns. Poker Flats had been the first of the roving show cities to take permanent root. Such settlements were all over the Free States now, said Paul Minct, but the biggest were still Poker Flats and Porto Cristo.

Paul Minct insisted they visit the shows and understand the nature of these dramas. 'Real or fictional, black or white, they represent a breed of our own kind that has successfully escaped the logic of the Fault, discovering new universes beyond our own. There, my dear friends, Chaos and Singularity perpetually war, are perpetually in balance. And sometimes one is no longer certain which is which. Philosophies become blurred and intermingled out there in the Second Ether. This was how I first learned that it was possible to move from one version of our universe to another and survive. We never die, my dear friends. We are, however, perpetually translated.'

What does he mean? asked Sam Oakenhurst.

He understands something of our condition, she told him, but not much of it. He is like those old South American *conquistadori*. All he can see of this secret is the power and wealth it will bring him. He is prepared to risk his life and soul for that.

Sam Oakenhurst grew fascinated with the legends portrayed on the stages. He talked about Pearl Peru, Corporal Pork, Little Rupoldo, Kaprikorn Schultz and others as if they were personally known to him. When the time came to leave Poker Flats, he bought several books of scenarios. As soon as they were back on the trail he studied them slowly, from morning to night, hoping to find clues to the versions of reality perceived both by Paul Minct and, in particular, Mrs von Bek. Perhaps the Fault was not the mouth of Hell, after all? Perhaps it was a gateway to Paradise?

Walking beside the Rose, he recounted the tale of Oxford under the Squad warlords. The alien renegades, furious at Oxford's resistance to their philosophies, informed the citizens that unless they immediately fell to levelling their entire settlement, colleges, chapels and all, they (the Squads) would eat their first born and bugger their old folk. 'And Oxford, Rose, went the way of St Petersburg and Washington, but not Cheltenham, which is still standing but which has lost its first born. And her old people rarely, these days, walk abroad.' The Squads had come in their black deltoid aircraft. Thousands. 'They told us they represented the Singularity and we were now their subject race. If we refused to serve them, they punished us until we accepted their mastery. They have conquered, they boast, half the known multiverse, and are destined to conquer the rest. Fearless Frank Force is their greatest ace. But nobody knows or understands the loyalties of the Merchant Venturer, Pearl Peru, whom he loves to distraction. His love is not returned. Pearl's passion is for Bullybop alone. And Bullybop is a thorn in the side of the Singularity. Nobody is sure of her secret identity. Honour demands that Frank Force issue no challenge to his rival, yet Bullybop is marked by the Singularity as an outlaw. Here now is the moral conundrum we must solve before we can proceed along a further branch. There is a road, after all, Rose. There are many roads. And crossroads. I can sense them. We can choose some which exist or we can create our own. But there's a formula, I know, and I must learn it.'

'This mania came over one of my men the first time we ever passed through Poker Flats.' Paul Minct was cheerfully dismissive of the Rose's fears. 'They either recover or they don't. In the end we had to shoot Peter Agoubi, poor chap. Lead on, Mrs von Bek. I'll take care of Mr Oakenhurst.'

'It will pass,' she said. 'He will regain control of himself soon, I am sure.' *For my sake, Sam, if not your own!*

This demand brought him, within a reasonable period, back to his senses, but his lasting emotion was of loss, as if he had been close to the secret logic of the multiverse and able, like her, to navigate a purposeful course through those quasi-realities. He could not make himself throw away his scenarios. He buried them deep at the bottom of his knapsack.

'It's unflattering to have a V character for a rival.' She pretended amusement. They had found some good beds in a ghost town about a hundred kays from San Augustine. She indulged her weariness, her poor temper. 'What is the actuality of this Pearl Peru? She sailed by accident through the Cloud of Saffron and that made her a heroine?'

In any circumstances Sam Oakenhurst would have decided that it was impolitic to show admiration for a character with whom the Rose seemed to be on intimate terms and whom she disliked. Such experiences were not, he told himself, helping his sense of identity. Once he caught himself yearning for the familiarity of the machinoix shutterbox.

Those people were real, he knew. But what he had experienced as myth, she had experienced as history. He vowed that he must never lose her. He was prepared to change most of his life for her. His curiosity about her was as great as his love. Now, he thought, they are impossible to separate. Our shoots are interwound. Our luck is the same. We are of the Just . . . He had a moment's understanding that he had given up his own madness in favour of hers. What had he accepted?

You are sworn to this, she reminded him. From now you must accept only what *I* determine as the truth. You will survive no other way. *Any independent decision of yours could result in my death.* You know this, Sam. You have dealt the hands. Now you must play my game, or we are both dead.

This is new to me, he said.

Play it anyway.

CHAPTER FIVE

Two Step della Texas

After they had traded the Ryman's and two Samsonites for ponies at the Flooding Whisper horse ranch just west of San Augustine they made better progress into Golden Birches, where pale light shuddered and huge crows flapped amongst the black lattice of the distant treetops. They arrived in Lufkin to discover that the Pennsylvania Rooms were still run by Major Moyra Malu, the shade of an elegant old swash-buckler who had fought with K'Ond'aa Taylor at Pampam Ridge and had carried the flag to victory for Charles Deslondes in '07.

At Paul Minct's suggestion she was to be their fourth, but not before another week's gaming had all parties apparently satisfied. She would draw her substance from Mr Minct. Then they took Major Moyra's good Arabs and headed through the milk tides down to Livingston where Paul Minct sought out Herb Frazee. The ex-president of the Republic was giving demonstration hands of 'Cold Annie' and telling Tarot to what was left of Livingston's polite society. He refused Mr Minct's invitation but suggested they look up Mrs Sally Guand' in Houston.

The road to Houston took them through Silver Pines. The strange, frozen forest was cold as death nowadays, said Paul Minct, but once there had been fires burning on every mound. They came out into foothills above a summer valley. 'There's Houston.' Paul Minct pointed. The huge city had recently melted and reformed into a baroque version of itself. Its highways made arabesques, glorious in the sunlight. Yet even here the uneasy terrain threatened to vaporise, becoming some-thing else, and Sam Oakenhurst yearned for California where Pearl Peru, he had read, was a living celebrity.

They passed under Houston's organic freeways. The Rose wanted to stay for a few days. The others insisted that they find Sally Guand' and press on to Galveston. But when Major Moyra Malu led them to Sally Guand's old offices above the Union Station, the buildings were melted shells and the rails had twisted themselves into one vast, elongated abstract sculpture disappearing in the direction of Los Angeles. Here, as everywhere, black and white lived as best they could, equals amongst the ruins, and miscegenation was not uncommon.

They lost the road some twenty kays from Houston, used up their provisions and were forced to shoot a horse before they got on another trace full of abandoned buses and pickup trucks, which took them across to Old Galveston to find Jasmine Shah, who had been operating a bar on the harbourfront until the local vigilantes busted her huge cache of piles noires. Her dark locks hiding a long, vulpine face, she was ready, she said, to do almost anything, yet she would only come in with them after she had whispered strict conditions to each one in private. She revealed that she, like Major Moyra, was now a shade.

Paul Minct had hesitated after she spoke to him, but then he nodded agreement.

The streets of Galveston were full of whiteys who had failed to fulfil the ambitions they had conceived in Mississippi and Alabama and were now desperately trying to get back to New Orleans, but could not afford any kind of fare. Black travellers were beset by scores of them, whining for help.

Sam Oakenhurst was glad when they got aboard the first schoomer available and sailed out into the peaceful waters of the Gulf. He and the Rose now had a better measure of the situation and yet he no longer had faith in his own good judgement. The thought of New Orleans was already beginning to obsess him.

The Rose begged him to rally. 'It seems Mr Minct does intend to sail into the Fault. Yet why would he insist on your finding us a meat boat?' (Paul Minct had commissioned Sam Oakenhurst to approach the machinoix.) 'Does he want us alive when he goes in?' Both agreed that Paul Minct had needed more partners only after Swift Thorn had stirred some memory. 'How does he plan to kill us?' Sam wondered. 'Perhaps he will not kill me until he has made sure of you, Rose. And you are necessary to him, I think. He knows you can help him.'

'But you, too, are necessary if he is to get the meat boat. You heard him insist. It must only be a meat boat. Has anyone ever volunteered to sail on such a boat?'

'It is forbidden,' said Sam Oakenhurst. 'He knows it is.'

'Then he demands of you a complex betrayal. Is this how he would weaken us?' The Rose began to brush her exquisite hair. 'Who would you betray?'

'Not you,' he said. 'Not myself. Nothing I value.'

'Betray the machinoix and surely you betray yourself. You have explained all this to me. And in betraying yourself you must betray me.

How will you resolve this? It is a problem worthy of Fearless Frank Force.'

She seemed to be mocking him.

'A moral conundrum,' she added.

There was a knock on their cabin door. A kiddikin bringing Mr Minct's compliments and looking forward to the pleasure of their company in a game of 'Anvils and Pins'.

'I have earned your sarcasm, I know,' Sam Oakenhurst said. 'But I am still willing to learn from you. What will you teach me, Rose?'

'You will learn that it is, space and time, always a question of scale.' She touched his lips. 'Meanwhile you must continue to risk your life. And you are sworn to serve me, are you not?'

'On my honour,' he said.

'But in demanding your help I exposed you to more than you ever expected,' she said. 'Perhaps you do not have the resources?'

'I have them,' he insisted.

'You must draw upon your archetype.' The Rose took his hand. Tonight her skin resembled fine, delicately shaded petals softly layered upon her sturdy frame. 'I have lost my home and must destroy the man who robbed me of it. We are only barely related as species, you and I, but it is Time and Scale which separate us, Sam. In the ether we embrace metamorphosis. You and I, Sam, understand the dominant law of the multiverse. We are ruled by multiplying chance. But we need not be controlled by it. I knew Paul Minct in another guise. Now, I think, he clearly remembers me. He can always recall a weapon, that one, if not a woman. This pair, these shadows, are an afterthought. His interest in the Fault could be secondary now. First he must deal with us, for we threaten his existence. Perhaps he is afraid to let us reach the Fault with him, lest he be cheated of whatever it is he has schemed for? Believe me, Sam, Paul Minct will be giving us his full attention for the next few days. These others, they are scarcely real, merely "1st and 2nd Murderers".'

CHAPTER SIX

J'ai Passé Devant ta Porte

The machinoix had sniffed his coming. Sam Oakenhurst stood at the rail of the great triple-hulled schoomer and saw through Major Moyra's glass that his brothers and sisters had assembled to greet him.

Their snorting, half-organic vehicles, dark green and brown with senility, drooled and defecated on the quayside, while neither citizen nor armed militia dare show disgust or objection. In their city, the machinoix were ignored for the same reason quakes were ignored in Los Angeles. They were unavoidable, uncontrollable and unpredictable.

Mr Sam Oakenhurst tasted their power as greedily as he embraced their kinship. His veins thrilled with the memory of long rituals under the shutterbox; his lingering initiations, his education in seduction. Beware, he signalled the Rose, for I am enraptured already. I love you, Rose. Only you.

The Rose held fast to him and gave him the strength she could spare. He knew there was no physical danger. Any decision of his would be accepted, for he threatened nothing the machinoix valued. This knowledge was insufficient to steady his nerve. He had to call on his every resource and never reveal a hint of his condition to Paul Minct and his colleagues. The Rose, understanding the importance of this deception to her own interests, gave him more support. She had no choice. He was her only ally and while he lived so did she. And she loved him, she said.

By the time they had clambered down the gangway to the lighter, he was scarcely able to disguise the signs of his massive emotional conflict.

With her help, however, he succeeded. He stood at last four square on the quayside, clutching her arm once before advancing towards the middle vehicle from which oddly tattooed hands beckoned, their fingers fractured and re-set at peculiar angles with inserted precious stones and gold. Gnarled as old hedges, the hands had the appearance of eccentrically made robot digits, jointed and decorated for their beauty rather than their function.

The Rose was casual enough as she turned to inform a nervous Mr

Minct that Sam Oakenhurst spoke machinoix perfectly. 'He is the only possible interpreter. He will get us swift passage to Biloxi.'

'It must be the meat boat.' Paul Minct was wheezing from his recent climb up the iron waterstair. 'I know they reserve it for themselves but it is what we must have.'

By arrangement with the ship's captain they were to stay in rue Dauphine at the Hotel Audobon, a collection of old iron slave shacks turned into elegant *cabines à la mode*. The uniformed whiteys who greeted them at the gates were not permitted to take the little luggage the gamblers brought.

These were cabins of choice, let only to passing visitors of their own high persuasion. When they were settled, Paul Minct told them, they must assemble at Brown's 'Bar Vieux' on Royale, where he would hire the backroom and a couple of simul-bottles. They could thus link up for a rough and ready run-through of their plan to enter the Fault aboard the meat boat. 'We'll be going in through Mustard Splash or Ketchup Cove.'

The bottles were the best quality the Rose had ever seen. Mere shades, Major Moyra and Jasmine Shah were nonetheless experts at handling and conducting the bottles, massaging unstable gases, nursing their milky energy into responsive motes.

Before they had arrived, Paul Minct had refused to tell her why they must go to this trouble when the Terminal's huge V resource was at anyone's disposal. He appeared to have reasons for not alerting the people at the Terminal to his intentions.

Her instincts told her that this whole charade was part of a complicated plot to trap her before killing her. It was unnecessarily elaborate, she thought.

But it was that which convinced her. Elaboration was Paul Minct's trademark. It was characteristic of his whole game thus to hide a simple brute intention.

Had he known she was in Guadalajara? If so, even Paul Minct's affectation for M & E was a part of his plot against her. She was admiring of his mind for detail. She had known him in many rôles, but usually he had not recognised her so quickly.

When Mr Oakenhurst rejoined them at Brown's he seemed introspective but carefree enough, almost euphoric. He told them that they had the machinoix blessing to take the meat boat to Biloxi. This was, they must all understand, a considerable privilege. Moyra Malu said she appreciated the implications. Only Paul Minct accepted the news casually, as if Mr Oakenhurst had done no more than act as a go-between. 'And how much do these great barons charge us, Mr Oakenhurst, for the privilege.'

'Nothing, Mr Minct. They act upon my word alone.'

'Flimsy enough, then?'

Sam Oakenhurst took a glaring interest in the screens, his mood threatening.

'I am not sure I can stand that smell for such a long voyage,' said Jasmine Shah. She had changed to red satin, she said, in honour of the occasion. She sported a feathery fan.

'We must endure it until Biloxi,' murmured Paul Minct, looking up from the bottles and retorts of his quasi-V, his mask reflecting the brilliant, ever-changing rhythms of the angry pastels. 'They are unpredictable, are they not, sir, these psychics? Sometimes they seem to need us more than we need them. But I expect they are agreeable people, by and large.'

Sam Oakenhurst knew he had nothing much more to fear until they were actually aboard the meat boat. He took his place with the other four around the viewing bowls which flooded them now in bright blues and vivid pinks, adjusting to a formal plum colour as Paul Minct stroked his back-upper to make shapes from the enlivened dust. Some of the images were familiar but many were not. Sam Oakenhurst found them obscene.

'We have agreed a common principle, my dears.' Paul Minct seemed a little sanctimonious. 'And must stick to the rules we form here tonight. Or we shall be lost.'

'Do we need to be reminded of that?' Sam Oakenhurst was irritable as he studied the bowl, finding some strands on the screen he could use. He wove a showy, challenging gambit. Planets and their histories formed and died.

'We are a team, Mr Oakenhurst.' Paul Minct seemed pleased by this offhand display. 'We can afford no weak links. No, as it were, anti-socialism.' Sam Oakenhurst guessed the fat man had found a tune which he must now rehearse for a while. Mr Minct searched under his veil and plucked at his hideous jowls.

Unusually alert, Sam Oakenhurst studied Paul Minct's companions and detected a tremor of victorious malice in Major Moyra's face. The Rose's warning was confirmed. Certain of his allies, Paul Minct was celebrating a premature triumph.

It will be on board the meat boat. That has always featured in his scenario, I think. I don't know why, save that he follows a personal aesthetic. Her shoulders set as if to disguise anxiety, Mrs von Bek gave her own attention to the bowls and began a detailed weaving, a story of a planet and its doom, a wonderful miniature. Sam Oakenhurst understood that now she, too, had issued a challenge to Paul Minct. These were the gentle beginnings, the courteous preliminaries of the game.

Upon Mr Minct's irrational insistence they began the first stage of their simulation, producing a reasonable version of the Biloxi Fault and some sort of boat in which to brave these self-created dangers. 'Now we sail into Mustard Splash!' declared Paul Minct, their captain. 'These murky walls will part, thus!' A magician, he revealed the blinding azure of a vast colour field. 'We shall follow a river – thus—' A hazier network of silver streams which, with his characteristic crudity, he turned into one wide road: 'This line will respond to the meat boat's unique geometry. And now we must do our best, dear friends, and make the most of our creative imaginations, for our quest lies even *beyond* the fields of colour – to find eternal life, limitless wealth! There one shall come in to one's true power at last!'

Later, in their cabin, Sam Oakenhurst and the Rose agreed that the exercise had been a complicated sham, a violent and exhausting process with no other purpose, as far as they could tell, than to display Paul Minct's artistic skills. 'That was not the Fault,' she said. 'Merely a surface impression and a bad projection. It was an arcadium, no more. Almost an insult. I wonder why? To convince us? To confuse us? To terrify us? He knows in his heart what truly lies beyond the Fault.'

They were lying together on the wide bed, the light from the swamp-cone turning her brown skin into semi-stable green and giving her face a deep flush. 'He still needs our good will, Sam. He had expected your challenge no more than had I.'

It had hardly been a challenge. Mr Oakenhurst, hyped on the sensations of his reunion, had merely wished to show that he no longer feared Paul Minct. He had risked their lives on a vulgar display and now admitted it.

She began to laugh with quiet spontaneity. 'I have a feeling he did not care to notice, anyway. He was preparing his talents for his demo. Let that hand ride for a while, Sam, and we'll see what happens.'

He marvelled at her beauty, the peerless texture of her skin, her natural, sweet scent, the ever-changing colours of her flesh, and he knew that his feeling for her was stronger than his bond with the machinoix. Stronger than with his own species.

'We are defenceless if he decides to kill us before the meat boat leaves,' he said. 'I'm pretty scared, Rose.'

'The best way to get out of trouble is to take a risk based on your judgement. You know that, Sam.' Her touch was a petal on his thigh. 'Take another risk. An informed one, this time. Make a change. What can you ever lose? Not me, Sam.'

She began to notice the tiny, symmetrical marks on his stomach, like stylised tears of blood.

He refused to tell her what they were.

CHAPTER SEVEN

Exitos de Oro

The meat boat left two days later from the quarantine dock, its brooding, over-decorated reptilian bulk almost filling the ancient channel. It was lying low in the water, giving the impression that it had just fed well.

In common with the others, Paul Minct had to steady himself against the smell from the holds. He held a huge nosegay of mint and rosemary to his hidden features, while the strength of the perfume sprayed about by Major Moyra was equally hard to stomach. Jasmine Shah contented herself with her fan and some smelling salts. She seemed lost in her own small fantasy.

They were led aboard by an obsequious whitey tattooed with the machinoix livery. The extravagantly furnished passenger quarters were clearly designed for the unwholesome comforts of the machinoix. It was a great honour, Sam Oakenhurst told them. The majority of quarters reserved for the machinoix were less comfortable. And there were quarters for the blankey slaves much closer to the meat.

He and the Rose stood together in the centre of Paul Minct's cabin while the huge creature prowled about the edges, the nosegay still pressed to his beaded veil, inspecting the peculiar cups and little needles placed everywhere for a guest's casual convenience. Sam Oakenhurst reached down to a tiny table and picked up one of the razor-edged shot glasses. He gently touched it to the back of his wrist.

'These colours are so muted,' declared the Rose. 'So gorgeous. So rich.'

'There's no one doubts the machinoix ain't *rich*, Mrs von Bek,' chuckled Jasmine Shah, crowding in with Major Moyra to admire the vast chamber. 'As Croesus, they say.'

'Could buy and sell the Republic of Texas, even in my day,' Major Moyra agreed. 'But they don't mess with human politics much. Ain't that so, Mr Oakenhurst?'

'That's so, Major.'

'Built for a giant and furnished for dwarves,' mused Jasmine Shah, making her own tour.

The atmosphere was one of general bonhomie as the would-be murderers saw their endgame laid out, already won.

Their adversaries' confidence could be useful to them, Sam Oakenhurst decided, and later in their own cabin, Rose von Bek told him she had decided the same. 'Their eagerness and anticipation can become our weapon. But it is three days to Biloxi. When will he strike, do you think?'

Sam Oakenhurst made a lazy gesture. He thought it would not be immediately. For the first time he was calmly ready for death. He did not much care how he died. He also knew that he could not accept death while his obligation to the Rose remained. He must make himself worthy of her.

She detected a certain heaviness in his manner. He assured her that he had never been on better form.

While a blankey, smelling strongly of meat, prepared their bed, Sam Oakenhurst said aloud: 'If Paul Minct hopes to seduce whiteys to his cause he cannot know the machinoix. This fellow and his kind are as loyal to their masters as anyone can be. Disobedience or treachery is inconceivable to them. They would be disgusted and terrified if it was suggested. The machinoix never put their own to work on the meat boats. They trust their whiteys absolutely. There is no reason why they should not.'

'Paul Minct must have some understanding of this. Does he think he can force them to divert the boat and sail into the Fault?' The Rose shook her head.

'Whether or not he plans to enter the Fault, he is without a doubt planning to trap us. He cannot see how we can escape and is happy to take his time. Yet why should he go to such lengths to kill you, Rose?'

'He must be certain. And it is in his nature to make such plots. He knows that I have pursued him through the myriad branches of the multiverse and that I am of the Just. I must put an end to him, if I can. Betrayal is a sophisticated and legitimate art which he practises merely for the pleasure it gives him. But he has another ambition I cannot fathom, as yet.'

'What did he do to you that you must punish him?' Sam Oakenhurst asked.

'He educated me to betray myself and thus to betray my people.' She spoke softly, economically, as if she could not trust her voice for long. 'The story I gave at Brown's was true.'

'And these other stories? Are they true? What we saw at Poker Flats?'

'Myths,' she said. 'True enough. They describe the truth.'
'And what does Paul Minct describe?'
'Only lies, Sam.'
With hideous dignity the whitey bowed and left the cabin.

CHAPTER EIGHT

Mon Bon Vieux Mari

'We were called the daughters of the Garden, the daughters of the Just,' she told him. 'We reproduced ourselves by the occasional effort of will. We understood the principles of self-similarity. I suppose you would call it an instinct. There is no particular miracle in being, as we were, part flora, part mammal. Such syntheses are common to the worlds I usually inhabit. Paul Minct made me cross so many scales and forget so many lives to reach him. The stories are always a little different. But this time, I think, we shall achieve some kind of resolution.'

'Surely, we are something more than mere echoes . . .?' Yet even as he said this Sam Oakenhurst felt oppression lifting from him and a rare peace replacing it. In combination with what the machinoix had given him, he found still more strength. He had reached a kind of equilibrium. At that moment nothing was puzzling. But was this merely an illusion of control? What she had told him should have dismayed him. Had her madness completely absorbed him?

'Our science was the science of equity,' she continued. 'We were the natural enemies of all tyrannies, no matter how well disguised. Our world occupied a universe of flowers: blossoms and leaves were woven between blooms the size of planets. Paul Minct allied himself with a devolved race whom we knew as the Bab Bab and these he ultimately unleashed upon our world. Just before he committed that crime he was my lover and I taught him all our secrets.'

'And your sisters?'

'Our whole universe was raped. I am the last of it.'

Until then Sam Oakenhurst had been unable to imagine a burden greater than his own.

CHAPTER NINE

Dans la Cœur de la Ville

'We are playing charades, do you see!' Paul Minct's mask glittered with a kind of merriment. 'Major Moyra is in the part of Little Fanny Fun, while Manly Mark Male is played by our own dashing Jasmine Shah! But who shall play the rival? Who shall play Handsome Harry Ho-Ho? You know this one, Mr Oakenhurst, I'm sure.'

'Those tales no longer fascinate me, Mr Minct.' Sam Oakenhurst stood just within the cabin door. The three would-be murderers had pushed away furniture and draperies and made a stage of a broad, ebony table, its legs carved with a catalogue of machinoix delights. It was on this that the two performed, while their superior applauded from an asymmetrical couch he had made comfortable with the sanctuary's afterlife cushions.

'This is disrespectful to your hosts.'

'Oh, Mr Oakenhurst, we shall not be going back to New Orleans! We're on our way to the Fault to find the Holy Grail, remember?' Major Moyra bawled in open contempt and unhitched her gaudy skirts.

The Rose stepped up, anxious to end this: 'Crude entertainment for a mind such as yours, Paul Minct. Or is this merely a *leitmotif*?'

'You are too judgemental, Mrs von Bek.' Paul Minct turned his glaring mask this way and that as if he could barely see through the holes. 'You must be more flexible. Only flexibility will enable you to survive the perils of the Fault. Come now, join our little time passer. Choose a character of your own. Pearl Peru? *The Spammer Gain?* Corporal Pork? Karl Kapital?'

'I have nothing further to take from this,' said Sam Oakenhurst. 'And nothing to put in. Play on, pards, and don't mind me.'

'Play for the hell of it, then!' Jasmine Shah sprawled her painted legs over the table. 'Play. Play. What else is there to do, Mr Oakenhurst?' Her yellow eyes were sluggish with guilty appetites. His anticipated death was making her salivate. 'Taste something fresh.'

The killing ritual was beginning. And so they sat obediently until they were called and Mr Oakenhurst was a somewhat wooden Harry Ho-Ho, while the Rose became Pearl Peru to the life, telling the first tale of *The Spammer Gain* and how her fishlings were stolen. Enough to distract Paul Minct a little and make him clap his pale hands together. 'You are a natural actress, Mrs von Bek. You missed your vocation.'

'I think not,' she said.

'There, pards, we've proved ourselves easy sports,' announced Sam Oakenhurst, 'but now we must come to business. We are here to discuss the part of our plan where we take over the meat boat. Are the whiteys bribed, yet?' Mr Oakenhurst again found himself speaking from impulse. His tone was sufficient to let the enmascarado know that Sam Oakenhurst was making a call.

'Not yet,' said Paul Minct easily. 'There's time enough, Mr Oakenhurst. Let us relax.'

'We no longer accept you as our director.' The Rose swung down from the table as Paul Minct, gloating in a supposed small victory, displayed his surprise. But he recovered quickly.

'Here's a better game than I anticipated.' Mr Minct calmed his two shadows with a casual hand. They were both thoroughly alarmed. Evidently they had not considered a play made at the opponents' convenience.

Caged light, fluttering in the woven flambeaux, cast the only movement on Mr Minct now. His body was as still as stone. As if he hoped to stop time.

'This is not like you, Mr Oakenhurst.' The Rose was amused.

'Not like me at all.' He turned to address the enmascarado. 'A surprise play, eh, Mr Minct?'

Eyes moved like quick reptiles behind the mask. The curtain over the mouth rattled. 'Just so, Mr Oakenhurst.'

Sam Oakenhurst hardly knew what to do next. He felt a rush of elation. He was in control of his terrors.

CHAPTER TEN

Aimer et Perdre

It had never been in Sam Oakenhurst's nature to decide the first move. Paul Minct had relied on that knowledge while certain the Rose would not make a play before Mr Oakenhurst. But now, equally unpredictably, Paul Minct produced the little OK9 he had once recommended to Mrs von Bek and he took a step back to cover them both. 'This is not my style, either, as you know. But I'm willing to change if you are. That's the basis of a relationship, as I tell my wife. No wands now, Mrs von Bek. This beam is wide and I will resort to brute murder if I must. I have a vocation to fulfil. An oath.'

'Ah!' exclaimed the Rose in surprise. 'This one has a conscience!'

'I had such hopes for your death, Mrs von Bek. Mr Oakenhurst would have appreciated what I made of you. We have a little time before we prepare the sacrifice. Not much, but we must use the best of what God sends us.' He signalled to Major Moyra and Jasmine Shah. Then suddenly he was still again, as if stabbed.

'That is the man,' said Sam Oakenhurst to the machinoix. 'He is not my friend.' He watched incuriously as one oddly jointed jewelled hand closed over Paul Minct's wrist and squeezed the gun free while fingers felt through the beads deep into Minct's mouth and throat.

Rose von Bek looked away from Paul Minct and, with Swift Thorn, brought Major Moyra and Jasmine Shah merciful deaths. In the last moments the game had been unpleasantly easy as often happens in a spontaneous endmove. When the Rose looked back she saw that Paul Minct had been returned to his seat. He was not dead, but his cold eyes begged for her mercy. The rest of him had been expertly snapped here and there. He was little more than a heap of broken bones but he would live indefinitely.

Mr Oakenhurst bowed low before his invisible kin.

The voice which came from the folds of drapery behind the table was musical but oddly diffident. 'We shall put those two with the other meat.' There was a long pause, then: 'The broken one is yours, if you wish.'

'Thank you,' said the Rose.

'No thankings, no,' said the machinoix. 'Not need. I am the same. Same. You. You.'

In the following silence the Rose said: 'Where has she gone?'

'To rest,' Sam Oakenhurst told her. 'She has used up pretty much all her strength for a year. What will you do with him?'

'Eventually I must kill him. I have that much compassion left. But it will take me a while to find the necessary resolution.'

Sam Oakenhurst stepped aside to let the whiteys drag the corpses off. 'Nature resists linearity. Why didn't you understand that, Paul Minct? What was your plan? What did you intend to sacrifice and to whom?' Approaching the couch he reached to Paul Minct's head and touched it in a certain way, allowing the lips to move.

'The meat was for the Fault.' His suffering made Paul Minct obedient now. 'The Fault is a sentient creature. Five times I fed it. This sixth time was to bring me my reward, for I would be sacrificing the Rose, my mortal enemy, body and soul! And what rarer sacrifice? The Rose is both the last and the first of her kind. Then I should have been permitted to sail through the golden branches into the Great Cup and know my whole power!'

'You must tell me the truth,' she said. 'It will make me more merciful. How did you plan to take over the boat?'

'I placed no faith in bribes or whitey revolt. I simply made adjustments to the steering gear. That is why this boat is now on inevitable course for the Fault, under full sail. We shall keep our original bargain, ma'am. But you never did confront me, Sam. Not really.'

Mr Oakenhurst silenced Paul Minct's mouth. The man's bravery was more impressive than his judgement. 'We are to be your sacrifices, still? I think not. Eh, Mrs von Bek?'

The Rose frowned at him. 'It is either the Fault or drown. Have you no curiosity, Sam?'

'There are innocent lives in this!'

'They will not die, Sam. That's merely a conception of the Singularity. You have already discovered the benefits of mutability. The Fault will either translate us or reject us, but it will not kill us. And there's every chance we'll remain together. We must have the will for it and the courage to follow our instincts.'

'I must return to New Orleans,' said Mr Oakenhurst. 'There's a debt outstanding.' He looked with hatred into Paul Minct's agonised eyes.

Again, he began to doubt his judgement. What good had his decisions been now they were heading helplessly into the Biloxi Fault? He turned to ask her how much time she thought they had, when the whitey bos'un shuffled down the companionway and crossed to the door, kneeling with bowed head before Sam Oakenhurst and the Rose and not speaking until Mr Oakenhurst gave permission.

'Respectfully, master, our meat boat is about to be a-swallered by the Biloxi Fault.'

'Remember!' she called, as she followed him up the narrow ladders towards the bridge. 'It is only a matter of scale and experience. You are not a fraction of the whole. You are a version of the whole! Time will seem to eddy and stall. This is scale. Everything is sentient, but scale alters perception. The time of a tree is not your time.' It was as if she shouted to him all she had meant to teach him before this moment. 'To the snail the foot which comes from nowhere and crushes him is as natural a disaster as a hurricane; it cannot be appealed to and is impossible to anticipate. The time of a star is not our time. Equity is the natural condition of the multiverse. There are things to fear in the colour fields, *but not the fields themselves*! Remember, Sam, we are God in miniature!'

Now he was on the top deck, heading for the bridge. The vast black sails bulged overhead as the freak wind took them more rapidly towards the Fault than ever Paul Minct had planned. The massive presence of the Biloxi Fault filled their horizon, all bruised colours and sharded light, yelping and gulping the ruins of star systems and galaxies as the meat boat sailed inexorably towards the lava-red glow of Ketchup Cove.

'I will remember all your lessons!' He took the wheel from the terrified whitey, but it would not respond to his straining movements. The boat dipped and rose on a sudden tide while the wind threatened to tear the sheets from her masts. Help me,' he said, as the whitey ran below. She came towards him. Then something soft had batted the meat boat into the middle of the bloody, blossoming field. Yet the vessel maintained her original momentum, travelling steadily under sail. They could see nothing but the surrounding scarlet. When they spoke their voices were unfamiliar and used new but coherent languages. Sam Oakenhurst felt his stomach peeling open, his entire flesh and bone skinless to the flame. He fell backwards.

He tried to look up beyond the sails and saw something moving against the scarlet. A huge owl. He shuddered.

Now the Rose had her hands upon the useless wheel. Mammalian only in broad outline, she appeared to curl her limbs and cast roots into the steering machinery, as if seeking the whereabouts of Paul Minct's tamperings. Her scent enraptured him. It was thicker than smoke.

Something vicious and insistent threatened nearby and was dangerous, some version of Paul Minct. The Rose pulled mightily on the wheel and this time the meat boat responded, gliding into a sudden field of blue populated with the black silhouettes of mountains shifting constantly in perspective, and then descending into a mælstrom of purple and white, soaring into field upon field of the vast spectrum, turning and wheeling until Sam Oakenhurst had to take his eyes from her to lean over the side and throw up into an infinity of lemon yellow spheres and witness his own vomit becoming another universe in which uncountable souls would live, suffer and die until the end of time, while the sounds that he made would eventually be interpreted by them as evidence of a Guiding Principle.

The Rose was laughing. Sam Oakenhurst had never seen a creature so filled with joy, with the rage of risk and skill which marked the greatest jugadors. He had never known a creature so daring, so wise. And it seemed to him that some new strength bound him to her, through all the colour-flooded fields of the multiverse. And then she began to sing.

The beauty of her song was almost unbearable. At once he started to weep and his tears were blinding quicksilver. It was as if she had summoned a wind and the wind was her voice calling to him.

'Look up, Sam! There, beyond the colour fields! It's the Grail, Sam. It's the great Grail itself!'

But when, his eyes now clear of tears, Sam Oakenhurst looked up all he saw was a lattice of light, like roots and branches, twisting around them on every side, a kind of nest made of curled gold and silver rays. And through this, with happy ease, the Rose steered the machinoix meat boat. Her hair was wild around her head, like flames; her limbs a haze of petals and brambles; and her song seemed to fill the multiverse.

The meat boat was a fat brazen lizard crawling over the surfaces of the vast fields, following the complex river systems which united them, replenished them, blending with new multi-hued mercury fractures running through a million dimensions and remaking themselves, fold upon fold, scale upon scale, until they merged again with the great main trunks, ancient beyond calculation, where (legend insisted) they would find the final scale and return, as was their destiny, to their original being: reunited with their archetype; no longer echoes. 'And this shall be called the Time of Conference,' said the Rose, bringing the meat boat down into a clover field of white and green. 'The Time of Reckoning. That, Sam, is the fate of the Just.'

He had managed to reach her and now sat at her feet with his arms around the stem of the wheel. He watched her as a new force took hold of the boat. A sudden stench came up from the holds, as if something had ruptured. She struggled with the wheel. He tried to help her. She sang to whatever elements would hear her but she was suddenly powerless. She shook her head and gestured for him to relax. There was nothing more they could do.

'We can't go any further now, Sam,' she said. 'We're not ready, I guess.'

'*Not you yet. No, no, no. The offering first . . .*'

Turning with sudden recollection they saw oddly shaped jewelled hands disappearing below. How long had the machinoix been with them?

'She must be close to death,' said Sam Oakenhurst.

'Can you help her?' asked the Rose.

It was only then that they saw the shapeless ruin of Paul Minct, its upturned mask a blazing battleground of brands, its eyes enlivened at last with the fires of hell.

The Rose made a movement with Swift Thorn. There came a jolt, like a mild shockwave. Sam Oakenhurst felt water wash up his legs and reach his back.

He heard the sound of a tide as it retreated from the shore and he smelled the salt, the oily air of the coast. He opened his eyes. The boat was gone.

Eventually his vision adjusted. He understood what had happened. He lay on his side in the water, as if left there by a wave. A little above him, on the beach, the Rose was calling his name. 'Sam! The Fault has taken the meat boat.'

'Maybe Paul Minct achieved his ambition?' Away in the distance were the tranquil skies which marked the Biloxi Fault. Mr Oakenhurst turned onto his back. He began to get to his feet. He shuddered at the state of his clothing and was glad there were no witnesses to their coming ashore. The Rose appeared unaffected by their adventure. Taking his hand she waded briskly through the shallows and brought them up to the tufted dunes. A light wind blew the sand in rivulets through the grass.

'The meat boat was accepted and we were not. Whose sacrifice?' She pointed. 'See! We have Biloxi that way. New Orleans the other! We shall go to the Terminal, Sam. I have a purpose there.'

'I cannot go there yet,' he told her. 'I must go to New Orleans. Is it too much for me to learn? Too much that is novel and incomprehensible?'

'Ah, no, Sam. You already know it in your bones. Come on to Biloxi, mon brave. Later, maybe, you go to New Orleans, when I can come with you.' Standing there against the yellow dunes, her hair still wild, a red haze in the wind, human in form but radiating the quintessence of the rose, all its exquisite beauty, Mrs von Bek made no indirect attempt to persuade him, either by gesture or word, and for that he loved her without reserve.

'You must go alone to Biloxi,' he said. 'There is a price for our salvation and I return to New Orleans to pay it.'

'Oh, don't go, Sam.' Clearly she found this request almost distasteful, though she had to make it. 'Are you sure there is nothing more to this than your own addiction?'

'On my honour, I swore to help you. On my honour, I must keep my bargain with those who helped me fulfil that pledge to you.'

She accepted this in silence, but it seemed to him that he had wounded her or that she disbelieved him.

He said more softly: 'I will meet you at the Terminal. It is not my life I owe them, but my respect. I must acknowledge their sacrifice. Courageously they defied their most powerful taboos to do what I asked of them. And here we are, Rose. Alive, thanks to their courage.'

'And ours, Sam. I would return with you now, but I, too, am bound to a promise. If I lived after my business with Mr Minct I said I would deliver a message to Mr Jack Karaquazian at the Terminal Café. So I must make my way there and, yes, I will wait for you, Sam, at least until the boredom grows intolerable.' She smiled. 'Then I will come and find you. Yes, I will meet you again, whenever our luck will have it so. Then, I hope, you will want to come with me, beyond the colour fields, beyond the universe known as The Grail, to the wonders of the Second Ether, where plurality forever holds sway. There you will discover what it is to be jugadors and paramours! What it is to be alive! There's more than me in this for you, Sam.' Her lips released a sigh.

'Well,' he said. 'I think you will not forget me, Rose. You know who I am.'

'By and large, Sam.' She turned away.

As he put the Rose, the ocean, and the dunes at his back and took the broken old road up towards Louisiana, her voice returned to him on the wind.

'*Ma romance, nouvelle romance. Ma romancier, muy necromancier. Ma histoire, muy histoire nouvelle. Joli boys all dansez. Joli boys all dansez. Sing for me, olé, olé. But they shall not have muy vieux carré. Joli garçon sans merci. Pauvre pierrot, mon vieux, mon brave. Petit pierrot, mon sweet savage. Le monde est fou. El mundo c'est moi.*'

There was to be a final miracle: it seemed to him that the distant yell of the Biloxi Fault took fresh harmonics from the Rose's song and amplified and modified it until for a while a vast unearthly orchestra played the old tune, told the old story of lies and truth, of betrayals and sacrifices, of quests and oaths, of love and loss and resolutions that are not always tragic. The old story, which is echoed by our own.

Corsairs of the Second Ether

Warwick Colvin Jnr.

THE STORY SO FAR:

Having at last followed the SWIPLING swarm through the unpredictable scales between planes and arrived at Ko-O-Ko, the Lost Universe, CAPTAIN BILLY-BOB BEGG and her famous CHAOS ENGINEERS are prevented from returning to the First or Second Ethers by the activities of AYESHA VON ABDUL, protectress of the Lost Universe, and her ruffianly slipling Corsair allies. Only seven other ships were successful in pursuing the swipling swarm all the way to Ko-O-Ko, including those of CAPTAIN QUELCH; of STERLING, Second Beast of the SKIPLING folk; of RA, First Beast of the SKIMLINGS and of the parasitically held renegade ship of BIG BALL and his unwelcome ally KAPRIKORN SCHULTZ, Banker to the Homeboy Tong. Two other ships are known to have reached Ko-O-Ko, but are at present unaccounted for. Although Captain Billy-Bob has tried to warn Ayesha von Abdul that her army of sliplings means no good to the Lost Universe, the Protectress refuses to listen, even after she has declared her faith in the common Great Mood and found true love . . . There seems no saving her, but then Captain Quelch suggests a meeting between himself and Kaprikorn Schultz, with a view to taking control of the slipling horde and conquering Ko-O-Ko in the name of the Singularity. There is nothing for it, Captain Billy-Bob decides, but to attempt the dangerous manœuvre known as the 'scale-flip'.

Her crew of famous Chaos Engineers are unanimous. It will mean a wild dive through to the old Mars station and an attractor so familiar the ship might just flow to like and re-organise in natal space. It worked once before, in the tale of the Mandelbrot Sidestep, but everyone had known it was the purest luck, and it would be purest luck once again, should they survive. Captain Billy-Bob is about to give the order when suddenly, blotting the fore-screens, Captain Quelch's *The Linear Bee* appears, casting a significant shadow into the equation. But can Captain Billy-Bob stop the progress in time?

Now read on . . .

CHAPTER ONE THOUSAND AND FOURTEEN

Hard A-Stern on a Rogue Branch

Captain Billy-Bob Begg strides through the instrument conference carrying with her the shadows and dimensions of all her adventures. Some now argue she has skipling blood. Her outlines leap in and out of her surrounding aura – faces, shapes, colours, gestures, long forgotten.

Her helmet boils with fractal dust normally left behind in any scale jump and she is contemptuous of disapproval ('They'll never take me or my ship to Reality Dock!' she swears) as she bleeds her screen to her enemy's co-ordinates, so familiar she makes no conscious computation. And there is the face of the Original Insect, whimsically superimposed upon the haggard, hatchet features of Captain Horace Quelch, still not entirely certain if he can afford to gloat just yet.

'Marm?'

'Horace!' burbs the revered Main Type of the *Now The Clouds Have Meaning*. 'You'll let us pass, I hope, for all our sakes.'

'Singularity is the only commonality I recognise, marm. I am never, I hope, *ad utrumque paratus*! I'll be obliged if ye'll edge off this branchline and stick to ye'r own roads in future.'

'You've been tongue tickling with Kaprikorn Schultz,' said Captain Billy-Bob with a dismissive eruption of a finger or two and her chief outline breaks into violent blue and yellow, then red and yellow, then pale green, alarming her enemy, who seems to shrink even from her image.

'There's a string of sapphires I can do nothing about,' declares Quelch.

'Another trick of the Master Banker.' Pegarm Pete and Professor Pop crowd about their Main Type, while Jhong de Bhong plugs into his new chest and begins to spark urgently.

'Kaprikorn is the most respectable creature in the multiverse,' declares Captain Quelch with a gashy grin and his eyes blob red, through some genetic fluke, they would guess, rather than a blip of the screen's 49.

'There's twelve other patterns to this,' murmurs Professor Pop, passing his calculations to his Main Type. 'He has considered eight. Those four are free. The one I have indicated gives us maximum roll, unfortunately.'

'A roll-and-fold manœuvre, as I'd feared.' Captain Billy-Bob applauds their instruments and busies herself with the fussy metaphysics of the problem. 'But have we any right to the luck we need?'

'We must pray,' says Pegarm Pete. 'Faith, darling, and the confidence of the Just is all that can guide us now.' He refers to his Main Type's secret Calling, for she is, indeed, one of the Just. It is her Faith, rather than her Luck, that these days her famous Engineers trust most.

'Very well,' she says suddenly, and bursts the crystal with a fierce, swift movement.

'You have blinded me!' roars her enemy.

CHAPTER ONE THOUSAND AND FIFTEEN

The Consequences of Pierced Scales

'We'll pour rum on their rear-folds before you can peep "claw-rat to a clam",' boasts Kaprikorn Schultz as he slips his stolen ship into a careless corkscrew guaranteed to bore into the heart of Ko-O-Ko and terrify the peaceful swiplings out of the all-protecting grid-nest. But he is still unaware of Dilly-Dee Begg, a stow-away, crawling even now through the nauseating gaps between the mighty walls of a Singularity Heavy Warper badly modified for folding and poorly maintained by Big Ball the renegade, who never planned to take her anywhere but into the Field of Indigo and make a living off the passing skimling trade. This is no retirement for an old creature, he complains, but by now he has been strapped into his brochette and glares moodily at the steel spike jutting upwards between his thickly scarred tentacles. 'This is not pain, it is mere indignity.' He has noted the whispering presence of Dilly-Dee Begg and has not betrayed her. He returns to his B-screen and its repeated images of Big Ball devouring Kaprikorn Schultz of the Homeboy Tong. 'Ah! Blood! Blood!'

But Kaprikorn Schultz turns suspicious glares on all his colleagues now, convinced that Captain Quelch has betrayed the original agreement. He is impatient with the sluggish controls and eventually explodes through the hull, spreading his blue wings against the wide paleness of Ko-O-Ko, the Lost Universe, determined to discover and leech the *Now The Clouds Have Meaning*.

. . . While Dilly-Dee Begg wrestles with the ruined controls!

CHAPTER ONE THOUSAND AND SIXTEEN

Return to the Amber Trail!

At the heart of a field of cerise and yellow flame gradually crystallising to form the familiar Home Dragon, suggesting they must be close to the Martian Scaling Station, Captain Billy-Bob Begg drew comfort from her crew. All the famous Chaos Engineers were cuddled to their revered Main Type, lending their Faith to hers in an eccentric act of prayer, since they could only, now, put their trust in the Great Mood. But more than one insect face had regarded them on their journey. More than one insect had shown them the horrors of singularity as if they were proud of themselves. The *Now The Clouds Have Meaning* was unfolding and unfolding at a leisurely rate, like a slow chrysanthemum, which was the sweet-smelling emblem of most Chaos Engineers and further improved their optimism, for they had expected more roll and less of this acceptable undulation in their fall through the scale-fields.

Little Rupoldo speaks of maps ablaze and fractal loops, desperately attempting to re-bond the garden housing and harmonise with the full ship, but Corporal Organ has almost lost hope.

'Sweet Rupoldo, sweet pudding. Plums for Rupoldo now! We will float now.'

'*She bangs like a firetruck, hee, hee, hee!*' The voice of Kaprikorn Schultz, the half-hume, still follows them down the scale, powerful obscenities guaranteed to agitate their garden and butterfly them to the Great Mood knew where.

'I am too tired,' sighs Little Rupoldo, no more than a shadow in Corporal Organ's soothing arms.

'Loop upon loop, branches that are all cul-de-sacs. How can that be? Nature abhors a cul-de-sac. Is it Kaprikorn Schultz or Captain Quelch? Is it the whole brute power of the Singularity? How can we succeed?'

'Hush, diddle, hush. Hush, darling little Rupoldo. There are no cul-de-sacs in Nature. Never fear. Never fear!'

'But the end is close for that one, I think,' murmurs Professor Pop in weary sympathy, unable to take any real attention from the up-screen. 'There's Mars. I can hear her!'

'*Tower to* Now The Clouds Have Meaning. *Tower to* Now The Clouds Have Meaning. *What is your present scale? Repeat, what is your present scale? We have searched all of the known Second Ether and found only ghosts and shadows. The famous old warhorse has screwed herself into Limbo and lies in a fold nobody can chart. Tower to* Now The Clouds Have Meaning. *We cannot locate you in the Plasma Vortex.* Please give us your present scale!'

But Captain Billy-Bob Begg and her famous Chaos Engineers are unable to respond to the Scaling Station. It seems they must drift off-scale for all eternity.

'Oh, behold! Oh, fear!' Corporal Organ flings a hand towards the R. They all know that sinister shape. Kaprikorn Schultz has re-formed *The Face of the Fly*!

(To be continued)

Part 4

Routes

The idea that a mountain is made of rocks and that each rock is like a small mountain in itself is an idea very familiar to mountaineers.

Friends of mine who climb mountains send me accounts . . . in which the climber was amazed to find that the top of the Matterhorn was like the entire Alps in miniature.

Benoit Mandelbrot
TV Interview
Fractals: An Animated Discussion

CHAPTER ONE

Der Colt is ihr Gestz

The distant yell of the Biloxi Fault took fresh harmonics from the Rose's song and amplified it until for a while a vast unearthly orchestra played the old tune, told the old story of lies and truth, of betrayals and sacrifices, of quests and oaths, of love and loss and resolutions that are not always tragic. The old story which is echoed by our own.

When her own old story was at last modified to fractured cacophony by the Biloxi Fault, the Rose struck out up the beach towards the Terminal Café whose lines shifted into focus against the lurid, uneasy funnel of the Fault.

The Terminal was a two-storey clapboard sprawl of dining room, gambling area and various rooms to let. A peculiarly patterned light billowed from the kitchens and the paint was blistered and peeling while the aluminium roof roiled with moody reflections. A sign over the main entrance announced the name of the Café and, in guttering ice-cream neon, proclaimed itself to have 'The Last Heat on the Beach'.

She pushed back the screen. The inner door swung easily and she entered, the subject of suspicious eyes.

She began to walk towards a raised area at the far end of the hall.

The horrible mælstrom of the Fault framing them, a group of jugadors had their whole attention upon a flat game. The air surrounding them grew cloudy and garish as they played, their eyes staring deeply into whole universes of their own creation.

Jack Karaquazian sits at his game, wagering the highest psychic stakes from a position conventionally known as the Dead King's Chair. His stoic back is against the whirling patterns of Chaos ceaselessly forming and reforming. His fellow gamblers know him as Al-Q'areen. There are shades amongst these players, men and women who by some chance have lost their own hold on life yet still wish to play at the tables – surrogates of the living gamblers, contributing their remaining experience and cunning to the game. They will do anything for even a hazy simulation of existence; the alternative is extinction. All these jugadors have the abstracted, dedicated ascetic appearance of a strict order. The Egyptian smiles on them, a kindly jackal.

There was once a story told in Memphis, when Jack Karaquazian worked there, of an upriver captain on the Missouri out of Saint Jo; an octoroon woman who could read currents and waters better than any pilot; who was keenly courted by owners, white or black. She had lost her own stern-wheeler to a pirate attack while waiting for steam in the Nebraska Streak and had caught up with the thieves only after they had broken the boat's back in the white water channel. She was said to have killed the pirates to a man, using a rapier. He seemed to recall she had some kind of Dutch name, a familiar one.

Well, that's her, thinks Jack Karaquazian as she stalks in to the Terminal, a wary stranger.

Her skin is the colour of dark olives tinged with pink, her hair a subtle red. Her eyes are brown-green and there is a vibrancy about her that reminds Mr Karaquazian of something that is not wholly human and when she tells him her name he offers her the respect he reserves for all legends.

'Captain von Bek, I am at your service.' He stands and bows. His long arms lift a little towards her, his gentle fingers, still holding a shimmering deck, extend almost as if to embrace her, and his smile is a thing to fear and to adore.

No matter how impossible he has set his handicaps and how high he has raised the psychic stakes, he never loses.

He marvels at unsought inspiration. The unwanted power, the unlooked-for streak of luck, had made an unhappy madman of him. All he ever desired was what he lost out past McClellan where herons flew like grey angels through the black cypress branches and three gold stains lay on the pewter water like ingots of purest gold driven into the deep heart of reality. He wanted what pride and blind folly had lost him when he had failed to follow his heart.

Rose von Bek, used to most recognitions, is unsurprised by his greeting. The ghastly colours behind Jack Karaquazian change suddenly so that his pale skin and long black hair appear almost in negative, an image which fills the Rose with more than a hint of nostalgic terror. She speaks to her fellow adept with great courtesy, explaining that she has a message for him which she has memorised. It is unwise to carry written language between the First and Second Ethers.

> 'Mrs Dovero presents her compliments to Mr Karaquazian and respectfully invites him to make his way into the Second Ether where we may be reunited. This lady, Captain von Bek,

will be his guide. Signed with enduring love and with faith in
a mutual destiny—

Colinda Dovero.'

The Rose is unused to the Terminal. Her attention wanders from Jack
Karaquazian's face to the agitated shadows, like doomed souls reaching
aimlessly into the emerald green electrics of the tables.

Jack Karaquazian sat back from his game, his delicate Egyptian
features giving him something of the appearance of a fox, in white lace
and black velvet, ready for any human trick.

'You would not I hope be making fun of me, ma'am?'

This response surprises the Rose. She has never before seen eyes
warier than her own and is impressed by the evident intensity of his
affection for her friend. 'I am not, sir,' she promises.

Jack Karaquazian stood up, slipping his lean arms into his black silk
jacket, abandoning the shades with whom he had been playing 'Old
Funny's Chopper' out of an obscure sense of charity. The shades
immediately fell into postures of near-stupor, no longer animated by his
generous will.

The Rose remembers her own recent brush with two malignantly
animated shades. She pities the half-creatures but she is never unhappy
to see the last of them.

Jack Karaquazian stepped down from the Dead King's Chair, his back
still firmly presented to the pink and yellow horror which was the
current manifestation of the Biloxi Fault, and which even the Rose
preferred not to confront. He took her arm and led her up a ramp,
sliding in a kind of reverse gravity helter-skelter to his room where the
light poured like blood into a dark blue pool. He apologised for his
careless shielding. 'It gives me comfort, this illusion of being at the centre
of the mælstrom. I can pretend to face reality here.'

He saw that she disapproved of his cynicism. He apologised. He had
become unused, he said, to well-bred company and had a feeling he was
mad. He shook his head like a dog and collected himself. 'You have seen
Mrs Dovero recently, ma'am?'

'Relatively recently. She awaits you. She believes you will want to join
us.'

'I am at her service, ma'am, as well as yours. Where do we travel?
How far? I must pack.'

'I fear there is no provision you can make against our particular
journey, sir.' It is as if the Rose imitates his own formality.

Again he paused. 'Oh, ma'am, you are not Old Death, are you, in a
fresh disguise, come hunting for my soul?'

'I earnestly hope that I am not.' She smiles a quick reassurance. 'Death, sir, is my enemy.'

Jack Karaquazian, rolling his booted feet in the rivulets of barley sugar which spilled upon his obsidian carpet, looked at her earnestly. 'As he remains mine.'

'Shall we go?' suggests the Rose.

She waits outside his unsteady door as he changes his linen. He shares Sam Oakenhurst's fastidious obsessions. The Rose is reminded of a bullfighter preparing to confront his opponent. And yet the way he moves like a dancer and holds his shoulders *à Flamenco* advertises no artifice. She believes he is naturally graceful, like her lover, Sam Oakenhurst, who is in other respects a very different individual. She wonders how Mr Oakenhurst fares with the machinoix.

'Do we go up the Trace?' Mr Karaquazian asked as they descended into the Terminal.

'Not to Natchez,' she tells him, 'but to New Orleans. We're waiting on Sam. You're familiar with the Quarter?'

'More than sometimes suits my peace of mind.' He acknowledged the significance of her question. 'But we can get a place where we'll be okay. If Sam stays in with us we'll not have to fear the machinoix.'

'I know where we shall be almost safe,' she says.

Boudreaux Ramsadeen performs an eccentric figure on the dance floor to the throb of his pilo zee-band while his tiny partners flock about him like monarchs, all red and black. He waves the two jugadors farewell. With a rare gesture of finality he watches them through the bright lattice of gold and fluttering copper, an expression of affection on his brutish face.

They leave for the stables where Jack Karaquazian always has two horses prepared.

Mounted, they returned to the blue and yellow beach, the garish Fault filling the sky to their left, capering and farting like an angry ape trying to take human shape; the air immediately above it is a serene pale blue but everywhere else are the bruised, sickening colours of ruptured reality.

'It's been behaving like that for almost a season,' said Jack Karaquazian. 'Death imitating life.'

CHAPTER TWO

Huron-Blut

The Audobon *cabines à la mode* on rue Dauphine would take them if they swore to observe the curfew. They promised they would obey the rules for now and, should they need to break them, they would confer first with the landlord. This last was a shifty whitey who picked his teeth with his thumbnail and betrayed all the worst characteristics of his race, mumbling his demands in a jargon they could barely understand.

Their shack within the compound was called Cardinal Cottage and lay only a few yards from the cesspit but they betrayed no disgust as the Rose took a velvet purse from her clothing and paid the man four guineas which he promised would be returned in proportion if they stayed less than a month.

Jack Karaquazian found the place oppressive, but it had two floors and could be defended. Upon a great obiché sideboard, carved in crude imitation of the machinoix style, he found piles of hand-coloured magazines, dog-eared and dirty from a hundred usings, in which were recounted the tales of the Chaos Engineers and their perpetual war against the Singularity. Jack Karaquazian had only seen these recently. Travellers had been bringing them in to the Terminal. 'But I had not realised they were so popular! These are real people are they? Originally?' He told her that the Terminal had been visited twice by what he had taken for a burned-out pilo who had announced herself as The Merchant Venturer, Pearl Peru. At both times he had retired to his quarters until she had gone. 'Do you know this particular Pearl Peru? Does she model herself on a V-character?'

'Not exactly,' was the only answer the Rose would give him then. 'These characters are followed everywhere now. In the South, both west and east of the river, and for all I know they're being read beyond St Louis. Do you enjoy them, Jack?'

'Oh, they are hardly my kind of entertainment,' he said.

'Well,' said the Rose, 'it is worth familiarising yourself with such things. Especially if you would know the secrets and comforts of the Second Ether.'

'You have yet to say where this place lies,' he said. 'Are we not going up to Natchez and following the Trace to McClellan?' To the gold Stains where he had last seen Colinda Dovero but, dishonoured, was unable to follow her.

'I said nothing of McClellan.' She sighed a little. 'We must find out first if Sam is still with us.'

'Then I suspect we must sweat it here for a while.' He slipped off his jacket and bending to his saddle-bag removed a hammock which he proceeded to sling on the hooks provided above the shack's only door. She could sleep upstairs if she wished. He preferred to swing in the shadows with his Sony handy. Testing the hammock's security, he put the weapon between his teeth and climbed into the net.

The Rose told him she had her own manner of sleeping and folded herself near the stairs, invisible to the unknowing eye.

Before he admitted sleep he told her that he longed for a place where he might rest and know peace and which was not the grave.

CHAPTER THREE

Der Diablo-Raub

Standing on the roof of Cardinal Cottage the Rose could see beyond the compound wall where at night the only illumination came from an orange moon and the guttering flambeaux, bubbling globules of viscous chemicals, marking the progress of the mechanish engines through streets over which they held unchallenged sway. After a certain hour, the stink of the wheezing, shrieking vehicles became almost intolerable, a mixture of charnel house and overheated electrics. She speculated on the nature of their mysterious attractors, the means by which they could draw energy from the air itself. Perhaps Sam Oakenhurst would be able to tell her. She had sent out a message to him.

Something rolled by, close to the gate. For a moment the air was filled with a marbling of grey, black and blue which dissipated like a falling wail.

Jack Karaquazian was beginning to lose patience. Now he spent much of his time down at Army Square with a few second-rate players, trying to ease his boredom in one-against-all hands of 'Guppy's Surprise', the featured game of the old Providence Bar and Grill. Often he would not be back until morning, when the curfew ended. He had hoped, he said, never to see another of those drooling mechanish again. He refused to discuss how Sam Oakenhurst could be spending so much time with the metalloids' masters.

To keep her hand in, the Rose had set up a few old Brackett's jars from which she coaxed a fairly complex main play, complete with pseudo-consciousness for most of the elements, including a detailed triple-logic frame. With some Brackett's she could often get quintuple-logic, but for the moment she was satisfied.

She played against herself. The setting was the Biloxi Fault and a universe she called the Grail, which was situated in the Second Ether and where her adopted home now was.

She called her world Sylvania and it was not dissimilar in many respects to the one she now inhabited, though most of the dramatic instabilities were not manifested there. She had risked a great deal in leaving. Even now there was no certainty she would return with her two charges; the man she herself loved and the man loved by her friend.

By nature more patient than Jack Karaquazian, the Rose began at last to fear that Sam Oakenhurst was no longer alive and his latest machinoix bargain had been for more than his time and his flesh.

With slender fingers she teased up the Brackett's, turning their fluorescent gases into simulacræ of whole universes, whole peoples, near-individuals.

She considered the dangers of recreating her own past.

CHAPTER FOUR

Gun-Slammer's Choice

(In which Mr Karaquazian is challenged by a youth from Tennessee, claiming right of dispute-by-blood according to the laws of his people, but Mr Karaquazian will have none of it. This scene ensues:)

THE YOUTH: (pointing boldly) YOU ARE THE COLD-BLOODED KILLER WHO SHOT MY BROTHER IN THE BACK UP ABOVE NATCHEZ ON THE DARK MONTANA!

KARAQUAZIAN: (politely) IF I KILLED YOUR BROTHER, SIR, I HAD NO INTENTION OF IT. (Significantly – he is trying to avoid confrontation) AS A RULE I SHOOT ONLY IN SELF-DEFENCE AND WHEN I DRAW IT IS USUALLY TO KILL.

YOUTH: (waving a huge Olivetti 41D) SHOT IN THE BACK, YOU BASTARD. YOU DAMNED COWARD!

KARAQUAZIAN: (softly) THAT IS YOUR OPINION, SIR. NOW I BEG YOU, LET US DISCUSS THIS RATIONALLY. WILL YOU TAKE A DRINK WITH ME? WHAT WAS YOUR BROTHER'S NAME, SIR?

YOUTH: (defiantly uncertain) BEN KAFKA – YOU SHOULD KNOW. HE WAS BEATING YOU AT 'DRUNKEN JEWELS' AND WHEN HE GOT UP TO ANSWER NATURE YOU SHOT HIM IN THE BACK.

MR K: WITH WHAT WEAPON, SIR?

BOY: WITH A REMINGTON 60/40 SUCH AS ALL THE VS SHOWED YOU CARRYING. I WATCHED 'MANSNAPPER' FOR TOO MANY EPISODES NOT TO KNOW WHAT HEAT YOU SLING!

MR K: WELL, SIR, IT'S A PRETTY WELL-KNOWN FACT THAT I HAVE NEVER BEEN BEATEN AT 'DRUNKEN JEWELS'. WHEN WAS YOUR BROTHER KILLED, SIR?

BOY:	MAYBE FALL. MAYBE NINETY. SOMETHING. WE AIN'T PAID MUCH ATTENTION TO DATES IN TENNESSEE. NOT FOR A WHILE. BUT WE STILL KNOW BLOODY MURDER WHEN WE SEE IT.
MR K:	WOULD THAT HAVE BEEN BEFORE OR AFTER WE GOT THE FAULT?
BOY:	AFTER, OF COURSE.
MR K:	THEN, SIR, I GUESS IT WASN'T ME KILLED YOUR BROTHER. I DID NOT CARRY A REMINGTON FOR TWO YEARS BEFORE THE FAULT AND HAVE NOT FOR A SCORE OF SEASONS SINCE.
BOY:	(hysterically) I SAY YOU ARE A LIAR! A COWARD, A MURDERER, AND A CHEAT!
MR K:	(levelly) I APOLOGISE IF BY AN OVERSIGHT OF MINE YOU HAVE CONFUSED ME WITH SOMEONE ELSE OR, INDEED, IF I DID AT SOME TIME DEFEND MYSELF AGAINST A RELATIVE OF YOURS, BUT I CANNOT ACCEPT THAT LAST REMARK, WHICH HAS TO DO WITH MY PROFESSIONAL HONOUR (he slowly raises his long arm, moves his hand towards his lapel – THE BOY thinks he's going for his Sony and levels his own huge weapon, but JACK KARAQUAZIAN lazily moves his arm back along the bar to its original position. Now THE BOY will be even less sure what to make of MR KARAQUAZIAN'S next move). I BEG YOU, SIR, WHY DON'T WE SIT DOWN LIKE GENTLE-MEN AND COME TO AN UNDERSTANDING?
BOY:	YOU ARE A COWARD, KARAQUAZIAN, AND A MURDERER AND A CHEAT — AND IF YOU WON'T DRAW I'LL SHOOT YOU WHERE YOU STAND!
MR K:	SIT DOWN, I BEG YOU, SIR. I INTEND YOU NO HARM, BUT I ALWAYS SHOW A WOULD-BE ASSASSIN THE RESPECT OF KILLING HIM OUTRIGHT. THIS BLOOD-FEUDING, SIR, WILL NOT DO. I'M NOT THE ONLY ONE BELIEVES IT A POOR AND UNWIELDY SUBSTITUTE FOR THE AMERICAN CONSTITUTION. PLEASE, SIR, PUT UP YOUR WEAPON.

(Whereupon THE BOY lets off an uneven stream of grey carcinogens which do nothing but blister the paint of the bar and alter the chemistry of some of the drinks while JACK KARAQUAZIAN almost reluctantly draws his Sony and slices twice, leaving a neat cross where THE BOY's heart once was. He turns away, reholstering his weapon, an expression of grim distaste on his face.)

MR K: THIS IS NO WAY FOR CIVILISED MEN TO LIVE. (From habit, he orders himself a double Ackroyd's.)

CHAPTER FIVE

Six Weeks South of Texas

After the Providence incident, Jack Karaquazian stayed with the Rose, building up a complex variety of energised gases into worlds and intelligences to match her own but his whole being could not engage and he admitted he felt the lack of edge which comes from playing the real thing.

'One day it could be both simpler and more exciting for you, Jack,' the Rose assured him.

After almost a week of this a kiddikin tapped on their door with news of a visitor at the courtyard gate. His name, said the kiddikin, was Captain Quelch and – fingertips to tittering mouth – he was a white man!

Jack Karaquazian's instinct was to refuse an interview. It was unseemly for whites to demand such sudden courtesies. But if this was the same Quelch who had also left his card at the Terminal then he guessed he was ready to confront him. The presence of the Rose was a comfort.

'For some reason I am nervous of this proud whitey,' he admitted to the Rose.

The Rose seemed only amused. And so the lantern-jawed, hook-nosed Captain Quelch was admitted. His skin as white as an alligator's belly, he swaggered in with a most condescending air as if he were their master. His hands were silvery, multi-hued, like the scales of a dying fish, and he offered one to each of his hosts. He was used to power. His old grey and gold leathers were scarred and splashed from a thousand battles and his face was lined with the evidence of a million betrayals, but his pallid blue, bloodshot eyes were humorous, as if he took relish from this situation, anticipating some of the uncertainty Jack Karaquazian must feel when confronted by such an apparition as himself, stepped over from the Second Ether and still giving off traces of spectral dust, large as life, saluting and chewing on a cold cheroot: the image of his V original. Or was he the original?

'Well, my dears – *quid hoc sibi vult*, eh? Good evening to you. I'm Quelch of *The Linear Bee*. It's not often I put in to New Orleans. Always hated the place and got out as soon as I could. You people like red tape too much for my taste.' He kissed the Rose's hand and winked.

For all its Latin quotation and hearty equity, its louche charm, Jack Karaquazian found the man's manner disagreeably insolent. 'Good evening, Captain Quelch. And where would you be from? And on what business here?'

Captain Quelch laughed. 'You know as well as I that I am from Old Reg, Chief Clerk of the Singularity, Secretary to the Central Ethic; Guardian of the Great Desk, Will of the Original Insect. You know that, sir! I tore apart whole scales to come here. You must have seen the wounds I made. The powerful shall devour the weak! I am the levelling scythe of the Second Ether! I will not waste my time on your children's strategies. What business, sir! Indeed! As deadly as your own, sir, believe me.'

'Mr Karaquazian knows almost nothing, as yet, of our Second Ether,' softly said the Rose.

At this, Captain Quelch relaxed, unbuttoned his uniform tunic, took off his cap and sat himself down in an easy chair on the other side of the Brackett's. 'Is that a flagon of Ackroyd's I see yonder?'

The Rose did not seem at all dismayed. She poured the strange white man a drink. He smiled at her as he put the glass to his lips, his eyes intimate for a second or two. Jack Karaquazian considered the extraordinary likelihood that they had once been lovers. This made him even more uneasy, though he continued to trust the Rose.

'Why are you here, Captain Quelch?' She replaced the stopper of the decanter. She was not welcoming.

Quelch delicately relished his drink. '*Quis separabit?* I was passing through, my dear Rose, and had heard you were presently in New Orleans. I had it in mind to look at some new recruits and to take a glance at yours, if you had the fortune to pick any.'

'I'm not impressing this player or any other, Captain Quelch. That has never been my practice and you know it. Mr Karaquazian is not a recruit and neither has he chosen to play the Game of Time. We field only volunteers. You would do well to return to your proper sphere, sir, and remember your situation. Here you breathe the same air as the living. Here you are merely tolerated. You are abhorrent, sir. You defy our laws.'

'Oh, madam, pardon a poor zombie for paying a sentimental call on one of his old home haunts, where he hoped to derive a little comfort from a more fortunate sister.' Captain Quelch was laughing. 'You are pompous, today, Rose. Not yourself at all.' This last was clearly a barb, but Jack Karaquazian did not understand it.

'Will you banish me, Rose? Back to my native Hell – our common ground? Will you exorcise me, Rose, or slay me with a spell as you slew Gaynor? Or seek the help of those diabolical machinoix as you did when poor unsuspecting Paul Minct sought to play a hand against you? He was never in your class, Rose. Few are.'

Jack Karaquazian found the white man more intelligent and entertaining than the average river rat but exuding an enormous sense of power and danger even as he joked with them.

The Rose was warily unafraid. She shook her hand at Captain Quelch. 'We'll meet soon, Horace. In more fulfilling circumstances, perhaps.'

'I'd enjoy a game again, my dear.' He licked a reminiscent lip.

'No more with me, my dear. I have done my service.'

'You'll never retire. None of us ever retires!' Captain Quelch cast a knowing eye over the shifting Brackett's. 'Nothing will keep you from the Second Ether, Rose, or the Game. It's in your blood as it's in mine. You could not exist without the taste of terror on your palate. Everything to lose! Everything to win!'

'There is one difference between us,' she reminded him.

Then something close to anger appeared on Captain Quelch's rugged reprobate's face and he said quietly, looking at his glass, 'You can wound a chap, Rose, like nobody else.'

'It's in the nature of the rose,' she said. 'It's in my blood, Horace.'

At this he stood up, placing his empty glass between the two Brackett's. 'Clearly there's no human warmth here for an old shade.'

'Not much,' she said. 'Not now.'

He left, after winking intimately at Jack Karaquazian. '*Sine era et studio*, old soul.' He paused to re-button his tunic. 'I trust we'll meet again, sir.'

'Looking forward to it,' said Jack Karaquazian. His own blood had quickened. He felt his body blossoming into secret and alarming vitality.

CHAPTER SIX

Formula for Fear

When Captain Quelch had gone Mr Karaquazian asked the Rose why her words had so hurt their visitor.

'He has no soul of his own,' she said. 'He must leech from others. For all his fine words he is a scavenger, like any who sail with the Singularity. They have no business here. They grow too bold. They are attracted by death. They are carrion. This planet is near its end, I think.'

Jack Karaquazian was taken aback by her venomous eloquence. 'He is your enemy, then?'

'He has made himself my enemy. I sought no quarrel with Captain Quelch or his damned twin!'

'There are two of him?'

'Two? Oh, no, Jack. More than two. But we'll take that in its best order, shall we? Synchronisation is the key to harmonic scale. Like putting each line in play. Believe me, Jack, our pasatiempo there is easier than any ordinary day's game of "Pretty Beginners" at the Terminal. It's only that the stakes are different.'

'Are they all white, like Quelch, those we play against?'

'Some aren't. But they happen to be the people who elected to make themselves conquerors of the Second Ether. The rest of us were merely glad to be granted its beauty.'

'What's wrong with them wanting to conquer you?' Jack Karaquazian felt antagonism. 'Do you not represent Chaos and the destruction of all sentience? Does not the Singularity represent Law and a secure, simple, predictable society unthreatened by chance? What does the Singularity represent? The unromantic desires of the common folk for a hearth, a home and children. This is the reality of the common dream, which the romantic denies. What am I to believe, Rose? I am given no arguments that I can grasp, no familiar maps. Show me how it's played and you know I'll join any game you like – but don't ask me to play blind. Or against my own people. Or against God. You won't do that, will you?'

'I said it to you one way.' She was patient. 'But I'll say it your way, too, if it suits you: it's an honest game I'll be offering, Jack, with honest winnings. And I promise I'll scroll the whole thing to you before I ask you to sit down at a table with me. You won't ever be playing blind, Jack.'

He accepted her word and considered the events. Somehow Captain Quelch's visit had confirmed an instinctive understanding that Jack Karaquazian's interests were linked with those of the Rose. Quelch represented something cold and loathsome in the lower levels of the human psyche. Something greedy and unwholesome. Something devolving, which served only the cause of the Old Hunter, which eternally plotted the reduction and ultimate destruction of the human spirit.

'Why,' he said, 'did you not tell me more of this earlier, Rose? I could reasonably suspect manipulation on your part. I am averse to being manipulated. If you say your game is straight I'll take your word, but I'll admit I'm having trouble doing it.'

'It gives me trouble keeping my oath,' she says. 'I keep it anyway. I was waiting for my Sam Oakenhurst to arrive so he might tell you in words you'd best understand. I'm not keeping secrets from you that will affect your actions, Jack. I promise. You can decide each play as we go. I don't even ask you to commit to the Game of Time. No mortal soul could reasonably do that for long. To guard against insanity we play together and we play in turns. And we make ourselves forget that we play at all. Don't pity yourself too profoundly, my dear. At least your true love's safe and sound, while I've no notion who or what has claimed the soul of mine.'

He was grateful for this reminder of his manners. He had been ungentlemanly. He would advertise his own petty feelings no longer. He felt he needed a good hand to play and an opponent like Sam Oakenhurst or Mistress Mint, whom he had also loved and who, for all her outward disapproval and even disappointment in him, had cared deeply for him and played a wise game. Almost as wise as Colinda Dovero's, thought Mr Karaquazian, and was glad to remind himself of what he stood to gain from this.

But then he frowned and shook his head.

Mistress Mint?

Surely she had been nothing more than his invention in a long game of 'Bluff the Shade' he had played in Alexandria even before he took the schoomer for Atlantic City?

For the first time since he had put himself in the Rose's hands Jack Karaquazian became afraid.

CHAPTER SEVEN

Sky-Pilot Cowboy

Sam Oakenhurst met Jack Karaquazian on Goodnight Street just below the old covered Marché Blanc where few respectable people ever ventured, even in New Orleans. It was where the whiteys found their whores. Daylight murder had become common above Rampart. The curfew applied even at these edges of the Quarter.

'You're looking well, Jack,' said Sam Oakenhurst. 'Your old self.'

'I'm feeling it, Sam.'

Mr Oakenhurst's irony, if that is what it was, he offered without inflection. His face was changed beyond recognition. He held out a hand. The thin bones had been broken and reset, then broken and reset again, each time adding (or growing) new bone until they were twice the length of the originals and had become what the machinoix considered handsome. His face, which had been the subject of a score of eccentric surgical exercises or rituals, now had the cadaverous appearance of a long-dead goat, yet retained a certain sad beauty reflecting much of what Jack Karaquazian knew of his friend's character. It cost him some self-control to shake the offered hand. It was like shaking hands with the Old Hunter himself.

'I hear you're in town with the Rose,' said Sam Oakenhurst. 'But they didn't know where you're staying. I thought she said she'd meet me at the Terminal?'

'Audobon,' says Jack Karaquazian, 'same as always.'

'I remember. My memory ain't what is was, though, Jack.'

'Mine neither, Sam. It's good to see you.'

'You recognised me?'

'Right away, Sam.'

Mr Oakenhurst sighed with relief. 'Then maybe she will, too.'

CHAPTER EIGHT

Kit Carson's Perilous Ride

The Rose had played many scenarios and so had not been overly disturbed by Sam Oakenhurst's appearance. She, like Jack Karaquazian, had a habit of looking at the bones first. The essence of her Sam was still there, as strong as ever, she thought, beneath all that tortured muscle and sinew, which had been blessed by the most skilled knives among his machinoix kin. She kissed him. He tasted at her like a man unsure whether he embraced a mirage. 'Mon grace, muy rosa, mio darling! I have dreamed of this for a thousand years!'

Jack Karaquazian went into the courtyard to stand by the old fountain which had always been dry. He lit a rare Romeo y Julieta and, looking up, searched among the heavy, hot clouds for the stars. New Orleans gave him the shivers.

Outside, a mechanish squeaked and gibbered, parting the crusty smoke and uttering that foul, flowing green viscous stuff they used for light. Jack Karaquazian was glad he had eaten little and early. It was impossibly hard to make sense of the events of the last hours.

'O, pierrot. Mon brave, mon beau!' sang the Rose and Jack Karaquazian was reminded how he had meant to come to Colinda Dovero purified by some spectacular heroism, some deed of mighty self-sacrifice. Instead he had learned only how to accept forgiveness.

There had to be more. He would earn her love, he thought. In his heart he already knew that love is rarely earned but given freely and without hesitation, one soul to another, with little logic or sense. It was for love of himself that he yearned for heroism. He was reminded of his purpose in being here, of what Colinda Dovero had offered if he followed the Rose, and his warmth toward Captain von Bek grew stronger again.

Now, he assumed, they would all be on their way to Natchez.

'Do we have another meat boat, Sam?' she wanted to know.

'I could not fairly ask for that. Then they offered me my caravel. I am not sure of it. They understand my goals and are glad of them. It took them many turns of the eternity cushions and the shutter boxes before they fully understood my needs and rose to fulfil them. In their own fashion, of course, which I in turn now understand. They insisted on preparing me for my journey. They have passed everything they know of the Second Ether into me. They, too, have been players in the Game of Time but have exhausted it and been exhausted by it. They are the missing fishlings, some say.' He became self-conscious. 'Or at least that's how the Chaos Engineers see things. I suppose you don't look at that trash, do you, Jack?'

'I am unfamiliar with your pseudo-Vs, nor do I recollect their originals clearly. My childhood was full of Ali Baba and those wonderful historical soaps for which Egyptians were justly envied. These are like creatures from the barbaric past, from the time of the pharaohs!' Jack Karaquazian was puzzled by his friend's unfading intensity. 'But I have heard of the one named the Merchant Venturer, Pearl Peru, for she came calling on me once or twice at the Terminal when I was in no mood for visitors.' He did not mention Captain Quelch.

'Pearl Peru herself! You're greatly honoured, Jack. She's one of the noblest and most beautiful of all the Paladins of Chaos. She is a paragon, Jack. Her only weakness is her kindly, trusting heart.'

'Sam!' says the Rose laughing. 'These characters from your V magazines are of no interest to Jack!'

'When those characters come a-visiting, Rose, as they seem to be doing fairly frequently, I believe them to be of some interest,' says Mr Karaquazian. 'Sometimes I have the notion that we are all trapped in a bad game of 'Old Tom's Last Roll'. Is something happening to the rules?'

'Not yet, Jack,' says the Rose, 'but we are playing for Time.'

It wasn't much of an answer.

'There's a man in Gulfport selling a boat that might suit us,' says Sam. 'We could ride over and look at her. Then if we like her it's a short haul to the Fault. Does she have to have sails, Rose?'

'It makes no difference,' says the Rose, 'so long as she steers and moves I can probably sail her. I'm getting used to those currents.'

'This here's a paddle-wheeler I guess.'

'All the better,' she says. 'I prefer a little steam.'

'Let's go,' says Jack Karaquazian, anxious to put at least the ambiguities of New Orleans behind him.

But Sam Oakenhurst must know what Pearl Peru said and what she had looked like. Was her body covered in multicoloured skins which moved over it like living things? Did the ether-dust pour continuously from her helmet and nostrils?

'Unfortunately on the occasions that the lady called,' says Jack

Karaquazian, 'I was otherwise engaged and could not meet her. To tell you the truth, Sam, I was weary of strangers just then. I had some thinking to do.'

Sam Oakenhurst's long upper lip almost trembles with disappointment and he turns away to recover himself. 'There have been periods,' he says by way of apology, 'when only those melodramas saved me from madness. But perhaps I wasn't saved from madness, after all?'

Jack Karaquazian puts his hand on his friend's arm.

CHAPTER NINE

Pilgrim From Tombstone

Boudreaux Ramsadeen was surprised when the three returned to the Terminal Café and sat down at the back bar, near the stage. 'That's a real pretty boat,' he said. 'What you mean to do with her out this way, mon amies?' He was nervous. It was his nature to create as much stability on his premises as was possible and he disliked talk of expeditions into the Fault. He had already heard a version of Sam Oakenhurst's voyage into Ketchup Cove. He desired no trouble of that sort.

'You staying long, Jack?' he wanted to know.

'Not long,' said Mr Karaquazian and made a reassuring gesture. 'We ain't going through the Fault now. We're going back up to the river. There's been a change of ideas.'

Somehow the machinoix had contacted Sam Oakenhurst on the journey from Gulfport and warned that the Fault was now dangerous to them. A kind of trap, they said. They had advised the trio to take the big flat-bottomed double-wheeler upriver and sail her to St Louis where they would find an entrance to the Second Ether which would accept the boat, *La Perle du Suede*, whose wheel the Rose had quickly mastered. So there she was, freshly painted, moored beside the Terminal, where the old pier once stood, while Boudreaux Ramsadeen, learning the good news that they were going on, welcomed them loudly with generous relief.

He offered them his best. He had a new cook from the city who would work only in the dark. 'He is blind! Mon Dieu! And ugly! Phew! Mama dell' God! But it is pure cajunish. You'll take some sup, mes amigos?' He smacked his lips and kissed his fingers, ogling them like an old husband.

Later, when they had gorged on the blind chef's magic, Boudreaux sat back from the table and offered the opinion that it was getting close to their end. 'Either that or we're going to be free again. What you think, Jack?'

'Free again,' says Mr Karaquazian. 'Free at last. What's the point of expecting anything else?'

'That's you, Jack. But my guess is it's finis this time.'

Mr Karaquazian shrugged. He had taken liberally of the Fröm. 'Who knows, mon ami? Danson, danson! Make that squeezebox stir us all, mes amigos! Ola, Patric – 'The Antelope' upon your autoharp, if you please. We have here all the power you'll ever know or need.' The musicians grinned uneasily through the fluttering shadows. 'Joli boys, alles dansez! Pretty amigos, bon temps, bon temps! Regard! Elle rollez! Play, my brothers, play. Tonight, at last, I am ready to dance.' Then, with the Rose on his arm, he stepped upon the floor, all poised and alive with danger. But it was Colinda Dovero he saw as they danced.

('God is life ruled by a moral principle and the Devil is death ruled by mere appetite,' says Jack Karaquazian to Colinda Dovero. 'There are however many states between God and the Devil.' They dance together on the deck of the *Etoile du Memphes* while Mr Pitre plays dobro and guitar and Sweet Steve, the blind kiddikin, runs his ghostly fingers over the buttons of his snaking squeezebox, playing all the grand old two-steps. Colinda Dovero sings in his ear: 'O, joy. O, joieux embracero. Mon beau, mon brave. Dancing till the end of time.' And there would never be, could never be another Jack Karaquazian, she sings. Her Jack Karaquazian.

'He hunts for souls,' says Jack. 'He hunts for yours and mine. They are what he feeds on.'

And the night currents of the Mississippi swim in the guttering lamps of the boat and reflect the mosquito candles in their little glass cages, dissipating the shadows of passengers taking an evening promenade as the great paddles lazily push them upriver. The pilot calls a halloo to invisible acquaintances along the sand bars. The boat heads for the broader waters above Oaktree.

Bats swarm suddenly in the darkening air, fleetingly framed against the great round disc of a sun bleeding like a ruby into an horizon where cypresses and pines in silhouette seem to spell a prophecy in an unknown alphabet, stinking of some richer yesterday.

And when the dancing was done they had taken their own stroll upon the deck, passing Oaktree Levee, invisible to port, and hearing the whiteys singing plaintive laments of wounded pride and cheating lovers, of lost power and paradise, to the strumming of primitive guitars. She had been moved by the sadness of the sound, that constant underlying elegy of defeat, and had wept for a moment before embracing him.)

It is the first time Boudreaux Ramsadeen has seen any of the three on the floor. He is surprised at what graceful dancers they all are –

handsome Jack Karaquazian, exquisite Rose von Bek, cadaverous Mr Oakenhurst. It is as if legends have come to an ordinary dance hall. The other dancers are inhibited not by the skill of these jugadors but by the willingness of myths to take the common floor.

Eventually the music recovered its confidence and the fiddle player came in. The ope grew thick and the measures became familiar, in spite of their flourishes. The others returned to the dance until all were making their wild points and elaborate turns amongst those terrible shadows, leaping as the flames of the Fault leapt, uncertain and unafraid.

Only when the dancing went on without cease did Boudreaux come to realise that this was their true farewell. It was, he guessed, how they honoured him. They were making the most of their days of life. When they went back to the boat they would begin a voyage from which, no matter what else occurred, they would never return.

CHAPTER TEN

Voodoo Slaves for the Devil's Daughter

She found me reading 'Spark of the Grey Fees' (the words were often familiar but the language itself a mystery, dependent on many secondary, even primary, references denied my limited intelligence and experience. But gradually I came to learn the rudiments of a kind of Second Ether pidgin until I grew skilful enough to enter into bond with my character and add her considerable store of wisdom to my own. Suddenly I knew the powers and near-omniscience of a demigod!). 'I have never seen a man so hungry for the Second Ether,' she said.

My name is Sam Oakenhurst. I am of the jugador persuasion, Mercie Marie, and until I met my love, the Rose, followed that calling in the First Ether until, after several adventures, I joined the Rose to play the ultimate game, the *Zeitsjuego*, the Game of Time, which I shall continue to play for the rest of my long life, for I have by unhappy accident joined the ranks of the dying.

As soon as we were first reunited and alone, we embraced. In my fever I had confused her with Pearl Peru. It was as if everything I had ever valued or desired was at once restored to me.

'Spark of the Grey Fees' tells this tale the best, with all the nuances, the moral ambiguities, the odd twists of plot common to the finest old Vs of the golden age. It is a terrifying thing to have to accept one reality in favour of the others. It is that moment of choosing which is so distressing. Extinction or eternal life on the throw of a die! And in the end the Game of Time engulfed me. I was addicted as I had told her I would never be. As she had never wanted me to be.

'Our black little souls, Sam,' she had said. 'That's all we have between us and the Pit. But it's enough to give us even odds in a game which, if you lose, you will live a billion glorious years or more and if you win, you live forever. Either way, Sam, suit yourself. You'll discover what you want in the Second Ether. And it's only rarely, muy compañero, that you find what you expected to find. Have you anything to lose by playing the big table, Sam? Playing for the power to change the nature of reality? That's what it means, when you control Time!' She pressed her warm rose lips against my hard, fleshless head. 'We're playing against Entropy and for Chaos. Against Singularity and for Law. For life against death. *We're playing for the power to change the human condition!'*

As the meaning of her words threaded into the dark places of my imagination, I experienced the kind of fear which had seized me when the machinoix first began their indoctrination rituals with the Gentle Scarrings. But now I knew one thing I had not known then – I would survive and I would profit from the experience. That, I realised, was why the Rose had chosen me as her consort at this level of the Game.

I feared neither pain nor death but only the loss of my love and my honour. And for those alone I was prepared to play to the end.

I lie.

I did not fear pain. I embraced it.

Pain was my positive proof that I lived.

CHAPTER ELEVEN

Vier Asse

The machinoix cleared their way past New Orleans and provisions were waiting for them on the quays, tended by whiteys in their masters' intricate tattooed livery, who efficiently stowed the goods and offered themselves as hands, if needed. Rose von Bek in particular was reluctant to have these strange creatures aboard. They appeared completely dedicated to the well-being of the machinoix, yet seemingly had their own customs and codes, independent of their masters. Only Sam Oakenhurst could explain the machinoix and he never spoke of his kindred, as if to reveal anything of them would be a betrayal. Sam Oakenhurst was casual with the whiteys, showing them a kind of veneration. The few he recognised, he asked after cousins and aunts. To his companions he argued that a couple would be useful, since nobody had any idea any more what was going on beyond St Louis. These whiteys, at least, wouldn't desert. At first Jack Karaquazian supported the Rose. Eventually, however, Mr Oakenhurst persuaded them to take four as stokers.

The Rose had explained the existence of the Second Ether and how the Game of Time was played in it, a story created by the Chaos Engineers and the Singularity but affecting all existence, as well as the fate of every individual and quasi-individual. In the *Zeitsjuego* one joined one's identity with that of an existing player. By adding one's talents to the whole one played for an advantage in the story, perhaps making a new character or developing a fresh plot thread, perhaps a beginning, a fresh echo to fill a void and set new patterns working, perhaps even adding to the pantheon? She had told Jack that whether he played the Game or not, he would certainly be reunited with Colinda Dovero in the Second Ether.

'What are they – these Chaos Engineers and their opponents?' asked Jack. 'Our creations?'

'It's not as simple as that, Jack,' murmured Sam.

'But we play for Chaos?'

'We play on that side for our own advantage. Sometimes for theirs. It is an acceptable symbiosis.'

'How is that?'

The Rose explained how the symbiosis became complete until there was no escaping the character or the Game. One played perpetually until one's dissolution. All characters were controlled by the laws of entropy. Ultimately they would die, their souls with them.

What the Rose and her kind played for was a chance to defeat the laws of entropy and create nothing less than a new reality. 'To mould the multiverse in our own image.'

To Jack Karaquazian that sounded very much like blasphemy.

'To find a way of living in the multiverse according to natural laws? The triumph of life over death! The triumph, Jack, of God. Nothing less.'

'And that's what you play for?'

'Pretty much.'

He said he could not refuse to play at least one game in the Second Ether. After all, they seemed to be trying for the same big win. But he had remained uneasy, even when Sam Oakenhurst and the Rose began to tell him the stories of the Chaos Engineers, the great epics of quests and revenge which were even now being enacted in the Second Ether. 'It seems little different from a good game of 'Oglala P.', though I can't imagine how it would work out, what moves you'd have to make. What do we lose?'

'That's easy, too,' she said. 'I told you. You lose your eternal soul. The demigods of the Second Ether are not immortal. Their longevity is vast, but ultimately they die. That's why Quelch was so bitter. And if you are not free of them, you die also. The dying demigods become increasingly desperate and greedy for life as they realise what is happening to them. They grow into demons. They prey on the living – their own kind as well as ours. They are death, Jack, determined to overcome life and see the whole multiverse an infinite emptiness rather than let others have it. It's that simple, Jack.'

'Not simple in the playing, I'd guess.'

'I reckon not,' she agreed.

Now Jack Karaquazian stood alone by the boat's blunt prow and looked out across the Mississippi River, broad and brown, splashing lazily against the jetties and wharfs, lapping about the useless oil refineries, mile upon mile of them, in untarnished silver alloy, their cryptic, slime-traced structures rising from water gradually re-claiming them. To Jack, they had an heroic air. What were these plants but the final despairing attempt of their forebears to impose linearity upon an environment which they themselves were increasingly fracturing?

'White madness' as they used to say. How many billions of people had been infected by it? Jack Karaquazian no longer found the pipelines and storage chambers, the processing systems and personnel sections, obscene or grotesque. For him they held a certain nostalgia. What grandiose arrogance! What magnificent confidence in the future they predicted! What vast folly! Mais ce n'est pas la guerre!

CHAPTER TWELVE

Prairie Paddles

Before they got to Natchez they learned how that city had blazed, her hills lighting up the Louisiana side as bright as day. The border war had lasted ten weeks before the combatants had united against a fresh enemy from the East and disappeared. Now it was generally reckoned safe along the river, at least as far as Memphis. There was little left to burn. At Mullens they wooded up and took on passengers, refugees including some Indian women and children who spoke of a massacre of the whites – and the Indians with them – by an insane army of disinherited petite bourgeoisie taking its revenge upon familiar victims. But now they had reached Jackson, the Indians had heard, fortifying the city against a rival army marching from Alabama.

Quivering paddles pushed the heavy waters up into spray which passed through the air like little pearls. Every town as far as New Auschwitz was blackened timbers, drifting ash and clinging, gritty smoke, so that the dark grey clouds cascading from their own stacks seemed pure in comparison.

One evening the Indian women got off at New Auschwitz. They said they had relatives to find in northern Arkansas but they feared to get too close to those larger settlements still standing. Cheated of other prey, a mob might again turn on them.

'It's the apocalypse,' said Jack Karaquazian, watching them stumble through the fouled ruins. 'The majority of us revert with terrible ease to the brute state!' Murder and rape had become the familiar norm. Doubtless the dinosaurs too had tramped decisively towards extinction, preying upon their own kind. He raised a hand to wish the women a safe journey. They no longer looked back but doggedly rolled their handcarts up the old trail joining the Vega di Tennessee which led into those beautiful blue pine hills where he and Colinda Dovero had spent a day or two long ago. As anger filled him, he could only curse his own folly in letting his lunatic notions of honour separate him from his soul's mate.

('It's slower there, Jack,' Colinda had said. 'There's more time. And they can reach agreements.')

'She told me it was just good luck got her to what you call the Second Ether.' Mr Karaquazian addressed the Rose as she joined him at the gangplank. 'But I told her I was of an earning disposition. I couldn't take anything that was free.'

'You got your luck free, Jack.'

'I didn't know that then. I should have imitated her generosity. Those Bergers were on my conscience. I guess I've discovered humility. It's of little use now. I am still separated from a woman I would kill to be near, to protect in any way she so desired.' He would no more think to impose upon her love than he would play a marked deck. His feeling for her surpassed even his sense of honour. His code had been his weakness. It had betrayed them both. It had divided them.

He heard her name in the soft wind blowing between the running lines. The wind slammed shut the wooden door of the wheelhouse, the texas. From somewhere below he was sure he heard a passenger murmur 'Colinda' and then laugh, but he knew this must be an illusion. When he found her would she still want him? He had changed. He could not recall the message she had sent but he remembered his own sentiments. 'When death comes, I want to be on the river.'

'It's simple enough.' The Rose was patient when he asked if Colinda still loved him. 'She's waiting, Jack. Yet you continually question her motives, examine her reasons and objectives – forgetting that simple truth. Do you question your luck? She loves you, Jack. She probably doesn't even want to. Colinda's love for you is direct and uncompli-cated. As enduring as your own. And never "earned", Jack. Accept it as innocently as you offer yours and you will thrive in the Second Ether, mon brave.'

She stood beside him on the upper deck. The cool evening air was warmed by two black stacks which sent whispering woodsmoke into the surrounding landscape. 'Truth and honesty are tested and proven and tempered in the Second Ether, Jack. In your world all is entropy. The lie is almost your only currency. Principle is martyred, raped and perverted. The truth is a dilute of uncertain memories.'

'You speak as if our dilemma here were a moral one. What morality has the Biloxi Fault?'

'Everything is a fragment of something else; a model for the whole. One thing echoes another. One thing mirrors another. There's a morality to nature, Jack. One we learn to recognise and sometimes emulate. Like recognises like. That's what you know already, Jack or you wouldn't be a jugador. You know the odds, the coincidences, the paradoxes, the repetitions which a true gambler senses and manipulates. Only the finest adepts can play the Game of Time with any hope of retaining and amplifying their own identities. With every game you play you increasingly become your own man.'

'You are daring to change God's plan?'

'We *are* God's plan, Jack. We believe that if we can bend time, we will have altered the nature of reality. Alter the nature of reality and you create any multiverse obeying any laws you choose – a multiverse wholly benign to our kind. Where death is banished.'

Jack Karaquazian was in no doubt of his opinion and spoke his mind. 'You are mad. And maybe damned.'

'Perhaps, but we are not the only people devoting our existence to this search. Others seek a return to their origins so that they might influence natural law. Any one theory or *all* of them will prove practical. Perhaps this race to seek our origins is common amongst sentient species? Perhaps the laws have already been changed many times? Perhaps the paradoxes and impossibilities we find in our worlds are merely fragments of a previous reality? Perhaps we are wrong and the multiverse is, after all, infinite. Perhaps the scales we know are only tiny motes in some vaster multiverse?'

'This is babbling folly. Mere visionary abstraction, Rose!'

'Madness is when you set yourself against infinity and inevitability. We believe we are not mad because we set ourselves against only quasi-infinity. Nature is finite. If the smallest fragment reflects the whole, then death is inevitable for the multiverse. But, by the same logic, *rebirth is also inevitable*. We wish to be present at that precise moment between the death of the old multiverse and the beginning of the new.'

'I have no such long view of things,' says Jack. 'In a world of reflections there are no evident causes – only effects. You stand in a hall of mirrors trying to determine which image was the original. Yet they are perfectly reproduced. Is it the smallest or the largest? How can you tell? You have dispensed with all measurement! And therefore with all morality!'

'Not so. The answer is to create what you seek. You triumph over nature by winning at the Game. Every time you beat the odds, Jack, you add further substance to your own individuality. Ultimately you will resemble nothing but yourself yet you will recognise others like you. Self-discipline and self-knowledge are the key. An individual becomes a unique universe, able to move at will through all the scales of the multiverse – potentially able to control the immediate reality of every scale, every encountered environment.'

She looked up into the darkening sky. 'We are magicians and ghosts,

Jack. We are goblins and visitations. We are future and past. We are memory and we are forgetfulness. Yet we achieve a kind of psychic density so that we remain coherent as we travel up and down the scales, back and forth across the multiverse, walking between the worlds on the silver roads people call moonbeams. Our existence is deeply dependent upon individual responsibility and will. That which our group conscience understands to be evil, is evil.'

'This is blasphemous arrogance,' says Jack Karaquazian without dismay, smiling. 'This is ungodly Satanism!' But he is curious.

'No, Jack. We are fulfilling the will of our kind and therefore the will of God. Consider, for instance, the intellectual rigour required, the careful debate between the wise thinkers of the day, the understanding of human nature, the willingness to listen to the testament of simple people, the ordering and re-ordering required, before those elders eventually codified the Ten Commandments. And if you believe those commandments came from God, so be it, for I believe God to be the sum of all that is humane in us, all that is logical and all that is, if you like, divine. But if God did give us the Ten Commandments through a relevation to Moses, what an intellect God must have! And if we fail to respect such a mighty intellect, we are fools.

'The world is full of more wisdom than destructive ignorance. Why then do we let our societies simplify and devolve? Look how we are reduced to warring tribes! How readily we offer up our own freedom to those who would destroy entire worlds for their immediate self-gratification. Why can't that vast majority of us band together to achieve peace and equity? What are we fighting, Jack, that has the power to conquer the will of almost every sentient creature in the multiverse?'

'You speak of the Original Insect.' It was growing cool. Down at the waterline the whitey stokers had come up for a breath of air and were staring with intense concentration into creamy water stirred by slow paddles, as if they divined their fate there.

'I speak of that life which is deadly, which exists only to devour and breed. Yes, and which we define as the Original Insect, inimical to our kind. It would reduce all life and thought to a few primitive functions, forever frozen in its development, thus achieving a kind of semi-immortality. But that is only death refusing the name, eh?'

'Doubtless,' says Jack, turning up his jacket collar. 'You make our opponents seem unbeatable, Rose.'

'You have the means of beating them, Jack, should you ever wish to play.'

He chided her for this. Both he and she already knew he was irredeemably destined to play the Game of Time. 'I have a habit of cool-headedness, that's all,' said Mr Karaquazian. 'A certain talent with the flat tables. A firm belief that God enjoys a roll or two of the dice now and again . . .'

'And a strong sense of what should be,' she added. She began to laugh at his mystification. 'And who you are.' She enjoyed walking away from him, leaving him to watch the Indian women descend a hill and disappear.

Tomorrow *La Perle du Suede* would push past Memphis. She had been warned not to stop in that wretched ruin.

CHAPTER THIRTEEN

Melody Ranch

Van Beek's gunboat was waiting off Mud Island as they slipped through the shallows at half-steam, their paddles thumping the water like a whitey woman's washing, with slow, laborious thuds. Pale light touched the city's tallest shards and revealed the gunboat, manned by gaudy ruffians, huge men armed with a tinker's wagon of weaponry, most of which looked spent. But they had a charge in the monstrous Cassion which bounced a ball of unhealthy energy off the paddle-wheeler's boiler deck and left two children coughing themselves to death as their parents watched helplessly from where they lay wounded under the forward awning, their skin shredding from their flesh and that flesh putrefying and turning to liquid which lay, unabsorbed, on the planks.

The Rose was furious. The texas foredeck bell was clanging. Waiting steam was belching in the safeties. The Rose climbed up to the wheelhouse and took over from a grim Jack Karaquazian. Without hesitation she put the paddles into reverse, bracing herself as the boat gave a ponderous roll. Already the remains of the filthy Memphis waterfront lay behind them. Deliberately she veered the big boat toward the channel edge where the current was less strong against them, watching as the gunboat came alongside their drifting bulk. She seemed relaxed but Jack Karaquazian noted the tightness of her grip on the wheel's kingspoke. Beneath them the *Perle* shuddered with the violence of her pent-up pressure. She had been ready to fly as soon as she had cleared Memphis. Now it felt as if she must burst apart. Jack Karaquazian turned a thoughtful eye to the stack safeties where bright lemon foam boiled down the dull enamel and the stacks beat like organ pipes.

Then his attention was drawn to the wheelhouse of the gunboat where a big whitey held the wheel steady. He was one of those whiteys who tried to pass for Indian by staining their skin with walnut and greasing their hair with black tallow to make them look like plains Blackfoot. The freshly healing scar across his naked, darkened chest betrayed his blood.

'It's Van Beek's big blanco pilot. And there's the Governor General himself. Paying us a courtesy visit.'

George Van Beek was easily recognised, his tiny bushman's features puffy with kargon implants and his right arm busy with a score of blinking bayley monitors, their lights reflected in his mild blue eyes. Teeth flashed violet as he grimaced, swinging down the starboard ladder which his men held steady for him. He dropped onto their main deck like an elderly cat.

He wore a grey and red uniform and was still used to authority. Without preamble he made his way up to the texas and told them he was their passenger. His own boat would follow behind to ensure his safety. He wanted the best suite they had and full service. He would disembark at St Louis.

Clearly Van Beek had no idea who they were or where the boat was going. He recognised none of them. Only Sam Oakenhurst had ever worked for Boss Van Beek and Jack Karaquazian had never known him well. After a silent discussion, they decided to let Van Beek believe he controlled them. They addressed the Boss with purring politeness in the archaic manner of the old gambling clans. They called him 'my handsome' and 'vardy sapisti' and Boss Van Beek became almost agreeable under their clever attention. He intended to recruit whites above St Louis and bring them back down to retake all his lost territory. There were enough weapons aboard his gunboat to arm a formidable force. And once the blancos had served their turn, they would make useful workers in the rebuilding. As he urged the trio to join him in his great dream it became clear that even in Memphis he had ceased to be a power and was now just another small-time warlord trying to carve out a few miles of territory to call his own.

The Rose was glad to let the paddles race and the steam take hold. Already the *Perle* was settling to a sustained purring rhythm, gathering speed as the whiteys stoked 'goldenwood' whose smoke was an oily, yellowish vomit.

The two men spoke of getting rid of Van Beek, but the Rose no longer seemed involved, She had a zee-band play that night and treated the Boss as if he were a king. They followed her example and not once did Boss Van Beek question them or do any more than assume that the trio were ordinary boat's officers on a regular scheduled run. The Rose said Van Beek was still dangerous while that Cassion was charged. It would cost them nothing to let him relax and think he was going to St Louis.

So they danced in the light of the mosquito lamps to the fiddle and the accordion, the guitar and the bass. '*Pauvre pierrot, muy pirogue vous rollez.*'

In his place of honour, his tiny feet not touching the deck, Boss Van Beek clapped his hands together, for all the world like a schoolboy at a pantomime. 'Bravo! Bal de mare! I have never seen better dancing. You will all be welcome in Memphis at the Governor General's mansion. We'll have some celebrating to do. We'll have some lively times.'

'Lively times ahead, Boss!' The Rose was a commedia coquette, openly displaying her ironic contempt for him before his brutal, unobservant eye. But he was used to fawning courtiers and had no time for flattering women, he said. He was not listening to her as he cast his thoughtful gaze back over the grumbling waters, alert for his gunboat's steady growl.

'Bad news, vola varde?' Jack Karaquazian pretended subservient intimacy.

'How long before we get to St Louis?' demanded Van Beek, refusing further questions.

'Two or three moons,' says the Rose, 'no more, sirree.'

'And it's a clear run, right? All the way up. Nobody in the way?'

They saw nothing wrong with offering him his required assurances.

Van Beek began rapidly clapping his hands, ordering the band to start up once more and the dancers to continue. They were less wholehearted now. Van Beek was disappointed. But scarcely puzzled any more, he confided, by the way some folks behaved. He invited Jack Karaquazian and Sam Oakenhurst to take a drink with him in the saloon. He said they had the look of gambling men. He himself enjoyed a game from time to time. He liked the real thing. They wouldn't believe the power he'd tapped in to! The games had been hard. But few had beaten him. Even the keenest jugadors. He wouldn't play these ersatz pseudo-flats.

They told the Boss they had two Brackett's aboard. Was he familiar with those? He became interested in a lordly way. They coaxed him down into the cabin. He played badly. They let him win and keep winning, wondering when he would realise what they were doing. He never realised.

'He fully believes he's lucky by divine right!' Sam Oakenhurst exclaimed when Van Beek had finally tired of playing and returned to his own cabin. 'Thanks to our efforts, Jack, things are coming out just as they should for Boss Van Beek.'

At Cahan the Rose went ashore to buy a few provisions while the boat was wooding up. The place was almost deserted and she was glad to find one small chandler's still operating down near the old jetties. The chandler was as glad to see her and was generous with his measures, warning her that just below St Louis the river turned around and began flowing north, becoming rapids and then a huge falls: 'Where Missouri used to be.' All the border states were one vast abyss of diseased and glistening rock, he said, which had parted like a rotten seam one afternoon. And pouring upwards from those immeasurable depths rose a kind of bloody vapour as if the last remains of the dead were striving for the upper air.

She remarked that he was of a poetic disposition and he told her he was once a singer.

'I know who you are,' he said. 'Captain von Bek, I have been in your company once or twice. I performed at the Kettle Kettle in St Jo.' And he lifted his head to remind her of his song:

> When your long, long journey's over,
>   Through the mountains and the snows,
> It's the seed you plant in winter
>   That in spring becomes a rose.

When she returned to the boat the Rose mentioned nothing of her news to Boss Van Beek. Later Van Beek locked himself in conference with a lieutenant from the gunboat. He had been abstracted, as if he had heard uncertain news. The Rose spoke of this to Sam Oakenhurst and Jack Karaquazian. They agreed that Van Beek's men might have picked up rumours but were probably discounting them. Such apocalyptic stuff was widespread these days. 'They get it from those magazines you read, Sam.' Half-serious, Jack Karaquazian teased his friend. 'It's spreading into the real world. People will believe anything.'

'You angry, Jack. What is it? Some disappointment?'

'If you like, Sam.' Jack Karaquazian began to cough softly and excusing himself returned to his regular suite which now adjoined Van Beek's. His disease had been in remission for some time but had returned last night.

He was careful with his measure of Ackroyd's. He hung up his silk jacket and brocaded vest, slipped off his bright black boots, loosened his belt and his collar and lay back in his best easy chair, on the arm of which lay a recent copy of *Captain Billy Bob's Monthly* relating the latest tales of the Chaos captains, in unstable power dyes which threatened to burn off the plastic and blind the viewer. The *Monthly*'s main story involved the search for a lost universe with an unlikely name. There was a further episode in the on-going 'Quest for the Fishlings' and a number of other stories involving minor characters from one series in major rôles. 'Professor Pop and His Speedshell' was for children while 'Pearl Peru's Recipe Book' offered conventional hints.

Mr Karaquazian could not believe these characters anything but fiction. Yet he had met Captain Quelch. Pearl Peru herself had come calling for him at the Terminal Café. Perhaps the magazines were only crude fictions invented for want of the real memories of these heroes and heroines of the Second Ether? No doubt they glamorised the truth like the old dime slots had glamorised N'Chaka, Ali Barber or Bumbum Wilson. There was no doubting Captain Quelch's reality, or his strangeness, much of which could be put down to an unfamiliar cultural ambience. But he had not seemed a demigod; merely a clever privateer.

Mr Karaquazian could not imagine the value of reading the magazines but he conscientiously went through a whole stack, page by page, following the adventures of the Chaos Engineers in their perpetual war against the Singularity, that mighty pseudo-universe enclosed by a vast wall of supercarbon which tore through the scales at a sickening and always increasing rate, ripping ragged holes in the delicate branches and colour fields; forever falling through seeming infinity, forever seeking to impose its simplified and sterile laws upon multiversal variety.

Control was their life. By means of ruthless conquest the Singularity believed they could overcome death. But death was all they ever won.

Mr Karaquazian soon realised to his dismay that the stories were beginning to engross him.

The remaining passengers disembarked at Osceola. Boss Van Beek displayed no surprise that he was the only one still aboard. The Rose noted how he showed little interest in his surroundings. He spent hours in his cabin consulting maps which no longer described the realities of his world.

Jack Karaquazian was strangely incurious about the man who had once enslaved Colinda Dovero and would have had her working for him in the North if she had not stolen his charts and gone up the Trace to seek out the Gold Stains. But Van Beek had never been interesting. Like every other tyrant, he was characterised by a stifling banality of mind and a blind devotion to his own greedy self-preservation, a baby. It was hard to imagine the dreams of such people whose desires were on a more primitive plane than those of the majority they controlled. Yet the majority soon became fascinated by them, began imitating them. Sought to become them.

At some point it might suit the Boss to try to take over the boat. He must certainly be keeping that option. He was too cautious at the moment. He needed their skills. Sam Oakenhurst had been for killing Van Beek and the crew of the following boat at night, when it would be easy enough, but the Rose had resisted. 'There's no harm in his going with us for a while. I want no unnecessary conflict. No bloodletting. We know where this boat's headed and he doesn't . . .'

They played a few more games with the Brackett's. Van Beek's strategies were so primitive and his goals so transparent that it was almost impossible to let him keep winning. But win he did and became more and more confident of his own superiority, openly contemptuous of the jugadors who, to ease their boredom, gave him displays of their most famous moves, identified with them by everyone who ever played a flat game, but which Van Beek still did not recognise, in spite of those same moves being used in a dozen games Sam Oakenhurst had played with him in the past. He could recognise neither pattern nor strategy. His only interest was in winning, which he imagined he did by wild, sudden, brutal plays, following an unconsidered infantile impulse he called his instinct. The impression, as Jack Karaquazian pointed out, was of playing against an aggressive, unintelligent ten-year-old.

Only once, as they sat with their Fröm after a game, did Boss Van Beek focus his eyes on Sam Oakenhurst and ask, with the intensity he usually reserved for self-reference, where the boat would be heading after St Louis.

'Oh,' Sam Oakenhurst offered a faint wink to Jack Karaquazian, 'I guess we're heading for Hell, Mr Van Beek. There's nowhere else for us to go.'

Van Beek had laughed heartily at this, repeating the observation several times. He rose to return to his quarters. 'You'll have to come and work for me when I get back to Memphis.'

'See you in Hell,' said Jack Karaquazian to Van Beek as the warlord closed the door on them. 'Do you think he plans to kill us, Sam?' He suppressed a cough.

Sam Oakenhurst's elongated fingers, imbedded with machinoix jewels, delicately touched his fleshless skull. He shrugged. 'Men like Van Beek simply see murder as an option. He'll probably work out that we're useful to him but then decide to kill us anyway. He trusts his instincts, don't he, Jack? They got him where he is . . .'

(When with Van Beek, Colinda Dovero had hardly talked about the man. There had been nothing to say. He was the usual kind of monster. 'We live in a world where casual injustice has become commonplace,' she said. 'In such worlds Boss Van Beek and his kind flourish. It's their job to finish what others began. They are like those creatures who used to follow armies after the battle. They are the slaughterers and scavengers, that's all. They fulfil a sanitary function.' He had suspected her of lack of candour but now he knew she had been telling only the truth.)

'Is it the end, Sam, when everything repeats itself forever?'

'Maybe for you,' Sam Oakenhurst said, 'but most people don't notice. They take comfort from repetition. So should you, sometimes.'

'I guess I'm too easily bored.'

'It was always your weakness, Jack. We get too hooked on that old adrenalin running high.'

(But there had been times when it was not so. When he and Colinda Dovero lay together in the drifting pirogue, watching the lattice of the cypresses reflected from swamp to silvered sky, when the water seemed thick and warm as oil on their bodies and they swam, careless of snakes, in the blood-orange light, gasping with pleasure. They watched the sun go down over the False River and the deserted timber shacks lining her far bank. There had been whiteys living there once, she had said. They had spoken a pure form of Swahili. Nobody knew where they had come from. Then the crows would appear, a great flock of them, lazily flapping through the twilight and cawing one to another like a cheerful congregation after a good sermon, all in Friday black.

He had recalled his mentor in Marrakech, 'Rabia Kul Amal, shaking her head in sadness and wondering why it was that in all her travels everyone she met, Moslem, Hindu, Christian, Buddhist or atheist, yearned for peace, for a harmonious life, yet were always seduced by demagogues. Van Beek had been powerful then. 'It is astonishing with what ease we allow others to profit from our pain,' she had said. Colinda had told him that there were some who banded together for the common good. Who were opposed to such exploitation. They were known, she had said, as the Nation of the Just.)

Some twelve days later, when they were just above Thebes, they noticed the ease with which the *Perle* made speed up the river. Then they realised that the current was running in the opposite direction. Though they still headed roughly northwards, they were now going down river. Yet still Boss Van Beek had not noticed, though his bravos were signalling from their boat, far ahead of the paddle-wheeler, having swept by in the night. They were reversing their own labouring engine, the bulky Cassion swinging eccentrically back and forth in its forward harness. Even the gigantic whitey steersman had a crazy look about him; now he drew desperate, wailing blasts on his whistle, trying to make *La Perle* heave to.

The Rose took *La Perle* past the gunboat as if she had not seen her. With their master invisible to them, even at this stage they would not attempt to fire the Cassion.

Jack Karaquazian went to find Van Beek. In his cabin the man wore a long jellabah. There was a strong smell of incense and ope. He was languid, almost amiable.

'Your men seem worried about you, Boss,' Jack Karaquazian told him. 'Maybe you should give them a signal to reassure them.'

Nodding abstractly, George Van Beek took his tiny body to the outer rail and offered his followers something like a benediction. Only slightly reassured they followed close to the boat, trying to be heard above the racketing paddles, bellowing garbled enquiries.

Boss Van Beek returned to his cabin while Sam Oakenhurst, his features less than reassuring, took a megaphone and told the gunboat's crew that everything was in order. He would meet them in St Louis.

The current remained gentle, but anticipating what was coming Jack Karaquazian thought he felt it tug a little more aggressively. He was profoundly uneasy. He wondered if Sam Oakenhurst and the Rose were completely sane. The Mississippi River was running backwards. It was commonly believed that an abyss lay ahead – into which all this water was pouring. They seemed unconcerned.

At what point, he wondered, did one universe impose upon another? He had hardly been aware of a shift. He had expected something more dramatic. Was the final slide toward oblivion always so uneventful?

He shrugged off his mood. Meanwhile Van Beek remained oblivious of everything. They let him borrow one of the Brackett's and he became absorbed in it, creating his own crude pseudo-reality.

The river was broadening. It was hard to make out the west bank now. Whole towns had already been engulfed, whole forests and mountain ranges. He again remembered his words to Colinda. When the Old Hunter came for him he wanted to be on the river. Maybe God was granting him this part, at least, of his unrealised dream.

He stood on the top deck, outside the texas, leaning on the brass rail and staring from side to side at the flat, grey expanse of water, mirroring an identical sky. Was the whole world slowly evaporating? He moved to look behind him. In the choppy waters of their wake the gunboat was not far away. Labouring to keep her speed down, she was in increasing danger of being swept on. The muddy wash of both vessels spread out in ever-diminishing ripples until they were indistinguishable from the tiny waves which the wind made on all that lonely water.

The birds were gone.

If the flood was upon them they were aboard an ill-equipped Ark. It seemed they had not been chosen to carry the race into the next world. Mr Karaquazian began to laugh. Then he began to cough.

A few hours later, when it was dusk, there was nothing to be seen but the water. The waves were higher, breaking against the paddle-houses and pouring over the lower deck. There was a wind, too, from the North. It carried an unpleasant sweet smell. And they could hear far away a kind of howling which was obscenely familiar to Jack Karaquazian, though Sam Oakenhurst and the Rose did not seem disturbed by it. 'It sounds human,' said Jack Karaquazian, 'like the Fault.'

In the darkness which came upon them quickly, as if they had entered a cave, Jack Karaquazian went to his cabin and lay on his bunk listening to the river. Its speed continued gradually to increase. When, at last, he got up, it was dawn and the steamboat was rolling violently in heavy waves. Outside, the spray was high and it was raining. Ahead to starboard he could just make out, through the shifting vapour, the gunboat. Its engine squealing, it tried to reduce the distance between them.

He joined the Rose in the wheelhouse and borrowed her glasses, glimpsing terrified faces before the gunboat sank again below his vision. They seemed to be lightening the boat, but the Cassion still bounced in its harness. They were beyond hope and should be praying for a quick death. The boat came up again and he saw the white giant, sweat making the stain run in thin streaks over his face and body, doing everything he could to keep control of the wheel. Jack Karaquazian would not be surprised if his own face had something of the same expression.

The Rose had just relieved Sam Oakenhurst.

It was always obvious when the boat came under her control. There was a steadier feel to their progress and she used the paddles astutely both to slow and to steer. The whitey stokers were performing heroically, tirelessly. She had been given the best. She was now grateful to Sam Oakenhurst for persuading her to take them on. No ordinary stoker would have remained with the boat once the river turned round. Most whites were hugely superstitious and would have deserted readily at the first hint of queerness. But these worked almost without rest, with an intelligent, ready response to her needs. Something in her found their obedience distasteful, but she was glad of it. She had a hint, however, of why and how the machinoix had trained their whites and to what impossible humiliations and horrors they had been exposed before the most useful of them survived. Now, of course, they simply bred true.

The voice of the abyss was growing stronger now. One vast human shout of pain.

Slowly the sky grew pink, then crimson, until the diluted blood of millions drizzled upon their decks and stained the cream filigree and confident brass and they tasted it in their bones until at last even Boss Van Beek emerged complaining and cursing, then stopped to gasp at what he saw.

'Where's my boat?'

'Your damned boat, sir, is over yonder,' said Sam Oakenhurst coming up from below in a yellow mackinaw and pointing.

The Rose's laughter was spontaneous. 'Mustard just ain't your colour, these days, Sam!'

He enjoyed her humour. In the last few days their relations had again grown relaxed and he was sure of her love. He had become increasingly cheerful as Jack Karaquazian had grown increasingly glum.

'It's okay once you done it, Jack,' Sam Oakenhurst reassured his friend. 'The first time's always hard for us.' He, too, began to laugh. This time it was infectious. Mr Karaquazian felt his spirits lifting. Then he laughed. Soon only Van Beek had not joined in their merriment. He was rushing back and forth on the top deck, darting down to the hurricane deck and back again. Something had happened to the other passengers! The boat was deserted! What was this? What was this? Where were his people?

The rain poured warmer and darker crimson and the horizon ahead of them boiled with brown vapour from which little tongues of oily blue and purple darted. Water was now roaring loud enough to drown the noise ahead, yet the Rose made no attempt to halt their progress towards the abyss. The rapids leapt and foamed. They were travelling at enormous speed. The awful horizon grew rapidly closer.

Then the water settled into a single, steady, spray-clouded rush. Boiling vapour filled the sky ahead and that sound of voices rose in their ears so they shivered with the pain. But Boss Van Beek paced and frowned. He had taken up the Rose's glasses and located his gunboat, helplessly whirling out of sight, its crew waving wretchedly and firing off the Cassion as if they thought they could challenge that frightful apparition and force it to retreat. Then, suddenly, the gunboat was lifted easily into the air: to plunge down again and disappear, in a fraction of a moment, into the pit.

Boss Van Beek began to scream as the yowling chasm dragged *La Perle* in the gunboat's wake. Then he stopped. For a moment there was a silence. The vapour cleared. They heard only the water rushing miles wide into a bottomless chasm. Beyond the chasm's edge was no horizon at all: the edge of the world.

The clouds boiled up again. The voices dropped to a soft moaning. The boat's prow dipped forward, her paddles clanking powerlessly. Even the Rose had trouble keeping her steering true, weaving with all the currents which surrounded her, selecting, rejecting, taking first one branch and then another until at last she had found a main vein and followed it. It was the best she could do.

The three of them were crammed into the texas. But as soon as he saw he was of no use Sam Oakenhurst went looking for Van Beek who had vanished below.

'I'm a fool,' said the Rose to Jack Karaquazian. 'I've let Quelch use me. Van Beek's one of his recruits!' She began to curse herself so intensely that Jack Karaquazian impulsively embraced her. He thought she had lost her mind.

Mr Karaquazian had never felt so horribly ill. *La Perle*'s twin stacks poured sparks and grey smoke into freezing air. Jack Karaquazian was reminded of the mint fields and date groves of Marrakech, capital of the Berber Empire, her dark green palms and glittering red walls raised against a royal blue sky, her minarets rippling with pearly colour and her pastel towers beginning to sound the day's fourth prayer. The city seemed to laze in the sun, yet her streets and squares swarmed day and night with the voluble, witty denizens of that least disappointing of fabulous cities. And he thought the paddle-wheeler sailed over the rooftops of Marrakech and he recalled a game played there, named after the famous square: 'Meeting the Dead'.

Sam Oakenhurst came in, shaking his head. The Rose's hands were firmly on the wheel. She had overcome her angry shame. The boat still moved readily to her command, flying out beyond the world's edge where the water crashed and shrieked, out into the bellowing storm, into the fractured air which broke like a slow mirror. When the cracks widened into rivers they flew down into a narrow vein of scarlet which bore them through pulsing violet rock and a blindingly vivid expanse of pale obsidian.

Obsidian became crystal and all that crystal was a great city, eerie in the distant fading vanilla light as they settled in calm water. Then the Rose began to curse even more violently, rounding on them as if they, too, were to blame for her dilemma.

'He used us just as he wished — Van Beek was Quelch's recruit! And thus we lost our own chance into the Second Ether! We are marooned here. Becalmed for eternity! Oh, my weakness! My fascination with my enemies! It has proved our damnation!'

'Van Beek's below,' said Sam Oakenhurst dumbly, staring out at the surrounding beauty, something neither he nor Jack had ever expected to see again.

'No he isn't! No he isn't!' The Rose left the wheel and pushed open the texas door to stalk about on her narrow upper deck. 'No, no, no!

'Van Beek paid for his passage with the blood of his people!' She groaned. 'No meat boat needed there, my lads. We do not deserve to call ourselves adepts.'

Sam Oakenhurst and Jack Karaquazian searched briefly for Van Beek. 'He must have gone overboard,' Sam called up to a still grim Rose. She turned her back on him.

But Jack Karaquazian coming from the stokehold said: 'Well, he took the whites with him.'

'They all went into the Second Ether, I guess.' Sam Oakenhurst shrugged. 'Or wherever it was we were. I'm reconciled to this, Jack. It ain't new to me. Whatever it is the Rose wants us to go to, it don't seem to want us. At least we got to keep the boat this time.'

'It's not back luck,' they heard the Rose say, 'it's bad judgement. What hope would we have had anyway? We're numskulls! The simplest trick in the world!'

Jack Karaquazian found it hard to share her mood. He had packed himself a rare pipe of M & E and was enjoying it as he leaned on the rail, looking out across the tranquil waters of a lagoon where herons waded in the reeds and huge catfish swam with calm purpose just below the surface, their ancient whiskered faces benign. The oaks in the meadow on the southern bank were beginning to take on a tint of russet and there was a rich smell of autumn in the air. In that scene of extraordinary peacefulness Jack Karaquazian found it hard to understand why the Rose should be so disappointed. They had fallen out of the mouth of Hell to land, somehow, in a corner of Heaven.

He asked Sam Oakenhurst what was wrong with the Rose. Mr Oakenhurst explained that they had been duped into carrying a passenger who was a recruit for their opposition, the Singularity. 'We didn't get close to our goal, a universe we call the Grail. We go through that before we have to make other moves and turns. You learn quickly. Like a game. It's hard to explain it any other way, Jack. There don't seem to be words for it.'

'It's like being a piece and not a player,' said Jack Karaquazian. 'That's what scares me, Sam.'

'Well, we're still players, Jack. But I think we needed desperately to get over there. We're running out of luck. That's why she's worried. My guess is we're just becalmed and can eventually make another attempt, but that ain't her way of responding to a set-back.'

Jack Karaquazian watched a kingfisher fly with swift, irregular wing-beats over the water to hover suddenly, sighting a fish feeding in the shallows, and dive, to flash upwards with a wriggling silver body in its triumphant beak.

'*The weak shall devour the strong,*' said the Rose to herself overhead. 'He could as easily have written me a note!'

Jack Karaquazian wondered how they had come to this peaceful limbo which reminded him, in indefinable ways, of his childhood in Aswan when he had waded amongst the rockpools and ponds of the cataracts while the bright white sails of the little boats, the masts at cryptic angles to the tall palms, went back and forth in the calms, plying from shore to sandy shore. The great grey rocks had glittered like the hides of ancient beasts cooling in the streams.

He had watched the ibis striking between the papyrus and he had wandered through the ruins of so many dead civilisations, learning their languages and their signs, learning their secrets until gradually he came to understand he must go to Alexandria to his rebirth, where the adepts taught at the so-called Musram Berberim. After three years his master had sent him west to Marrakech, red city of storks and miracles. There was no finer training. He had arrived back in Alexandria a proud and full-fledged mukhamir. A jugador of the first class.

He had returned, at length, to Aswan.

'Mukhamir,' he told his father. 'They say we are the chosen of God. That only we understand his complex logic.'

'Then you are an angel,' his father had said. 'Or you blaspheme and are damned for eternity.'

'We are merely his soldiers,' Jack Karaquazian had said. 'Defending God's honour and our own.'

But the Civil War had begun, one sect against another, one mosque against another, and, untended, Egypt's monuments had collapsed. The Nile had grown so clogged with the dead they said you could smell Luxor as far as Nairobi. What was happening to him now was in that sense no worse than what had happened to all his family after the Turks arrived, but by then he had taken the schoomer for America. They had told him you could make a lifetime's fortune working just a year on the handsome Mississippi steamboats, but they had not told him what bad losers some men and women could be. Thus he had learned to defend himself. Now his reputation with a weapon was as considerable as his reputation at the deep table. They had been heady years, playing life against death; risking all he had on the quickness of his mind and the speed of his draw until only the biggest gamblers or most powerful bosses would play against him and he had joined the small group who dominated the river queens in the years when society was still gripped by the madness of white power and was profligate with its energies.

The lean times had come with energy unaffordable to common folk, but still the landowners and industrialists, who wanted the thrill of playing against the best, would pay for all the feed the colour demanded.

Then they had drilled the Fault and the odds changed radically, became harder to calculate, yet still they had congregated to play, this time at the Terminal Café, to which the old jugadors from many parts of the world had come, sooner or later. Now it was all done, thought Jack Karaquazian, watching a family of brown pelicans rise out of the middle of the lake and fly towards the west into a pale yellow sun. All the energy had been used up. The game was over. He regretted it but could think of worse places to end his days.

'I can't change! I'm useless! I'm the most gullible idiot in the multiverse! I deserve to die!'

The Rose was now out of Jack Karaquazian's sight, on the other side of the texas, but he could hear her stamping. He was only remotely sympathetic. He wanted little more than what he had at this moment. He did not believe they were stranded.

As he stood dreaming into the water, he caught a distant sound in the sharp fall air, like a polite murmur, then a drone, rising to a whine, then falling again to a steady purr. He cleared his throat, realising that he was no longer coughing. Looking up he saw a huge old-fashioned flying boat sailing swiftly over the horizon, her wings at a swaggering rake as she studied the paddle-boat.

He heard the Rose break off in mid-curse and utter a loud whoop of joy.

'It's a turning world, Jack,' says Sam Oakenhurst coming up beside his friend and watching as the white Dornier, engines sputtering and booming on her upper wings, makes her dignified approach to the lagoon.

CHAPTER FOURTEEN

Zwei Rechnen Ab

Sam Oakenhurst had seen the plane once before but was surprised. Jack Karaquazian was mindlessly resentful of its appearance. He grumbled of vulgar waste.

Mr Karaquazian's prejudice was confirmed when, under his angry scrutiny, a white man pushed back the cabin panel, waving cheerfully to their boat before returning to his controls and taxiing close enough for the two men to throw him a line, allowing him to move from wing to boarding gate in a few elegant steps. Jack Karaquazian was struck by the pungent, chilly wealth of the air and breathed in deeply, as if it might be his last.

Stripping off his pigskin flying gloves the pilot offered a manicured and effeminate hand.

'Good afternoon, gentlemen. I am obliged to you. I'm Rudy von Bek. I believe my sister-in-law is your captain?'

It was only then that Sam Oakenhurst realised Rose von Bek had married a white. The possibility had simply not occurred to him. There was an awkward moment or two before he shook the visitor's hand. He had forgotten how to judge his fellow creatures by skin or sex. (He had admitted this more than once to a doubting Jack Karaquazian.) Mr Oakenhurst did not seem to notice their visitor's astonishment at the set and length of his fingers. 'I guess the Rose is glad to see a relative at this particular moment.'

'I thought I'd lost you.' Noting that Jack Karaquazian made no attempt to shake his hand Count von Bek looked around. 'It's pretty rough going in these parts, eh?'

Jack Karaquazian nodded. 'We've had a few upsets. Lately.' He asked the white man where he had come from.

'Mirenburg most recently. Do you know it?' Von Bek seemed heedless of Mr Karaquazian's frank disapproval.

Jack Karaquazian said that he had spent six or seven months in Europe as a youth and found it depressing. He wasn't sure what he had hated most, the poverty or the climate. He had been to Mirenburg but he did not remember it especially.

Von Bek seemed amused. 'Well, most Europeans are rather proud of Mirenburg. Even if her architecture is a little extravagant.'

Jack Karaquazian had found the buildings hideously and fussily barbaric and the streets only marginally cleaner than the inhabitants. Ruins and beggars, he thought. 'I have not had the privilege of your perspective and familiarity,' he said.

Then the Rose came glowing down from her cabin and embraced him. 'Rudy!'

Von Bek began to unbutton his flying jacket. 'Do you have anything to eat, old girl?'

Jack Karaquazian could not bring himself to accompany them to the dining table. He remained on deck, smoking his pipe and studying the birds.

Events had grown too strange for him. He felt deeply uneasy. Neither Sam nor the Rose had said anything of a plane or its pilot. He was almost convinced of his companions' mental instability. He was a fool for getting caught up in this. The sun set over the lagoon and he looked back at a saloon lit by warm orange lamps, by a cool, silver moon, and he felt lonelier than he had ever felt before. He turned up his collar against the cold but did not go to his cabin. For a long time he stood listening to the sounds from the water, reassured by the familiar calls.

Until recently his habit of following his professional code had served him well. That code had allowed him to make his way fairly comfortably through a harsh but largely familiar world; one he had rarely questioned.

Now his world grew steadily unfamiliar. While the physical disruptions were as nothing to a jugador of Jack Karaquazian's experience, the rest, like these arrogant whites, was disconcerting.

Mr Karaquazian was used to knowing who his friends were and to picking his associates. The Rose should have warned him to expect these events. His very identity was threatened. He was distressed to realise how much of his inner life was influenced by the actions of the outer world.

He had always tended to be solitary. He wished he could have made this journey alone. His love for Colinda Dovero had led him to agree to the Rose's plans and engage in her adventures. Had she used his love to manipulate him as she manipulated Sam Oakenhurst?

For most of his life Jack Karaquazian had lived the disciplined life of an adept, according to a few certainties and principles. But he had already made a nonsense of his honour once. Consequently he had lost

Colinda Dovero. Now that everything he revered was in question he did not know if he had manhood or character enough to survive.

Pulling himself together, Mr Karaquazian decided to seek out Sam Oakenhurst as soon as possible and put some questions to his friend. He trusted Mr Oakenhurst to answer as honestly as he could.

Meanwhile he let the ope engulf him as he told himself their story of the Gold Stains and his encounter with the brothers Berger and their pa in The Breed Papoose.

He recalled her leavetaking, how she cupped the drops of his blood in her hands before carrying it into the Stain. 'If you stay I shall not return. You're growing old here, Jack.' He remembered his game with Ox Berger and what the man had done for him. He had never met a more generous nor a better player.

Mr Karaquazian had learned to question the pride he took in his honour and his altruism. But Ox had taught him to accept another's forgiveness. Jack Karaquazian told himself his story and Colinda's. He was preparing to come to her an honest man.

And now, he thought resentfully, the Rose was his only hope.

CHAPTER FIFTEEN

Kein Talent sum Geierfrass

'Er fand keines,' Count von Bek called over his shoulder to the Rose as he settled himself behind his instruments. They had been speaking that harsh language ever since they left the paddle-steamer.

Jack Karaquazian thought the seats' luxury almost obscene but he had to admit an extraordinary sense of security. The interior of the aeroplane had felt cramped as they brought their luggage aboard. Now it seemed spacious. The decorations were intricate, lavish blues, yellows, golds, greens and reds. Some European notion of the Egyptian original. The garish vulgarity seemed appropriate to the vehicle.

On the other side of the aircraft Sam Oakenhurst's strange fingers explored details of brass and chrome. 'This whole thing's a work of art.' He had always been fascinated in what most people saw as the extravagant expression of a corrupt and degenerate civilisation in its final years, before its descent into mere savagery. 'Paul Reeve, almost certainly. The cost of materials must have been enormous. The machinoix possess great collections of these things, you know, in their bunkers. Most of their capital's invested in art.'

Jack Karaquazian had little curiosity about the machinoix or their taste. Like this bizarre white art, it related to nothing he understood or felt at ease with. He feared he lacked the imagination for the Rose's Game of Time.

Sensing his friend's mood, Sam Oakenhurst stopped his enthusiastic explorations and came to sit down. 'It ain't scary once you get there, Jack. No scarier than anywhere else.'

Sam Oakenhurst had explained everything he could to Jack Karaquazian. He swore the Rose was not deceiving them. Apart from his own instincts, he trusted the word of the machinoix. They had once played the Game but now chose not to. Though weary of the Second Ether themselves they assured him she spoke only truth.

'We'll know how to play when we get there, Jack. It's the same as the games we're used to, only with more scale changes. It should be easy for you.'

'I doubt that, Sam.'

Mr Oakenhurst persisted. 'I've had a taste or two of playing, Jack. There's nothing to beat the thrill. The way your blood quickens. Even the likes of us, Jack. It makes you young. Believe me, Jack. The Rose is on the square. You'll get what you want out of this. As will I.'

With a slight gesture of his fingers, Jack Karaquazian acknowledged his friend's concern. 'I guess I'm used to relying on a few basic rules, Sam. I always saved complexity for my work. I always wanted my private life to be simple. Maybe I should have let a little more uncertainty in? I guess that's how I really lost Colinda.'

'Maybe,' said Sam Oakenhurst. 'I don't know.' Jack Karaquazian and Colinda Dovero were probably the best gamblers on the continent. Mr Oakenhurst hated to see his admired friend experiencing regret. 'You don't have to do any of this. You can just go to her. You deserve that. Play later, when you feel like it. But Jack, I want to play bad. It's what I've been training for. I just want to taste the Second Ether, know the characters in the Game, maybe get to link with Pearl Peru herself. But you think I'm crazy.'

'You always followed your enthusiasms through, Sam.' Jack Karaquazian began to grin.

'You can have Colinda without playing the Game, Jack. She hasn't played it. She will think no less of you.'

'I want a taste of it, too, Sam. I don't have your obsession with it, but I do have a little curiosity. I'd like to find out where I stand as a player. Find the centre of all this, maybe.'

'Maybe there ain't a centre, Jack? Not in the way you mean.'

'Maybe not. Maybe I'll just have to make one for myself. Next time I see Mrs Dovero I want to be pretty sure of my bearings.'

'You're scared she won't want you?'

'Mainly that's what I'm scared of,' Mr Karaquazian agreed.

CHAPTER SIXTEEN

Ace Among Aces

PALE KINGS

Conventional Gambit

Level 990

OPEN:

First player (1) to E. Quadrant, slide at yellow, slide at green, turn left to Parrot, cross yellow, cross green, hover on 55, proceed at Lilac.

Second player (2) down scale to 10 < but slice > 7 and cross. Slice to West Quadrant. Slide on green, cross on yellow, turn right to Lizard, slide green, slide yellow, hover on 55. Maintain.

(1) Up to 19> and turn on GGF to yellow 4000, down to> 7 and cross. (2) To orange plus and reverse into spiral ⅄⅄ (switch to Runic 66), release and tap up to 10>. (1) Radical close scale. Slide on green, cross on yellow, maintain. (2) Fold to seven-seven, green slide, yellow slide, orange slide. Down 5>.

Thus towards achievement of 040 to fix.

CHAPTER SEVENTEEN

Pass des Verderbens

Until he looked out of the porthole Jack Karaquazian did not realise they had left the familiar world. What he saw was a mass of roughly circular dark blue shapes which grew smaller and lighter as they moved towards a pale yellow haze. The effect was of peering down an endless tunnel. He turned away and saw the Rose at the plane's controls, a black figure against the pulsing red and orange kaleidoscope forward. The far porthole revealed an identical phenomenon of blue circles at which Sam Oakenhurst eagerly stared. Jack Karaquazian became aware of the engines grumbling on the upper wings.

The vibrations increased as the plane dipped to enter a jagged shard of faded green and from there soar above a field of enormous poppies.

He felt as though he had been absorbed by a Brackett's. The light and colour had a similar soft vividness. There were no shadows. Everything glowed with equal intensity as if from inner fire. Steered with extraordinary sureness, certain to have been this way before, the flying boat banked and then nosed into a sky coruscating with multifaceted moonstones.

Now he understood how she had come by her reputation on the Missouri. His teeth were like metal. They ached. He was glad he had not eaten with the others. Bile leapt into his mouth. He heard the Rose laughing, saw Count von Bek get up from the co-pilot's seat and stroll past him towards the stern. Sam Oakenhurst took von Bek's place. Jack Karaquazian watched while faces formed in harsh purple tapestries.

They were insect faces. He found them abominable.

Russet oak leaves, becoming brown streaked with silver, fanned out and dismissed the faces. He breathed the scent of lilies.

'Sometimes,' he heard the Rose say, 'I think we're shown a glimpse of the beginning. But maybe it's only the end.'

It seemed to Jack Karaquazian that the plane banked again and began to spin: he became dizzy and the plane dissolved. He stood, naked and defiant against the firmament, his flesh fierce with brazen light, his destiny charted before his eyes, his spirit full of song. He was possessed of a noble certainty of purpose, ready to make his own way to the Second Ether and choose his role. He was consumed with a vibrant sense of physical well-being.

'Easy, Jack.'

The plane's engines slowed and there was a sound of rushing air as she began to descend.

Jack Karaquazian wiped mist from the porthole and saw recently mown wheatfields, vineyards, rooftops and chimneys.

Then the flying boat was dropping towards a large artificial lake flanked by totems carved in marble and granite, figures of boys and women in absurdly stylised poses, the old pseudo-realism of a white civilisation which in its day had ruled half the globe before collapsing under the weight of its own self-deception. Beyond this ornamental lake were the crenellated walls and towers of a barbarian city, its domes, steeples and votive columns rising high into an early morning sky.

The plane banked, straightened, coughed, coughed again, and hit the water smoothly with a loud thump which shocked both men. Up from the rear came a jaunty Rudy von Bek in holiday clothes, a pale grey suit and lilac accessories, including the traditional topper of his tribe. He carried a carpet bag. 'It's a wedding,' he said apologetically. 'I'm the best man. Goodbye, my friends.' He shook hands with them both as he paused by the main door in the middle of the fuselage. He would pass through this onto the lower wing. He would take the inflatable on a cord. They would retract the boat as soon as he reached the shore. 'I'm leaving you with the finest ether-pilot since Renark of the Rim. You are lucky men.'

'Which is why, I guess, we're here.' Sam Oakenhurst was warmer to the white man than Jack Karaquazian was able to be. 'We'll be seeing you, Rudy.'

Von Bek went forward to embrace the Rose. They spoke in that same guttural language, full of granite vowels and steel consonants, which Mr Karaquazian believed resembled the tongue used by bull baboons battling for kingship. All those European dialects sounded the same, which was doubtless why Europeans preferred Arabic as their common language.

Watching Count von Bek rowing himself rapidly towards the bank, Jack Karaquazian took deep breaths of the autumn air. The light was red-gold and gently fading, even as the sun rose upon the flashing copper and tiles of Mirenburg's roofs and gave the whole city the gaudy grandeur of a carnival. It was impossible to see any beauty von Bek and the Rose claimed for the settlement.

Momentarily Mr Karaquazian wondered why, at the last moment, Sam Oakenhurst had handed von Bek a folded sheet of paper, probably a letter.

He sought desperately for his bearings. He had had no time to gather himself, to take stock of what might be happening to him, to recover control.

The Rose watched von Bek through the plane's forward windshield. 'You are wondering, Sam, why I would marry someone like that. Rudy is almost the opposite of his brother, though both had courage. He has rescued me more than once. There was no escape from that stasis until he arrived. And from here we shall easily fly through the Autumn Stars up into the Grail. I know the way.'

And from there, thought Sam Oakenhurst, with a sensation in his groin which threatened to overwhelm him and yet did not seem entirely sexual, it will be a short step to Pearl Peru and the Game of Time.

He kissed his soul mate and dreamed of extravagant adventure.

CHAPTER EIGHTEEN

High Noon in Holtville von Ringo Hurricane

THE MORALITY AND PLURALITY OF NATURE
An Alchemical Treatise

by Dr. Jrmh. CORNELIUS, MB,
late of the Universities
of Prague and Alexandria.

London, The Scientific
Press, Bow Street, E.
1867

Author of:

THE VARIETY OF
CHOICE IN NATURE

THE MORAL PURPOSE
OF CHOICE

AN ORDERING OF CHAOS

THE RETREAT OF
MEMORY

&c &c

WITH CAPTAIN BILLY
BOB IN CHINA

by Warwick Colvin

CAPTAIN BILLY BOB AND
THE ELECTRIC KETTLE
by Warwick Colvin

CAPTAIN BILLY BOB'S
RADIO OVEN
by Warwick Colvin

CAPTAIN BILLY BOB MEETS
PROFESSOR POP
by Warwick Colvin

PROFESSOR POP AND HIS
SPEEDSHELL
by Warwick Colvin

PROFESSOR POP — TRAPPED
IN THE BOOMWAP
by Warwick Colvin

&c &c

Dear von Bek,

*Above is my 'want List' of books
which you might find in Mirenburg while
browsing. Don't ~~look~~ especially, mon ami,
but ~~thanks~~ for the other.*

Votre pard
JA

CHAPTER NINETEEN

Das Rote Universum

By the time we had found the Grail again and ridden effortlessly up the scales to the heart of the Second Ether, the Rose had convinced Jack of his sanity. Both he and I were almost through vomiting.

Jack says to me that I was right. The beauty of it is enough to die for.

'But we don't have to die, Jack,' says the Rose. 'That's the real beauty of it! We have a chance,' she says, 'and we've damned all to lose given the odds against us. Change the nature of Time and you alter the terms of the human condition.'

I understood better than Jack what she meant. They were trying to make some sort of just world! They were playing from faith, with the power of their trained wills. Giving their best in an effort to create an ideal.

From somewhere the Rose had obtained co-ordinates and a destination. We could rendevous with our chosen patrons in the lower colour fields where 'Cuttlefish and her Paramour' was being played, with all characters present – Fearless Frank Force, Kapitan Kaos, Manly Mark Male, Little Fanny Fun, Corporal Pork, Karl Kapital, Straight Arrow and the others for the Singularity. Opposing them were Captain Billy-Bob and all her famous Chaos Engineers, Kaprikorn Schultz and some who were entirely for themselves.

With the legendary *Spammer Gain*, Pearl Peru was one of the few truly neutral adventurers. But Pearl's weakness was for Bullybop, believed dead in the Blue Ice, searching for the Lost Universe of Ko-O-Ko, and this distracted Pearl from following her conscience, which told her to go to the aid of the *Spammer Gain*, whose quest for her fishlings had led that mighty benignity into the power of the Original Insect.

Jack was still uneasy about playing in the company of so many whites, particularly taking on a white's rôle. I told him his distaste was a weakness which would do him no good in the Second Ether, where issues of blood had long since ceased to concern us.

He agreed. 'To make a judgement according to race or gender is ungentlemanly and uncivilised, Sam. I know that. But that white battyboy freak still gives me the willies.'

Von Bek had not seemed a freak to me. Perhaps that was because we were all freaks there, save Jack himself. The Rose for instance was only half human and maybe me, too.

'I'm way out of my depth again,' says Jack. 'The same as I was when I lost Colinda. It's colouring everything.'

'Wait until you're playing,' I told him. 'Then you'll feel good again. You'll understand.'

But he was not entirely convinced. Twice, in the last little while, he had lost to me and the Rose at the Brackett's. We had been stunned. Jack had treated the events fatalistically, as if they were expected.

I told him this was a bad time to start getting demoralised. He agreed.

At this rate, I said, you'll be taken out of the Game in the opener! It was as if he was deliberately trying to sour his luck. And his luck, I said, was the best thing we had on our side. I wasn't fooling. Only as Jack weakened on us did I realise how much we were depending on his famous luck. But luck could go in seconds and never come back in a lifetime. We all knew that. Both the Rose and I were getting scared that Jack's luck wasn't around any more. We could have one of the walking wounded on our hands.

I took to reminding him of his own stories, of his legendary fights and risks, his unprecedented winnings and extraordinary losses: of how he had faced five bigwigs fixing to bushwhack him down on the Colorado, just outside Austin. How he had been hanged and never even gotten a bruised neck.

In Baton Rouge he had beaten Old Mums Bonchance at her own game. She had ruled the tables for as long as anyone remembered. And Jack Karaquazian challenged her and won. There was no one like Jack Karaquazian, Al-Q'areen, in the whole of the States. With his Marrakech training and his true Egyptian blood he was the very model of intellectual Africa; independent and self-disciplined, refusing the obvious and partial solution in favour of the whole; conscious of the common good; courteous to ladies and his social inferiors and able, if called upon, to defend his people and his honour to the death. He was, I reminded him, the inspiration of a thousand outstanding jugadors on his adopted continent alone. He was courted by the most beautiful women. Anyone who had ever sat at the flat table with him boasted of it. Why was he upset by the experience of being a piece in the game rather than controlling everything?

'You're too used to knowing all the moves ahead of time,' I told him. 'You'll have to take this thing move by move, as she comes. At least for a while.'

He asked me if you ever got used to it enough to read the currents of the Game without thinking. I said I knew this happened. The Rose could do it. But you couldn't get too experienced at it. There was a point where you lost spontaneity. That was when you gave up or retired. If you refused to admit your condition, you lost, sometimes instantly, and were no more.

'Extinguished?'

'I guess so,' I said. 'I only have a hazy idea.'

I knew a little more than I admitted. I had trembled, after all, as the tongues of the machinoix relived their ecstatic moments at the Game of Time. So *bébé*! They had taught me how to discover the Second Ether on the Path of Pain. You had to be fully alive to survive the Second Ether and play the Game. But I had followed the wide, red paths between the universes, borne above them on wings of pure silver and calling out the songs which took me through a confusion of grids and vapours, following the long, winding roads, dusty in the summer's heat, between the rolling, wooded hills or coursing into the heart of stars, flying naked against unguessable miles of dark blue silk and green clouds and the smell of warm rain, threatening a storm.

'You are alive and free in every element,' I added. 'You are fully alive. Aware of every individual vein and organ. Every blood cell. You have the whole multiverse at your disposal. You can go where you like and be whom you wish to be at any scale you choose.'

'But not if you play the Game of Time.' Jack grinned. 'If you play the Game you do what Pearl Peru should do or what Karl Kapital would do. You must obey the rules, however subtle. You must play their story and not your own.'

'No,' I said, 'you play your own story through theirs. That is what the great players do. That is the secret of winning at the Game of Time. You must hope to put your own stamp upon the tale, to leave it permanently altered. She is of the Just, as am I. We are hoping to bend the multiverse to our will and destroy the rule of the beast. It's in their logic and their alchemy as it is in ours.'

Jack said it was superstitious blanco nonsense and was disbelieving. 'Cheap fairground mumpo-jumpo. The kind those poor damned whiteys thrive on.'

'You'd be surprised what you can learn from their mumpo-jumpo!' I was angry with his deliberate ignorance. 'They have an old wisdom, Jack.'

'It didn't do them much good,' he said.

I saw no further point in talking to him and went forward again. I could feel those gorgeous archetypes down in the lower colour fields; I longed to hear the voice of Pearl Peru. I could sense them almost as strongly as they sensed me. They radiated an astonishing aura; mighty heroes and heroines playing out their lives with an intensity never captured even on the original V.

I had relived Pearl's early adventures. As human as myself then, she had sailed upon the oceans of Venus, trading between the soiled worlds and the fresh, knowing only slow, succulent sensations.

Lured into the Limbo on the edge of the Second Ether by a powerful demon, all that remained of an earlier hero called Koo-Aga, Pearl had been forced to play crude games and make humiliating moves at remote provincial termini. The demon had inhabited her body so that he might gain the Second Ether and rejoin the Game of Time. But Pearl had learned her lessons and determined to make her own mark on that famous Game. She aspired to become a major player in the struggle between Chaos and Singularity but remain neutral. She would earn her place in the pantheon not by joining one side or the other but by her daring trade journeys and explorations.

So she became the Merchant Venturer, Pearl Peru, having exorcised the last of Koo-Aga. Her story grew to be an integral part of the larger saga, the Tale of the Fishlings, itself part of an even larger saga known as the Fifth Lay.

The stories were endless but fell eventually into familiar patterns. The trick was to anticipate or provide innovation. It could come from anywhere and from anyone.

That was what I tried to tell Jack. It was no good being suspicious of the unfamiliar when everything was strange.

I was never at any point actually alarmed by Jack's lassitude and resistance, though I pretended to be. I knew he was the best of us. I knew that, once engaged with the Game of Time, he would play like the professional he was. At least, while his luck held.

But I knew I had to play the best I'd ever played if I was to have a chance of ever getting back together with the Rose. The irony was that, while Colinda Dovero placed no condition on Jack, the Rose would not be mine unless I had played the Game. She had to know my measure if I was to go with her. That at least was how I rationalised my decision and justified my fascination.

In a sense I was glad of Jack's situation. It meant I did not have to concentrate on my own.

Soon we would be choosing characters and I prayed to be accepted by Pearl Peru, to marry my soul to hers and become both a player and a piece in the Game of Time.

I did not anticipate my fate at all, which was to be rejected by Pearl Peru and taken in to the person of Captain Billy-Bob Begg.

It would strike me as a tragedy, a betrayal.

CHAPTER TWENTY

Die Furcht Lahmt Broken Wheel

CAPTAIN BILLY-BOB'S FIRST SCALE JUMP
by Warwick Colvin Jnr.
CHAPTER 900/1432
Trapped on the Yo-Yo-Flo

All was silence as Captain Billy-Bob indicated the scale-screens and explained what she had learned from the mysterious 'Professor Pop'. 'We call it "folding" but actually we are dissipating and concentrating mass in ratio to size, going "up" scale or "down".'

'But what's the urgency of your summoning, Cap?' called out Little Rupoldo, high in the fold net, voicing the question in their hearts.

'We have just learned that the force which conquered the remains of the First Ether, and made a quasi-universe of it by means of their secret super-carbon science, is now bent on conquering the Second Ether!'

'But surely such primitive science cannot threaten the integrity and freedom of the Second Ether?' put in young Lieutenant Kaprikorn Schwartz, the ship's accountant.

'Threaten it does, dear Kaprikorn,' Captain Billy-Bob assured the delicious boy. 'But you are wise to be dismayed. Let "Professor Pop" explain—' and she stepped aside for the huge greybeard as, the ether-dust powdering his tonsure, he addressed the crew and their sweethearts.

'My dears,' began the eminent oldster, 'it is now believed by some that the power of the Singularity to put its stamp on Chaos is so considerable that the Second Ether has scaled herself to its laws rather than their adapting, as we do, to the sometimes whimsical conditions of nature. The only power presently great enough to challenge the natural order of creation, the Singularity, is, in the eyes of most intelligences, the personification of pure Evil, and Old Reg, the First Voice of the Singularity, Satan Incarnate. Yet the secret of victory still lies, it is believed, in Ko-O-Ko, the Lost Universe, and that is why we are, no matter what detours we take, always on that quest, that journey to Ko-O-Ko. We believe that what we find there will save us from extinction.'

There was a gasp from every throat as the enormity of their task was revealed to them. Yet not one raised a voice against the captain. Instead a cheer broke out and Bumbum Wilson jumped into the scale harness shouting: 'We'll follow you to the ends of the multiverse and beyond, Cap'n Billy-Bob, if it's for our homes and dear ones.'

The proud explorer stepped forward, laughing with the joy of their confidence in her to steer them through the scales and win victory over the Singularity. She had drunk deeply of the Red Cup and now felt the power of the machinoix seeping into her bones.

Later Professor Pop addressed them all over his special 'Omniphone' which broadcast to a range of a hundred thousand scales. They had suspected but were now certain that the Singularity's quasi-universe had begun to fall away from natural gravity . . .

(These creatures are one with the multiverse, Sam. Only we resist its logic. Only we believe that love can defeat entropy and change the nature of sentient life. We, who so readily recognise our own slender grip on immortality and understand that we face extinction at any minute. To the majority of your near-immortals death is a very distant prospect. To ourselves it is more or less immediate. All a question of scale, Sam. We're merely taking advantage of our situation, the way we little humans will. We are, if nothing else, the creative force.

He smiled and rolled towards us. 'Yesterday you said you weren't human.'

'As human as you, Sam. But a rose is a rose.')

'If the key to Ko-O-Ko lies within the *Spammer Gain* and the only way to contact her is to join the quest for her fishlings, then quest we must,' Captain Billy-Bob was saying. She was grateful for this renewal of energy.

But now all eyes were on the scale-screens which were beginning to tremble with an overload of readings as the odds were measured and each player assigned their chances.

'What are the fishlings?' Professor Pop smiled at Little Rupoldo's innocent question. 'Originally hardly more than miscellaneous fractal dust moving through the scales in the wake of the *Spammer Gain*, then an ordinary Chaos free-scaler. Just as *Spammer* had, her fishlings gradually assumed a generic form and, with a spark of sentience, became the creatures we seek today.

'They swarmed around *Spammer* like pilot fish and made no distinction between themselves and their mother ship, who, in turn, had known them so long and through so many transitions that she believed them to be her natural children.

'She protected them as fiercely as she protected her crew. In particular *Spammer*'s Captain Wopwop loved her fishlings. They were her sublime optimism personified. Captain Wopwop still sails with *Spammer*. They are oddly interdependent now.'

And in answer to Little Rupoldo's inevitable second question: 'Ah, the *Spammer Gain*. Now there's a story all its own!'

CHAPTER TWENTY-ONE

Zydeco Gris-Gris

Jack Karaquazian had swivelled the co-pilot's seat. The view out of the flying boat's forward windscreen was now only in his peripheral vision. Laughing at him the Rose took the ship down an avenue of strawberry-scented, crimson columns which fanned into gold-laced polyanthus, blossoming then engulfing them in a tunnel of glistening jade stinking of rosemary.

Mr Karaquazian was growing used to these radical changes of colour, scale and image. He had begun to detect similarities, correspondences. It was an extraordinary kind of logic but its basis was not unfamiliar to a jugador of his rank. What had at first seemed disordered now betrayed the possibility of design. Each field unfolded its own scale, repeating its unique image with minor variations for something resembling infinity. Primroses enfolded and enfolded them, pink fading to yellow, fading to green, fading to deeper yellow, fading to black, fading to pink, enfolding and enfolding them as the flying boat poured its way decisively through the Second Ether, seeking the concourse of Chaos Engineers and Singularists which awaited their coming before beginning a further round in the Game of Time.

'We inhabit the same point in space but on a different scale,' she explains. 'We call this "folding". It is how we take newcomers through the multiverse. Where required we have other means of travelling, but I have always preferred this wonderful old flying boat. It serves its turn and it isn't nearly as extravagant as your disapproval suggests, Jack. The batteries in those restored engines will last forever. They are Swiss.'

'Look!' Sam Oakenhurst leans forward in excitement, peering through a sudden eruption of grey-blue auriculas becoming clouds and dissipating as if on a great wind. 'Look, mes amigos, it is the Grey Fees at last! And see – our heroes and heroines take their ease before the next step of the Game. I can feel her. Pearl Peru needs me! They wait for us to join them.'

'You're as eager as a virgin on his marriage night, Sam,' says Jack

Karaquazian, who had mistaken the hills for waves. He looked out at the grey river winding under a grey sky. But the charismatic physicality of the Chaos Engineers and their equally powerful Singularity foes battered at them like a furnace, threatening to engulf them. Through the closed windows of the Dornier poured the stink of archetypes and demigods; the vital, acrid scent of feral mammals. They reeked of the Minotaur. They triggered ancient terrors and delights. The Dornier descended into Babylon whose pagan pantheons celebrated an exquisite consummation.

Their senses alert to the presence of strangers, the great lords and ladies of the Second Ether looked up incuriously as the plane flew low over their concourse. Their chief attention was reserved for the cosmic energies against which they must soon be pitted.

Here were the mighty creatures of Hindu lore, of Egypt, Assyria and Persia. Mr Karaquazian was enchanted at last. 'Are these not our lost originals?'

'Possibly. But they are further from the angels than you or me, Jack.' The Rose speaks softly.

Mr Karaquazian's unwilling attention was wholly absorbed. He had no method of resistance. He watched frozen, uncritical. Those gorgeous phantasms floated lazily in the brilliant power fields beyond the Grey Fees, splashing waves of boiling multi-hued colour across their encrusted and corroded torsos, as if ceremoniously bathing.

Sam Oakenhurst was searching eagerly for Pearl Peru. Jack Karaquazian could have recognised none but Captain Quelch. The lords and ladies of Chaos and Singularity bore only the crudest resemblance to their magazine representations. Moreover the adversaries had grown to resemble one another, as occurs in any marchlands, in any long-disputed frontier, where adversaries become almost indistinguishable.

All these monsters displayed bizarre coral-like formations on heads and bodies. Irregular spurs and growths frequently gave them an insectoid or reptilian beauty. Carapaces of jade, brows of crystal, faceted eyes of jewellish brilliance; helmets fused with bone, metal with flesh, veins with display systems, bearing witness to their million encounters with the less congenial aspects of Chaos. Some had taken on the characteristics of the higher molluscs, resembling multi-coloured calimari, all sensitive tentacles and huge, enquiring eyes, yet still indefinably mammalian.

The magazines and even the original Vs had formalised and made more humanoid the appearance and identities of the Chaos Engineers and their enemies. Here, even Captain Quelch gave off unlikely vitality. His very outline seemed an elaborately artificial disguise, too human for the company.

Despite the variations of shape and limbs, each mighty being moved with a certain balletic formality clearly conditioned by its environment and perceptions, but which seemed ponderous to Mr Karaquazian.

The same fractal dust played about their bodies. They spoke the same language and often had similar names. Both favoured bizarre and awkward prosylactics. It was impossible to know how they distinguished friend from enemy.

But, when Jack Karaquazian presented this opinion the Rose put her finger to her lips.

Too late, for he had been heard. This was punishable blasphemy.

The surge of their anger struck him with physical force. For the first time he realised how thoroughly the creatures were aware of his presence, his very thoughts! Yet he remained bewildered by their disapproval. He was told that this struggle was the way of things. There was no changing it. This was how the fabric of the multiverse was maintained. How all life was sustained. He would be punished at once and for an indefinite time. The last to question God's evidence and authority had been taken in irons to a vault. This was demonstrated to Jack Karaquazian as he was taken in irons to a vault – scarcely a dungeon. The vault was vast and for much of the day was filled with sunlight which entered from stained-glass windows set in the roof. The glass and the sun made ever-changing patterns of colour and these patterns eventually communicated something to him, touching a sense that had been almost dormant.

It was impossible to be bored. The patterns and the pain were a wonderful aid to memory.

For one month he was left alone, experiencing profound remorse for his past; for the second month his mother was brought to speak with him every day. By the third month he had figured out the basics of his situation and could make relatively minor alterations to it. He had hope of success, of some kind of redemption. He considered his history.

At last Jack was able, by his own efforts, to take the rôle of page in the entourage of Lady Mo, but was captured by a powerful pirate called Oot-Rajoo who employed a number of minor demons, and who forced Jack to play crude games and make humiliating moves at remote provincial terminals until the chance presented itself one day on Venus, to escape his disgusting master and become, within the year, the Merchant Venturer, Pearl Peru, famous on all the seas of the Green Planet. Whereupon she was Pearl Peru, combining Jack Karaquazian's own experience with hers and Jack was hard-pressed to maintain his own identity under the archetypal force of her personality.

*

My terror of this unfamiliar existence, which seemed to have absorbed years of my life and yet not physically aged me, I deliberately keep alive. My terror is original to me. It identifies me. But Pearl Peru refuses to be moved by it. Instead she calls upon my gaming skills, for she now defies the whole Singularity as she enters her ship, *The Smollettsphere*, and orders her crew to set course for the First Ether and home to Venus. 'We'll take the old Solar Scaling Station. It's still the best. Set the controls for the heart of the sun.'

'You will,' the Rose tells me, even as this goes on, 'experience sensations of extraordinary well-being, Jack, and a belief that you have "come home". You will believe that the yearnings of your soul have been answered at last. That you have found the perfect equation. You have never been so at ease, so profoundly confident of your power. So *complete*. It is an illusion. This illusion will pass with familiarity. Pearl's crystallising bones ache with the weight of her peculiar carapace.

'Only when absorbing something close to an equal can she feel, again, those familiar sensations and emotions you enjoy. This is why she welcomes you so greedily. That is her hunger, which you must not fear. For the most part Pearl's brave enough in her pain. But you must be wary of her taste for melodrama.'

'She's Sam's, Rose! She's for Sam!' I could not turn my guilty head to look for my friend who had yearned and suffered for this union with his heroine.

'For a mysterious reason Pearl's rejecting Sam even as she accepts you. He will feel bitterly betrayed and this, of course, will be of use in the Game. Anyone else would be proud to be taken by Captain Billy-Bob. Sam believes he could have helped Pearl channel her pain to positive effect. But clearly it has always been you she has wanted, since she came seeking you twice at the Terminal Café. And Horace fears you. Don't you, Horace?'

From somewhere came the garbled sounds of a Latin quotation.

The Rose seemed to be teasing both the invisible Captain Quelch and me.

'Well, then,' I said, 'I must play her I guess.'

I gave my soul up to my legendary self.

CHAPTER TWENTY-TWO

The Politics of Turbulence

By releasing all control, by defying every instinct which until now had ensured his survival, Jack Karaquazian was almost immediately disembodied, as was the multiverse.

Aware of inchoate, seething Chaos all around him, knowing it to be the primal material from which all else was created, and direct evidence of a sentient will, he was at last unafraid.

He understood that this sentient will was only rarely capable of conscious self-direction upon any moral course. More often it manifested as little more than a blind urge to survive at all costs; the inheritance of the Original Insect, the mark of the Minotaur. What therefore was demanded of any trained jugador was to apply their own will, to use their own experience and intelligence, together with their own moral sensibilities, to create from that formless ether both shape, substance and a natural, enduring order which would be benign to the humans, or those of human origin, who played the Game of Time. It was their business to create, in short, more justice and greater predictability. To improve the odds for human survival.

All are players in the Game of Time. All have their parts, their place, their destiny. All have their chances.

That fragile combination of mind and conscience which was Mr Jack Karaquazian hung in turbulent ether; a void without scale, direction or coherence. Jack Karaquazian felt the terrible pull of it. It tempted him; offering him rest, forgetfulness and comforting death. A kind of power. A kind of confirmation. A kind of honour . . . It called to his blood.

The call was the most seductive Jack Karaquazian had ever experienced. As dreamily he let it claim him, he felt his very soul begin to lose substance. To dissipate. So, too, with his mind. Only by a vast and remarkable effort, struggling with an enemy without form or identity, was he able to reclaim himself. Then he understood that his act of self-reclamation signalled the beginning of this new Game. He had, as it were, taken hold of the Grail.

'*Colinda, I love you.*'

She had reached to him and she had cupped his blood in her hands. 'It's better there, Jack. Come with me, Jack.'

He could not. Not then. Not until he had understood and confronted the forces which had brought him to this pass.

She had spoken of the Rose; of a world at peace.

He understood that the same struggle was taking place on every scale, at every level of the multiverse, a struggle that was infinitely complex, fundamentally simple; a struggle between life and death. Life was this unfamiliar, formless ether-stuff, without intelligence or means of self-reproduction. Death was the empty void into which all life, undirected and without consciousness, gradually dissipated.

He recalled Colinda's talking in the early morning as the boat picked up speed past New Auschwitz.

'We came into existence by some accident, Jack. But now that we exist it is our moral duty to maintain our existence, to guarantee the existence of those who follow us. Our will is always, inevitably, the will of God. It is a will towards creativity, towards order, towards equity and justice and the rule of love. Some of us believe we are as much created by God as creating God but there can never be any meaningful dispute in the matter, since we live only to be united with God and one with God: the true reconciliation for which all life strives. First comes the senseless primæval struggle of form against form; then the conflict is structured to prevent useless waste; then the conflict is structured again, so that all shall understand its rules, then structured again so that the element of direct violence is removed; then it is changed into games and from games into mathematics and stories until the stories and the maths grow more and more to represent the complexity that is a reality comprising an almost infinite number of individual sensibilities. What we call "reality" in every meaning is the consensual will (unconscious, perhaps) of the Majority of Souls. The Will of the Just. All form struggles for consciousness, Jack, for it is through consciousness that form survives. Those who employ the instincts of the Beast are ultimately devoured. Yet often they are the ones who seem to triumph.'

He recalled every moment of her conversation now, every nuance. It was as if she had been preparing him, so long ago, for this time.

'Oh, Colinda,' he said. 'I love you. I will not perish.'

Jack Karaquazian could remember the sound of her silk dress in the hush of the Mississippi summer night, when the moon was high and the flat waters of the bayou mirrored every star. He could bring all that back – her scent, the touch of her, the beautiful, delicate tensions of his uncertain love.

'You can make it come out however you like, Jack. Make sure you keep a little confidence in your luck.' She had kissed him on the cheek, the sweet intimacy of a moth's wing.

In the Medersa Jack Karaquazian had studied earlier musical ages. For a while he had developed a perverse fascination for the weird whitey jass of the 1920s and 30s, not his usual taste at all. He remembered a Roy Summers Band recording from October 3rd '31, with the saxophonist Dan Donovan singing 'This Is The Day Of Days'. In the background, the distinctive chords of Tommy Blade's Xylo-Phone.

Note by note the exaggerated syncopation and rapid beat came back to him, and as he recalled the tune, the instruments and harmonies, all the colours of the music, it seemed to Jack Karaquazian that his love for Colinda Dovero grew into an enormous symphony which absorbed and amplified every sense until both he and his music filled the entire multiverse. As he looked about him, his own hands reinvented before his own eyes, he saw movement in the surrounding chaos, hints of shapes and colours and even scents and sounds, which gradually began to take substance, slowly at first and crudely, then faster and faster, the stuff building into a towering pyramid which disappeared from sight overhead.

There was space, thought Jack Karaquazian with hope, so therefore there must be time.

He saw that the pyramid was made of flesh. It was composed of millions of separate beings – and such beings!

'They are angels,' said Jack Karaquazian to himself. 'They are God's angels taking their battle-stations in the Game of Time.'

Choir upon choir of angels rose above him accompanied by the most blissful music, the most astonishing perfumes.

Winged and scintillant, with weapons which burned with all the glories of Paradise, with instruments of mysterious function, their robes swirling and waving as if in some heavenly wind, they rose. They rose towards the Godhead.

And each angelic face was the face of someone Jack Karaquazian had known or loved or admired. He saw his father and his mother, his teachers, his brothers and sisters and friends and every woman he had ever betrayed, every man he had ever killed.

It seemed to Jack Karaquazian that he stood upon a wide, grassy plain. Above him was the silvery pallor of an evening sky into which a huge, pulsing red sun bled its light. And on either side of that globe, filling every horizon and rising into distant invisibility: rank upon rank of angels – Lucifer defying God – the forces of Chaos and the forces of Singularity ready for war: ready to begin the great story that was the Game of Time.

[223]

It seemed to Mr Karaquazian that every soul in creation who had ever lived and died, or who lived now, was represented in that ultimate equation of sentience.

But even as he watched, the character of the two angelic armies changed – the one growing bizarre and complex, with individuals taking on increasingly idiosyncratic shapes, like the Hindu pantheon, the Egyptian or the Chinese, and somehow blending together to form an extraordinary and beautiful whole – while the other army grew steadily more austere, resembling the ascetic warriors of his boyhood reading; its colours fading to lustreless greys and blacks and pale browns, its individuals assuming an unholy similarity, no face different either in feature or expression, forming itself into a single wedge of power, a phalanx which threatened Chaos with the cruel ambition of its Singular nature.

Here were Chaos and Singularity taking the purest forms of their opposition as they prepared to fight a battle neither would or could ever win, but which could destroy the multiverse and sacrifice everything living to the infinite void.

What hope was there? Jack Karaquazian wondered, and then turned to watch as, between those two vast, assembled armies, a great cloud boiled, lazy and opulent and radiant with vivacious strength, creating its own music and harmonies as it rolled slowly through the ether, seeming to sing.

Gradually it became possible to perceive the size of the cloud and also its form. This was the *Spammer Gain*, tolerant and invulnerable, content with her fishlings around her, a mighty organism swimming carelessly through the gathered armies of the Apocalypse, glowing with constantly changing colours and planes, turning eyes which were the size of galaxies to regard the combatants with sorrow.

There were few amongst those two angelic hosts who did not seem shamed by her distress.

'But the stories must continue!' cried the Rose. 'The conflicts must be structured and explained. There can be no cessation to the Game of Time. That will mean the cessation of existence itself.'

Jack Karaquazian denied this. At a particular moment, he brought the multiverse back into the void. He and a million souls like him. Spontaneously, unconscious of all others, he recreated the multiverse in order at last to be reunited and know peace with Colinda Dovero.

The Rose had understood his power. His power and his luck is what she herself gambled upon. It was what she had promised him.

'Ah, Colinda! I will conquer this inchoate infinity. I will give it form. I will do whatever is necessary to ensure that I stand beside you once more.'

Chaos reared and was again a pyramid of glorious variety, a host which flashed with all the colours of the spectrum, with brass and gold and silver and copper, with platinum and steel. And through it all those same familiar faces in uncountable numbers rose in a great scintillating tower of creation, pulsing like living jewels, their beauty rich enough to breathe, strong enough to sustain all human need. They rose surely to the Godhead, to challenge that phalanx which was the bleak threat of the near-invincible Singularity – firm ranks of hard-faced soldiers, countless numbers of them, trained to demand only victory, disciplined to serve only one idea, embodied in one human master, one Greater Being comprising the Singularity, Old Reg, the Original Insect. Only the latter's reality was ever disputed amongst them; the former, never.

They prepared for a battle which, when in some unguessable future it came, must ultimately determine the nature of reality.

Jack thought again of Colinda. How could such cosmic actualities depend so much upon a few familiar human emotions? Upon love and faith and luck?

As Jack Karaquazian gradually reclaimed his physical identity from the ether, he took a deep breath, like a new-born child, and inhaled with a shock the fœtid stink of the Beast. It was only then that he truly understood how not all life survived through superior intellect or knowledge in the Game of Time. Other kinds of vitality had been drawn into this fresh reality by the psychic gravity generated by himself and those who had, individually and without mutual influence, between them somehow recreated the cosmos. A multiverse of possibilities obeyed the new laws Jack Karaquazian and his kind had built from the stuff of chance. But the new was still threatened by the old. Still threatened by the Beast.

Only through playing the Game of Time could Mr Karaquazian make sense of this struggle. They formalised their war, just as the laws of chivalry had once determined the stages of a battle. Without those laws, the complex mathematics, conflict itself was almost impossible. It was the means by which the parties could avoid stasis, establish a time, a place and a prize. Thus wars were turned into tournaments and tournaments into sports. And so too the Beast was tamed but never banished.

Now all he could do was play.

Even as Jack Karaquazian watched, listening to the opulent dis-harmony that was Chaos and the steady, horrifying drum beat of the Singularity, he saw them swirl suddenly and change into complicated patterns of raw, violent energy.

Chaos was no longer flesh. It had become whirling golden leaves and green, blossoming clouds. It had become hectic and whimsical, trembling through the entire catalogue of colour, a measureless palette of shade and nuance . . .

While the grey Singularity, stark and cold and consistent, as simplified and specialised as a shark, hovered, ready to strike at the very centre of the blood red rose, at the very heart of Chaos, to devour all that wild energy, tame it, enslave it, pervert it to the service of the Original Insect . . .

'No! Colinda!'

Where was she? He existed only because his desire for her to exist was stronger than his own will to survive.

(She had found him once, when he had tried to avoid her, in their early days, standing by the bar of the Lazarus Saloon on rue Royale. 'One day we shall dance together, Jack. And that dance shall determine our destiny. And it will be a destiny which joins us together for eternity.' He had smiled and refused to understand her, pointing out the virtues of the zee-band which had just come up on stage. Soon her words were drowned by 'Les Flammes d'Enfers'.)

Again Jack Karaquazian yelled into the void, defying death, refusing defeat and still claiming his Colinda. All he wanted was that she should exist: that she should survive. And he would die if necessary to achieve that end.

Now the battle was once more transformed.

He saw all the races and nations of mankind, people upon people, army upon army, race upon race, with their bold banners and armour, their chariots and horses and their war-machines, their ships and their fliers, all the people who had ever existed and all those who might come to exist.

This immeasurable army represented every stage of the human journey. It marched, it seemed to Mr Karaquazian, into a mirror. People against people, army against army, race against race, individual against individual, forever at war, forever marching into the mirror. Forever swallowed up in the Game of Time. And yet this struggle could never be determined by conflict. That was obvious to Jack Karaquazian.

'There must be some means of resolving this,' said Jack Karaquazian, 'some compromise which could be reached. Some sublime equation.'

He knew exactly what he was testing and that this time there would be no punishment. The gods had lost their power over him. He had successfully challenged their mathematics.

'Colinda!' In Jack's lonely voice was a hint of his old confidence, his old vision. 'Colinda . . .'

Again Jack Karaquazian saw the Angelic Host mounted in a great pyramid, saluting the pinnacle where a gold and silver figure, St Machaël as Jack Karaquazian knew him, lifted a burnished blade as if recognising the source of all creation, the Godhead itself. Once more that indescribable music filled Jack Karaquazian's soul. Had he been able, he would have wept.

Jack Karaquazian understood that God had created an enemy when he had created the profoundly mysterious idea of free will, which was the ultimate triumph of Chaos, a reality sustained entirely by conscious consensus.

It was not for God to reconcile us, Jack Karaquazian would say, when he told the story, it was for all of us to achieve reconciliation. But Old Reg would have none of it. The idea of shared and equal responsibility sickened him he said. How could existence be controlled, examined and predicted? Civilisation would decline to savagery in a matter of decades. The majority of beings, Old Reg's orthodoxy insisted, were still in a state of childhood and needed guidance, not power. Stability came only from a common leader, a benign father who would stop this petty squabbling and end the spread of spiritual pestilence, the inroads that chance had already made upon their lives.

Old Reg's arguments made sense to Jack Karaquazian. Why risk more bloodshed, more agony and horror? Where was compassion?

When it became clear to him that he was, by nature, better suited to serving the Singularity. Jack Karaquazian was not sure why he supported the cause of Chaos. Colinda had spoken of slower time, of security and peace. How could Chaos possibly achieve such a state? It must be the Singularity that Colinda served.

He looked and he saw the face of the Original Insect. There was a cold, rational wisdom there, but he saw no compassion at all.

Why not play for the Singularity? Play for the rule of law and the security of simplification?

'Jack,' said Colinda, standing beside him as the cool dawn came up over the roof of the Van Beek Hotel and the crows went crying into the air above Mud Island, 'you should give it up, Jack. You should conquer this urge of yours to control. It can lead only to damage and destruction. It can lead only to decay.'

Jack Karaquazian watched those massed angelic ranks, winged and splendid, moving in a dance which was some kind of conversation. Their spiritual and intellectual development was inconceivable to him. They were able to speak a thousand languages, and were fluent in at least as many mathematical systems. They were learned and wise and courageous beyond the imagination of any mortal, belonging neither to past nor present but undoubtedly to some miraculous future when he and his people would reach at last some further stage in their unsteady progress towards a state of grace.

Swords burned against the heavens; supernatural horses reared and bellowed. The multiverse was filled with the scent of roses as the angelic armies opened their glorious mouths and cried out their joy, cried out in the fulfilment of a prophecy which told how Chaos and the Singularity must be reconciled and how only through that reconciliation would order come to the multiverse of mankind.

But when would this reconciliation come? Was it not already too late?

Banners blazed! The horses snorted and their breath was white fire. Their hooves struck gashes into the very fabric of existence and revealed the terrible, empty regions of limbo, which even now threatened to gulp down their fragile wall against reality.

'Colinda,' said Jack Karaquazian. 'It must be you. You are my inspiration.'

And it was as if the armies had heard his voice and they drew back from the conflict. And as Jack Karaquazian watched he saw each angel, one by one, foes and friends, kneel and bow their heads as if they understood at last what thin barriers separated them from endless death.

They kneeled, arrayed upon the brink of Time, upon the very ledge of darkness beyond which was nothing and beyond which there never could be anything. They had arrived at the Gates of Entropy, through which all sentient life must pass at last.

The angels kneeled, apparently in prayer. A hush fell upon the multiverse. They must decide now if they will pass through those gates or turn and compromise. One way leads to pride and death, and the other to humility, love and life. They must decide how much they value life.

But first there must be further moves made in the Game of Time. The complexities as well as the simplicities must be reflected and celebrated.

Sam Oakenhurst must be sacrificed. The Rose must achieve her victory. Jack Karaquazian must play his best and final hands.

Jack Karaquazian is sleeping. He is dreaming. 'But now, Jack,' Colinda seems to be saying to him, 'now you must rejoin the Game. There is much for you to do. Take your place again. It is your duty to steer the destiny of Pearl Peru.'

With melancholy reluctance Jack Karaquazian returns to the Game. Now he understands exactly what it is he will lose should he fail.

CHAPTER TWENTY-THREE

It's Hard to be a Saint in the City

THE STORY SO FAR:

In order to make effective moves in the Game of Time (*La Zeitjuego* as it is called by the Singularity) Jack Karaquazian has been forced to accept their logical overview (but also clings to his own, making concentration on the Game doubly difficult). Meanwhile, Sam Oakenhurst has been absorbed into the greatest of the Chaos captains, Billy-Bob Begg, who believes she has taken his power and wisdom by drinking from the Red Cup. The Rose refuses the Game but remains in her ship, eagerly interested in the outcome and observing much of the play through her scale-screens, which have been adapted for the purpose. She sniffs for those connecting scents which will help her form a picture and witness Jack's learning the story of the fishlings:

CHAPTER TWO

How Kaprikorn Schultz Betrayed his Great Main Type and Abducted the Fishlings

In the course of her extensive ether-travelling the *Spammer Gain* had become completely organic, nowadays resembling at stable scale a well-fed sea-mammal, sweet-featured, trailing impossibly long mustachios of glowing baleen and glittering coral-coloured tentacles, her forequarters resembling a vast tropical cuttlefish a million miles wide, her lovely eyes full of wise astonishment.

Her intellect was in a constant state of activity. She existed in deep co-dimensional symbiosis with her crew whose well-being was her motherly concern. Her crew loved her with unreasoning loyalty and an almost childish passion.

The patterns of these linked emotions were a powerful natural talisman protecting the *Spammer Gain*, with the result that she had virtually no traditional enemies.

Even the Singularity had to treat with the *Spammer Gain*. The fishlings, who had conjured themselves into sentient existence around her, created in her a profound maternal pride which added to their mutual invulnerability. In all their ether-travelling, all the dangers of their deep explorations and high-scaling adventures, they were protected by the massive power of their mutual love and their relish for existence.

The love between the *Spammer Gain* and her fishlings was celebrated throughout the multiverse. Captain Wopwop of the *Spammer Gain* was an admired merchant venturer in her own right, courageous and clever and shrewd and risky as a rolled rat. She too had changed conspicuously under the fluid logic of the Second Ether and her face had come to look almost purely piscine. Hers was perhaps the most sublimely beautiful face in all the multiverse, while her generosity and active sympathy were a watchword amongst even those munificent and profligate Chaos captains who spoke of her in the same reverential breath as Captain Billy-Bob Begg, their exemplar and, upon appropriate occasions (for all the Chaos captains were fiercely free), their mentor.

Ultimately the fishlings began to form simple societies, separating into a number of tribes. The leaders were identified by the name of their tribe – thus Perch was Chief of the Perch tribe, Bream, Chief of Breams, and so on. There were at least fifteen tribes, each with distinctive appearance and customs, including Roach, Grayling, Salmon, Tench, Chubb, Charr, Eel, Zander, Barbel, Pike, Rudd and Dace, but their rapid evolution was to prove their downfall and Kaprikorn Schultz would set a false attractor to lure them over, using the boomwap he had stolen from Professor Pop: *and everyone's wrecked on main street from drinking unholy blood* . . . His plan was to win the confidence of the infamous Homeboy Tong and become their chief accountant.

Schultz departed, the fishlings swarming behind him, all but Chief Tench, a singularly intelligent creature who, having failed to warn the others of its misgivings, had elected to stay with *Spammer*, even though it had almost torn his soul apart to do so, for the false attractor was unusually convincing and had created all kinds of seductive secondary realities.

Delivered over to the evil ministrations of Mrs Reg, co-desk to the Instrument, the fishlings would be fed into the maw of the Original Insect and thus, the Singularity hoped, bring their legendary patron to their aid in the conquest of the Second Ether. Only blood could activate the necessary equation. But through carelessness and an innate sporting sensibility, Kaprikorn Schultz lost his stolen charges when he failed to refold his boomwap, causing his false attractor to dissipate. The fishlings vanished. Now not even the infamous Banker to the Homeboy Tong knew where they had gone.

'My fishlings!' cries the wretched monster. 'O, bring me back my fishlings!'

And so loved is the *Spammer Gain* that almost every Chaos Captain, wherever they are, on whatever business in the multiverse, rallies to her cri de cœur. And for love of Pearl Peru came Fearless Frank Force, Hero of the Singularity, to dare the Lavender Field and face the risk of massive psychic re-ordering. Five times Fearless Frank Force and his ship *The Right Course for Recovery* had corkscrewed down the misty maze of tunnels ripped through the fabric of the multiverse by previous Singularity voyagers. The tunnels' boundaries were announced only by the subtlest changes of lavender shades. Following crude charts and hearsay, Captain Force survived to enter the *Poppy and the Poppies* where a kind of civilisation had developed. It had made Frank Force its king and bequeathed to him his uncanny Fold Suit which allowed this paragon of all that was virtuous in the Singularity to pass along the megaflow without damage to his surroundings. He was heading for Ko-O-Ko, the Lost Universe, in the belief that the fishlings had found a home there.

Meanwhile evil Freddy Force, whose machinations allowed him to become Old Reg's Favoured Number Two, believes his noble twin to be dead and has captured Little Rupoldo. 'I shall try my luck again,' he declares. 'And next time I shall bring you back the *Mangootr* they put your father in!' Chuckling, he departs on his stolen Vespa Vortex Navigator. He hopes to trade information with Kaprikorn Schultz at an agreed rendezvous. (In those days Kaprikorn's rank was only temporary.)

'*My fishlings! Where are my fishlings?*' The whole multiverse reverberates with her agonised plea. 'Bring me back my *fishlings*!'

A scarlet cloud billows out from the *Spammer Gain*, a spume which rages, with painful yellows and dark, rocky greens at its dissipating edges. She scales recklessly down towards the dangerous demon-worlds of Limbo where echoes alone rule, their meaning forgotten, their origins lost, where all that is left of our former gods is a heartless appetite.

Deeply she dives down-scale, all her screens alive with rapidly growing and fading perspectives and formulae in every level of the spectrum, astral rays blazing a path through the roiling fractures of dissipating Chaos, pale blues and golds, pale lemons and pinks, teasing their way into the spaces which always grow between proliferating matter. Deeply she dives, as if the pain of it will replace the pain in her heart. Her recklessness terrifies even Captain Wopwop who begs her for all their sakes to change course and go upscale again, at least until they have discussed their predicament. Ghosts lick at their souls. Forgotten godlings taste the scent of them. Greedy echoes, longing for the substance *Spammer* can provide in such magnificent quantity.

'They begin to hunt us,' says Captain Wopwop. 'Here, our love has no power.'

'What?' *Spammer* is dreamy, lost, drowning in her sorrow.

'If the fishlings are in Limbo, *Spammer* dear, there is no saving them, just as we cannot save ourselves.'

'What? Are you frightened Wopwop, dear?'

'Aye, *Spammer*. Never more so. Is this not fruitless? Tell me you think it is! Do not extinguish us like this, *Spammer*. Feeding the damned at last.'

But, before *Spammer* can answer, news comes over the experimental omniphone. Little Rupoldo has escaped Freddy Force's captivity and has stowed away on a Singularity ship. He has overheard many crucial conversations. Fearless Frank Force has discovered Ko-O-Ko, the Lost Universe, and is even now seeking the fishlings there.

The *Spammer Gain* quickens with hope and she begins the long, exhausting scale-jump, via the old Mars Scaling Station, which will return them to the Second Ether. The Singularity will try to block her way. She will disguise herself as one of their number.

CHAPTER TWENTY-FOUR

Muy Poissonettes C'est Vrai!!

Sam Oakenhurst made his play and sat back to take a breather. He suspected the Rose of having something to do with Pearl Peru's failure to accept him. The Rose has always been jealous of Pearl. He remembered how ill-tempered she had become when he had first taken an interest in Pearl's adventures. He was not sure of his feelings. He still loved the Rose, yet he had yearned so long for Pearl Peru! Now that he was denied her, he believed himself betrayed.

I could do nothing but offer her my best, he would write in his journal. I had acquired the key to positive pain. This permitted me an almost limitless power, which was sought by Captain Billy-Bob Begg herself, whose own strange carapace had endowed her with peculiar aches and agonies. I was able to translate all this pain into daring battle-plays and counter-moves, with nothing to fear but death and no longer fearing that! We had the whole multiverse to play for, with immortality the pot of the day! This understanding brought her a certain ease and sometimes wild joy. Initially I could find no links to help me reveal the deeper solutions she needed, yet sometimes I felt as if she were eating me alive – but absently, as one might chew upon a forgotten piece of gum.

'It's a game with all winners or all losers, depending on their luck and judgement,' I told Jack.

I will admit that I was bitter that he should have the rôle I so coveted, but if one of us was to be a winner, rather than both, I accepted that he was the better player. When we had first parted to go to our identities and play *La Zeitjuego*, the Game of Time, I had told him spitefully that his identity was obvious – he could always look in the mirror. In my case all I had left of myself were my original eyes, now mere optic options.

Captain Billy-Bob was paying attention to the screen where Little Rupoldo had successfully hooked them into the Singularity's senders. I leaned forward, over Little Rupoldo's pixing shoulder, and watched.

Old Reg, his toothbrush moustache bristling with urgency, his round glasses angry with cold reflections, his tie a tight knot at his throat, addressed the Singularity's noblest hero. 'There are five freescalers of hume origin and three Chaos Engineers with the power to freescale. You, Frank Force, against all eight humes (and we do not know how many followers of the First Beast, all those sliplings and swiflings) – you, Frank Force, are the only Singularist with the means of emulating their skills. You achieve this wholesomely, through rational scientific, rather than metaphysical, method. Your mathematics are clean. Fate and the *Poppy and the Poppies* have provided you with an uncanny Fold Suit which permits you to roam almost at will through the Second Ether. I therefore adjoin you to seek the fishlings wherever they have flown, even to Ko-O-Ko, the Lost Universe, and return them to the *Spammer Gain*. Thus we shall ensure that powerful freescaler's loyalty to our cause, guaranteeing our conquests! You are further adjoined to avoid the presence of the Outlaw Venturer, Pearl Peru, at cost of Withdrawal of the Desk, leaving you unprotected against the lust of the Original Insect and consigned to Perpetual Shame.'

Excommunicated!

Fearless Frank Force received this news with considerable dismay. His whole purpose in convincing Old Reg to let him seek the fishlings was so that at length Pearl Peru would look on him with favour, turning her attention away from the loathsome Bullybop. He was not to know recent events had overtaken him. Bullybop had used his lover's power over Pearl Peru to try to bring her to Kaprikorn Schultz's confederacy. This had sickened her and at last confirmed her common sense, which she had been ignoring. In disgusted rage she had freed herself from his emotional glamour. His loathsome influence was broken. But her caution towards the Singularity and its servants remained.

(Furious and frustrated, Bullybop takes the Blue Cup and absorbs Paul Minct. A further mistake. He rushes to join Pearl's enemies but is incautious and is in turn absorbed.)

'See,' I told Little Rupoldo, 'under the deadly authority of the Singularity Frank Force becomes a creature unable to follow its conscience or its desires! This, Little Rupoldo, is the path of death. This is what would conquer us and win the Game of Time. We must throw ourselves into the turbulence of unknown scales and seek the Lost Universe of Ko-O-Ko. We must seek and survive the pain.'

These words were relayed. There was a silence in the great control room as the crew considered the meaning of my decision. Then, in accord, they offered up a cheer. 'We're with you, dear Main Type, to the ends of the multiverse, if need be.'

I gave orders for rapid angular scaling, simultaneously moving through time and space as well as scale. It would be agony for us all.

Frank Force passes us by, his uncanny Fold Suit pulping and repulping as he chooses the notorious underside. He considers fresh equations.

'She will not take it kindly,' he says, 'if I kill Bullybop.'

Frank Force does not realise that Pearl Peru has had her last encounter with Bullybop. This encounter will become legendary as The Conflict at the Field of the Blue Pearl Crocus:

Bullybop had returned, he said, with Pearl's spare livershield which he had borrowed:

It was a ruse. He was Bullybop in appearance, but already the half-demon Baron Pin was in control of him. And Pin favoured the taste of Minct.

The moment they were alone amongst the crocuses, Pearl's instinct (actually Jack's memory) told her Bullybop retained nothing of his original character. Paul Minct's features, still masked, gloated at her, horribly familiar to Sam Oakenhurst, now linked in. Nothing had warned him of Sam Oakenhurst's memory and experience. Such a combination was unimaginable to him. Baron Pin did not reveal himself but let Paul Minct blossom and define the character, with the result that Pearl's sense of loathing increased enormously. She immediately developed a physical aversion for the creature who had once held her with the power of a deep addiction. She craved now to destroy Bullybop. Jack's experience and instincts rescued her.

Still linked to Captain Billy-Bob but drawn temporarily to Pearl, with Jack's active help, Sam Oakenhurst remained terrified of his old enemy. Paul Minct had not long preceded him into the Second Ether. Only through this unprecedented double equation was Mr Minct resisted. At the end, employing furious force, Sam Oakenhurst almost killed himself and his whole *gestalt*. But at last it was done in a moment. Raging and vicious, Pin Minct fought these unnaturally novel mathematics and lost.

'Much obliged, Sam,' says Jack Karaquazian, while Pearl Peru stares coldly down at her ruined ex-lover. And Sam Oakenhurst, whose co-option to Pearl's cause can only be brief, which was only possible because of his enduring obsession and Jack's talent for innovation, returns wholly to Captain Billy-Bob Begg. 'Much obliged.'

I am relieved. I have no liking for such daringly unconventional moves. My admiration for Jack Karaquazian, however, increases. We are short a Bullybop, a Minct and a Baron Pin and that cannot be a minus. We have taken control of the logic. The angels are devouring each other. I can still hear echoes of their conflict.

'Don't mention it, Jack,' I say.

Jack had taught me the crossover technique which was to seal my fate.

I had occupied two characters at the same time, playing them in harness. An impossible triumph.

CHAPTER TWENTY-FIVE

The Masked Buckaroo's Leap for Freedom

It was impossible to be a freescaler and a Chaos Engineer. That was the received wisdom before Little Rupoldo cleared the Great Gnat and raced home on a barrel stave. In order to travel, the engineers manipulated the multiverse, following the ether patterns and the scales and some-times bending them a little. The freescalers, on the other hand, took their chances and went all the way with whatever flow was fastest or what seemed to be going in their direction. Blown like dandelion spores on the cosmic winds, using their wits only in self-defence, they sometimes bleated like Easter lambs in their helpless terror. Their philosophy – if such it was – could not be understood by Corporal Pork. His attention was still on the screen where the freescalers had left their trails. But this was something new. 'I'll stake hell to a herringbone if it isn't a sniffer sidling in at last,' he declared. 'What news, my snouts?'

'The Singularity's Freescaling Ace, Fearless Frank Force, is approach-ing the *Now The Clouds Have Meaning*, ship of the famous Chaos Engineer, Captain Billy-Bob Begg,' whiffled the little fellows. 'There, it is said, they will parley.'

'Unprecedented! Could this be the beginning of Peace between Chaos and the Singularity? An agreement to hold the Balance by other means than this life-devouring rivalry?'

'Love will conquer, Porky,' promises his new paramour, Little Fanny Fun. 'Love will conquer. It is what we play for. But how else shall we consume Time? Loyalties are changing suddenly now. I am helpless. I have no side!'

'Love is our friend in this,' says Corporal Pork. Captain Quelch, who is their prisoner, snorts with contempt.

'Nar! Nar!' he bellows, in mockery of the First Beast, whose brother he has so recently ripped up. 'Let this loving peace develop and we shall cease to exist! You foolish dullards! It is your own doom you'll bring with this sentimental lust, this feeble guff. Love is never our friend!

Should it triumph, we shall have no further purpose!' He is drunk on super-refined carbons, filling their quarters with appalling fumes. He has already devoured an entire flagon of Ackroyd's Vortex-Water. 'We'll be redundant. All we can do is play our bloody Game. We're specialised creatures. If we succeed in establishing and holding the Balance we're done for, my dears. We go straight to Limbo, darlings, believe me. *Sat sapienti* – you think I'm the cynic? Who set us up for this? God, do you think? Or people like us, but a couple of million scales bigger – doing just what we're doing now? And maybe somebody's doing the same with them. Where does the Game end? Maybe it's infinite. *The strong shall devour the weak*. That is the only law of nature I understand. How long does it go on for, my dears? How far does it go? Why question the unanswerable? Why don't we enjoy the Game and play it forever, my darlings? If we're bound for Limbo it's inevitable. Death is a natural consequence of life. Since death is inevitable we might as well make the most of life while we have it. Taste each moment. There isn't anything better than this for us. And it isn't that damned bad, either! The Game has been good to me. If the Game stops, corporal, so do we.'

'Love cannot be our enemy,' says Corporal Pork.

'Love is our salvation,' says Fanny Fun.

'Our doom!' Captain Quelch gulps the carbons like a goose gobbling smoke. 'Admit it, Pearl. Your creed must damn us all to inevitable and immediate death.'

'We shall change the nature of the multiverse and therefore the terms of the human condition,' says Pearl Peru from the shadows where she rests. Her war against Bullybop has exhausted her and she yearns for Frank Force, wondering why he does not come to her. 'We *shall* change the nature of reality. We *shall* change our own fates. The secret lies in our power over Time. We can order reality so that love truly *does* rule the multiverse.'

'A tall order, dear.' Captain Quelch pretended to return to his V. He had noted uneasily Jack Karaquazian's eyes peering out from Pearl's glittering head. He had gambled on the Egyptian being as upset by change as himself. Yet Mr Karaquazian was taking untypical risks. Was even strengthened by them.

Was it time, Quelch wondered, to desert the Singularity? '*Iuppiter ex alto perjuria ridet amantum*, as Ovid would have it.' The very small talk of these people sickened them. How could they draw strength from such insubstantial whimsy? At this moment however their grip on their power seemed far surer than his own.

What sort of minds, Quelch asked himself, could make sense of all that slithering, constantly regenerating and proliferating primary ether-stuff, that untameable slime? He shuddered. He was revolted, even now, merely to be in their company. His temper had not been good since he had lost his peabody in the crude opening round as they had reached the Grail. He longed for the clean, open seas of the life he had left behind, the warm scents of the tideless Mediterranean where they had all been born, so long ago, where Europe met Asia and Africa. He even felt nostalgic for Kent.

Pearl groans. 'Where is Frank Force? Will he ever return from the Lost Universe? O, Frank! My love! Is he gone with the fishlings?'

'Look,' says Corporal Pork, all his little eyes upon their brightening screens. 'Look, my friends! I think we are rescued.'

Something has holed the Singularity's false-universe. Its hectic momentum has been reversed. It is the *Spammer Gain* bright with supercarbon filings which swarm to her motherly gravity. Another new development.

'Fresh fishlings for her, I think,' says Pearl Peru in satisfaction. 'But what became of the others?'

Only Captain Tench, venturing alone and determined into that vast and uncongenial universe, will ever discover the truth.

Spammer has inadvertently blown up the Martian Scaling Station, causing a flux-twist which, in turn, has given Captain Billy-Bob the co-ordinates she needs.

The news comes through on the omniphone – in her ship, the *Now The Clouds Have Meaning*, Captain Billy-Bob has freescaled the length and breadth of the Second Ether, returning with fresh, detailed charts locked into her logic banks. It is just the knowledge the Engineers need to develop much-needed new mathematics.

Now they can, with confidence, challenge and perhaps even defeat the Singularity!

But still no news of Frank Force. It seems the rumour of his rescue by Captain Billy-Bob was false. Pearl Peru begins to weep.

Captain Billy-Bob does not return in triumph. She is broken with shame. Having fallen through thousands of millions of scales in her wild search for the Lost Universe, her adventures have taken eons of subjective time. She and her crew have suffered impossible agonies and transformations, only through luck retaining a rough equivalent of their original psyches. But they failed to find the fishlings. Sam Oakenhurst blames himself.

'And where is Frank?' demands Pearl, ungenerous in her desperation, careless of her friend's terrible burden.

'Frank is safe,' says Captain Billy-Bob, shivering with the enormity of her guilt. 'Frank at least is safe. He is with me.' The voice on the omniphone became a dissipating echo. Pearl would learn the implications of this soon enough.

①

Acting spontaneously, Captain Billy-Bob Begg, in order to save her ship and her crew and pull Frank Force from the plasma vortex which Kaprikorn Schultz had erected in their path, had repeated the impossible double-up manœuvre, this time irrevocably combining both her body and her spirit with Frank Force's, melding them together into one permanently enjoined being! The power of Chaos and Singularity, combined with the ingredients of the uncanny Fold Suit broken into a rich and near-lethal fuel, had brought the *Now The Clouds Have Meaning* home.

②

'Sam Oakenhurst is dying,' cries the Rose. 'Quickly, Jack! He is dying of shame. He has lost control of his own logic.'

'Forgive me,' begs Sam Oakenhurst of them all. 'I set my sights on pain when I should have set them on love. It was my fatal confusion, Rose. Forgive me.' But he will live for countless millennia, united with Captains Begg and Force: a tiny part of them.

③

Fearless Frank Force is helpless, bewildered by his co-existence with Captain Billy-Bob. They share identical space and scale. Frank Force is not sure what to do or say now. Is he still alive?

It had been Sam's decision. He had known it would kill him as an individual. But Pearl and all the others were saved. Jack Karaquazian would live to win where Sam Oakenhurst had lost.

Jack Karaquazian looked at Sam Oakenhurst, their identities wavering, focusing, seeking one another out. Pearl's wonderful arms embraced her lover.

'So long, Sam,' she said.

④

It had been an act of extraordinary self-sacrifice and cleverness, taking great courage on Sam Oakenhurst's part, making himself the medium

[240]

through which Captain Billy-Bob and Fearless Frank Force joined their strength together. He had reconciled Law and Chaos through the power of his loving sacrifice. No such act had ever succeeded in the history of the Game. He has changed the rules.

The Rose had not anticipated this. 'Sam!' She is at her friend's remains. He lies on the vibrating floor of the Dornier while a violent storm crashes around them. Silver lightning glares against the windows. His strange skull lifts itself.

'Sam! Come back! You had some bad luck, that was all. You don't have to go. Look! Jack's released himself from Captain Peru!'

'It's a question of honour, Rose,' says Sam Oakenhurst. 'I pushed Captain Billy-Bob to the decision. I guessed wrong and I took them all with me. I caused them impossible agony and for nothing. I said we were exploring but I was really escaping. I owe this to them. I owe this to the Pearl, to bring her lover home. Goodbye, Jack. I did my best. You still have a game or two to play. But I think I've improved your odds a little . . .'

'Have you learned nothing, Sam?' asks Jack Karaquazian, his grief turning to anger against his old partner. He looks back from where he sits at his controls. The windows are full of uneasy blackness slashed with crimson. 'Your honour will destroy you as it almost destroyed me. Your chivalry is the Old Hunter's finest disguise. His last resort. Don't you understand what you achieved?'

'I had a duty to Captain Billy-Bob. I could not let her down. She is my Main Type.'

'What about Pearl Peru?' Jack Karaquazian tries mockery to sting his friend back to their company, to save his human soul. 'Was she not also your Main Type once?' He rises from his seat and kneels down.

'Goodbye, Pearl,' says Mr Oakenhurst. 'Frank Force and Captain Billy-Bob will find you. God is, after all, a tree.' And he lets himself go.

Sam Oakenhurst's mortal body dies in Jack Karaquazian's arms. What is left of him has gone to play in the service of entropy; to roam the quasi-infinite, a demigod blessed by death's eternal simplicities. A gloriously doomed soul.

And the Rose falls weeping upon Jack Karaquazian's weary shoulder.

⑥

As she comforts her friend, Pearl Peru keeps half an eye on the controls of *The Smollettsphere*, waiting for a blink-up from Professor Pop who has installed his latest omniphonic equipment in the disused bellows chamber. This is a moment of grief and she respects it. Pearl feels for the Rose, feels for her friend, but she must remain vigilant now. The Singularity has pursued Fearless Frank Force and is desperate to reach him before he consummates his love. They are confused by his readings and do not understand that he has been united with their greatest enemy through Sam Oakenhurst's noble act of reverse entropy.

Old Reg's mystified grumble comes over the omniphone. 'I smell some perverse equation. Obscene mathematics. Can they have *eaten* our noble hero?'

'It could be their tradition,' says evil Freddy Force, equally baffled. 'But they cannot be allowed to break any further rules. Our whole existence is suddenly at risk.'

⑦

OAKENHURST'S LOOP: THE 'BLUEBONNET'

Based on Karaquazian's gambit, a significant round in the Game of Time, with far-reaching consequences, achieved thus:
  SO to BBB and hold; BBB to FF and hold;
  FFF to PP; PP to JK. JK releases.
  (Resolves to BBB+FFF and a Significant Wedding:- BBB+FFF=A+ PP, where Chaos=Singularity (CS). And held stable. An unprecedented resolution which will be recorded as a classic, the famous Cosmic Balance. It will be spoken of in legend.)

⑧

Sam Oakenhurst has been the catalyst for the chemical wedding of Fearless Frank Force and Billy-Bob Begg. That alone was a daring move risking extinction of his individual soul. He learned the move from Jack Karaquazian who had already established the precedent and the odds. Mr Karaquazian had set the scene, visualising the chances of the best outcome and his gamble had paid off. It was probably the greatest success of his long career.

But now the action was alarming even Captain Billy-Bob. She speaks urgently to Pearl Peru. 'We cannot afford to deny tradition further. I am carrying too heavy a cargo. You have witnessed the consequences. This new logic could destroy us. We have no notion of its power or effect!'

Nothing will remain of Sam Oakenhurst in the First Ether but his memory and his deeds.

While Pearl Peru has great respect for Captain Billy-Bob she keeps her own counsel. She is confused by the strange attraction she now feels for the famous Chaos Engineer. It is the emotion she felt for Captain Force. It is almost uncontrollable, unmistakably sexual. Yet, for all this rising lust, Pearl cannot agree with Billy-Bob. Pearl now knows tradition is death and orthodoxy will always cause the destruction of those who embrace it. That is the fundamental logic of the Game of Time: by refusing its logic, one alters its nature. It is thus that a round is won.

'Congratulations, Jack,' says the Rose. 'Now we can rest.'

Jack Karaquazian knows that he survives and owes it to Sam, together with the conquest of his own preconceptions. He is free. He feels an equal measure of triumph, humility and grief.

Not knowing why, Captain Billy-Bob has developed a reciprocally overwhelming desire for Pearl Peru. 'Has anyone ever mentioned how you look like Captain Wopwop in the face? Are you related?'

As the news comes over the omniphone, announcing Old Reg's peace proposals, we leave Pearl Peru joined in sexual congress with Captain Billy-Bob who had absorbed a partner to be alive again.

It is how a god survives.

CHAPTER TWENTY-SIX

A Moral Multiverse

What Sam Oakenhurst had lost to his honour, Jack Karaquazian had gained over his presumption. The Rose kept a light hand on the wheel but still wept for her stolen love, envying Jack his courage, his dramatically successful grasp of the Game. 'You are a jackal,' she says. 'You have the sweet hand of a grand master. Clean, simple and ruthlessly definitive. I'm proud to know you, Jack.' It was clear, however, that she wished he had died and not Sam.

He looked for mockery and was surprised to find none. He tasted the triumph of his victory. He licked his handsome lips. Grateful for Sam's sacrifice, he had also helped engineer it.

The Dornier began to descend through pale wisps of lavender cloud beneath which, Jack thought, he could see the ocean, bright and calm in the sunshine, blue as his native Mediterranean.

'*Video meliors, proboque; deteriora sequor*, as the poet says. Ovid seems pretty perfect for this moment, don't you think, old boy? O, the wild rose blossoms on the little green place. Literacy is our most valuable gift, the source of memory and enduring myth; the wellspring of all we now call civilised and the means by which we pool our commonwise. Communicating thus from Past to Present we improve our understanding of the world and our multiverse. I came to appreciate the true value of literacy when I tried to imagine the emotions of the first human being realising the implications and the potential of a written language! *Video meliors*, old chums.'

And here came Captain Quelch, wearing a stained linen suit, a gaudy gold watch chain in his waistcoat pockets, a slightly faded carnation in his lapel, his battered white cap at a rake, a bit of unlit cigar in his mouth, a small carpet bag in his hand, trudging from the back of the plane. 'My motto, anyway.' Smelling faintly of cognac, he leaned over the Rose, staring down at the gentle waves which ascended to meet the flying boat. 'Good to be home, eh, Rosie?'

Jack Karaquazian saw that she was grateful for Quelch's company. She reached up and took the old pirate's arm. He chuckled affectionately, almost embarrassed.

Mr Karaquazian felt something like a cold knife cut and he was free of Pearl Peru. She fell away behind him, intent on her fresh ambitions, her new love.

The war amongst the angels was not over. Even now monstrous forms were moving through the colour fields, treading the silver roads between the worlds, their armies reassembling as they prepared for a further stage in the struggle. One reconciliation, no matter how impossible it had seemed, did not mean that the struggle was resolved, only that those who fought, those who played the Game of Time, were aware that it was possible to establish new laws. Jack Karaquazian and Sam Oakenhurst, through their mighty alter-egos, had changed the assumptions of the Game forever. They had left their mark upon the multiverse and the struggle between Chaos and the Singularity would never have the same character again. Mr Karaquazian understood that there were many games to be played and that perhaps he would be called upon to play again. But meanwhile he was content. He believed that he had earned his respite, his chance of tranquillity and fulfilment. His reunion with Colinda Dovero.

The Rose let out a sigh. 'You always did know what surface your bread was buttered on, Horace.' She touched her lips to Quelch's pitted wrist.

'*Medio tutissimus ibis*, dear girl. Any chance to dodge the old *tempus edax rerum*, you know. I say, Jack! Look, old boy – down there – that's our island!'

The Rose was smiling, perhaps retrospectively. She brought the boat delicately to the waves and landed almost soundlessly in a little bay whose rocky walls were terraced by cream and white houses trimmed with royal blue or ochre, an entire town built up three sides of verdant cliffs which tumbled brilliant streams of silvery water straight into the sea. Men, women and children leaned over balconies to witness their arrival. Dogs barked. There was a quay and a white stone mole. Beyond these were the red and blue striped awnings of cafés and restaurants. The harbour bustled with returning fishing boats seeking lanes amongst slender yellow yachts and fat black sailing dinghies.

Expertly the Rose taxied her massive flying machine into a mooring at the mouth of the bay. She switched off the engines. She pointed at the rich tumble of villas, apartments, churches and public buildings clustered above them; a natural pyramid . . .

'Colinda will have seen us arrive. She'll be waiting for you on the quay, Jack. There's a steamer sails from the mainland next week, for New Orleans.'

'What is this place?' Jack Karaquazian trembles intensely with the dawning realisation of his release.

'Las Cascadas, dear boy,' Quelch tells him. 'Our island paradise. Our home. That's my old girl, over there!' Captain Quelch points at a handsome white yacht anchored near the mole. She bears the blazon *Hope Dempsey, Casablanca*. Quelch removes the stub of his cigar from his lips. 'Where did you think we were? It's home, old boy. Smell that air! Cleanest in the world. There's nowhere to beat the Med, Jack. You know that.'

Captain Quelch unbuttons his collar and yawns. 'Would you believe I used to teach at a school in Kent? I was thinking of going over to have a look at the old place. I left under a bit of a cloud. I never could abide red tape.'

'Please tell me where we are,' begged Mr Karaquazian, rising unsteadily.

'You're safe enough, Jack. You helped create that security. The Fault's only a legend here. A fading echo.' The Rose unstrapped herself, got to her feet and began to collect her things from around her seat. 'This is an old city. It has always welcomed the likes of us, Jack. You might not want to leave.' She looked up, offering him a quick grin.

'How did you find it, Rose?' he asked.

'I was brought here by a lover, long ago.' She swung a duffel bag over her elegant shoulder. 'Better get ready, Jack.'

Near the flying boat's door Jack Karaquazian stands before a full-length mirror. He is preparing for his love. He wears his tight-waisted black silk jacket, his best linen and fancy vest, his black trousers, his silver-studded boots. His long hair hangs straight to his shoulders, framing his handsome face. Al-Q'areen is a kindly, clever jackal. He slips ancient rings on his fingers, scarabs and vultures, and, for luck, puts a fresh deck into his breast pocket. He smiles as he adjusts his cravat and remembers herons flying against the cypresses, the pale sun burnishing the waters of the bayou where three gold stains lay upon the surface. *Pauvre pierrot, muy petit beau*. He clears his throat, unsurprised that his disease has not returned. He has defeated it. He remembers how she scooped his blood in her palms before she disappeared. Is that how she brought him here? By old-fashioned magic? But where else has he left his blood?

The Rose is now joyfully eager to disembark. She makes her way past a whistling Captain Quelch and heaves open the big door.

Already a boat, powered by an old-fashioned outboard, bounces across the calm waters towards them. Jack Karaquazian no longer disapproves of such engines. In an extraordinary act of self-renewal he has rejected all his earlier certainties and prejudices to win a handle on his own salvation.

He begins to hum the strains of 'Grand Mamou', recalling how he and Colinda danced on the deck of the *Etoile du Memphes* in the warm, drying air, when they had first declared their love.

Then he adjusts his cuffs, sets his hat on his head, glances one last time into the mirror and steps out again, brave as ever, to claim his heart.

'I'm feeling it, Sam,' he says.

Thanks to Los Tigres del Norte (Musivisa), Mamou (MCA Records), The Movies Sound Orchestra (Yel) and the bands at Michaut's, New Orleans; to Garth Brooks, Doug Kershaw, all the artists on Swallow Records, Ville Platte, LA, and friends in Porto Andratx, Marrakech, Atlanta, New Orleans, Houston, Lost Pines, TX, West Point, MS, Hattiesburg, MS, Oxford, MS and Oxford, UK, where this was written. Thanks also to Ed Kramer and Brother Willie Love . . .

Thanks to the German Silber-Western *and* Western-King *magazines,* Adventure *maga-zine,* Planet Stories, Startling Stories, Thrilling Wonder Stories *and other pulps. Very special thanks to Dave Garnett, editor of* New Worlds, *who originally undertook to get this going.* Blood *is the first of three books. The other two will be* Fabulous Harbours *and* The War Amongst The Angels.